GHOST PRISON

Ghost Prison

Herbert S McKinney

Contents

Chapter 1. The Reformatory

I am William Sidney Porter, formerly Inmate #30664 at the Redmond Reformatory. "Old Big Red" was her nickname among old-timers. It wasn't out of fondness for the place, I assure you, but rather revulsion. My time at the Reformatory was inspirational, but I wouldn't want to repeat it. Today, I'll be your narrator during parts of this strange collection of stories. Stories that will chill your blood, captivating your mind with tales of spirits, tragedies, torture, and blood. These words best describe the tragic events before the construction workers laid the foundation of the Redmond Reformatory so long ago. It's also the best way to describe the many strange events that occurred years later at Redmond Prison.

Redmond Reformatory, constructed in 1886, likely evoked thoughts of Dracula's castle for the inmates who had the misfortune of being stuck there. All the while, its colossal granite stones gave off a church-like aura, leaving many of its visitors in awe and its unfortunate inmates trembling in fear. Even the style of the place was awe-inspiring, intimidating anyone who stood in front of its massive walls. This was because of the mix of Romanesque and Victorian styles. The building's size and other features simply amazed onlookers. The Reformatory sits on land soaked in the blood of the restless. However, one wandering soul was more troubled than the rest, a Native American killed unjustly in cold blood.

This Native American was among the first to arrive in the area. However, he wouldn't be the last person to die there tragically. He was only trying to flee an unfamiliar setting of being amongst Europeans with unknown customs.

On a sunny day, his daughter marveled at the fall foliage, while he waited silently, biding his time to flee with his daughter. He mistakenly believed he'd go unnoticed, with everyone distracted by a wedding. If only he had more time. Maybe, just maybe, he could have avoided being discovered running for his life with his daughter in tow. However, a bullet will find you if it's meant to, just as a bullet found him, sealing his fate. The ball swirled in the air, almost in slow motion, before piercing his skin, creating a small gash and leaving no exit wound. As his lungs filled with blood, it became harder and harder to breathe.

Time passed, and infection set in. He could feel a sharp pain spread throughout his body. Blood seeped from his wound, while on reflex he applied pressure, desperately trying in vain to slow the bleeding. Despite running for his life, he wasn't fast enough. His run slowed to a crawl when he collapsed. The pain subsided and the cold set in. He tried to use every ounce of strength to crawl until he could go no farther, breathing becoming harder and harder. He knew then his life was over. His blood soaked the ground beneath him as his daughter escaped, never to be seen again.

Since the ancient law of blood revenge went unfulfilled because he had no sons, his blood stained the earth, demanding revenge. His soul drifted aimlessly after death. Denied his desire for revenge, he lost the peace he deserved in death. The few who cared buried his body in a shallow, unmarked grave only remembered by posterity through the accounts of bystanders. Sometimes, under the moon's glow, people swore they saw the silhouette of a man prowling around at night with a feather in his head. Some believed this land was sacred; however, nearly everyone else thought it was haunted and cursed.

Considering the long, sad story of this place, it likely seemed both haunted and cursed. Cursed by the dead who linger. People who had no peace in life and suffered from violence, disease, and mental illness. Worst of all, these restless souls also received no peace in death.

So why was the new Redmond Prison, located nearby, also cursed? Some think construction workers used materials from the old prison by accident to aid in the construction of the new one. This created a spiritual link between the two that allowed the ghosts from the old Redmond to roam the corridors of the new one. So the prisoners housed there, unfortunately, are not only serving time with other inmates, but likely with ghosts as well.

Meanwhile, miles away in Columbus, Ohio, at the Correctional Institution Inspection Committee, loud snoring radiated from the office of Committee Chairman, State Rep. Douglas Hardiman through his office door.

The setting sun was near the horizon, casting an orange glow on the capital as Chair Hardiman sat at his desk, slumped over, sound asleep in his statehouse office. Committee staff covered his brown mahogany desk with oversight reports on the state prison system. When a loud knock on the nearby door startled him, disoriented, he looked up from the reports he was supposed to read, scrambling to remove one page that was stuck to the side of his face. He could hear a low but muffled voice calling out to him but knocking hard.

"Hey, you're knocking like you're the police." Recognizing the woman's voice, he yelled, "Come in!" As the door to his office gradually opened, an angry but beautiful woman stood in the doorway: Rep. Kimberlee Townsend. She had flowing blonde hair down to the collar of her navy-blue blouse.

Her blue high-heeled shoes brought attention to her shapely figure. Rep. Townsend also left no doubt in the minds of her colleagues that she possessed beauty and brains. However, at that moment, she was mad.

"Chairman, have you seen this report on Redmond Prison?"

"No, I haven't. I kind of fell asleep."

"Strange stories are coming out of the place, and in-custody deaths are outrageous."

"Ms. Townsend, I've been serving the people of this state for a long time! No one can explain the crazy shit that goes on at Old Big Red in a report."

"Aren't you going to schedule hearings about it?"

"Why would I do something so dumb and idiotic? I'm a moderate Republican in a caucus filled with right-wing lunatics. Two years ago, those lunatics voted to privatize most state prisons despite my warnings and objections. My colleagues believed the promises those smooth-talking executives from the for-profit prison corporations made. Guarantees they could deliver cheaper and smaller government through prison reform and privatization.

"Everyone knows large companies operate in an atmosphere of shareholder demands for ever-increasing profits and fat dividend checks. They couldn't deliver then, and they can't produce cheaper now. They couldn't offer better because those state contracts have a minimum occupancy clause under the privatization agreement. The state must consistently provide them with enough inmates to prevent revenue fluctuations. The FBI has uncovered evidence that these corporations knew how to meet this quota. It turns out they were providing generous campaign contributions to our elected judges. Those judges then provided a steady pipeline of poor minority convicts who couldn't afford criminal defense lawyers. Black youth and young adults who broke misdemeanor-level laws, many of whom didn't break the law at all, are now doing serious time.

"They tell me mysterious interests are pulling the strings behind the scenes. People who have curried the favor and enthusiastic support of elements of law enforcement holding racist attitudes. You'll also be interested to know that the United States Justice Department's Office of Civil Rights is snooping around. FBI agents are going to be crawling all over us. Friends in the know have warned me of many open FBI investigations with multiple State, House, and Senate targets whom they refuse to reveal.

"We've got enormous political and criminal storm clouds forming."

She looked at him with a frown, confused at what he was saying. "Why are you telling me this?"

"I've been here longer than you, but you just got here."

"It's wise to avoid staying too long in public office. I'm considering early retirement. My contacts at DOJ insist on remaining anonymous and have assured me I have nothing to worry about or fear. However, they have advised me to walk away. People I trust say I don't need to be here to deal with this mess and the stress generated from these investigations, especially since I've got a heart condition."

"They tell me I'm better off spending time with my grandkids."

The clock ticked past 5:30 am on May 12, 1971 the day of the bank job, as Jessie Bowman settled into the stolen car, feeling the worn leather of the seat beneath him. Beads of sweat rolled down his face, his heart pounding with a mix of anxiety and determination. He gripped the steering wheel tighter, determined to do his job. The wait for the crew to leave the bank felt endless. He was not supposed to be there, but he was desperate. His one-year-old son was a handful, eating constantly and going through diapers like crazy. When he held his son, Jon Bowman, whom he called Jon Jon, in his arms, the baby's big brown eyes brought tears of joy to his face. Lately, he was experiencing premonitions. Dreams of a future nightmare, too real to ignore. Days before the bank job, uncertainty about his options consumed him. His criminal record limited his job options and made him more determined.

This job stood out from the others. Because on this job, an odd feeling came over him that maybe, just maybe, they should take a break. He warned them to let the heat die down from the other jobs for a while. However, the other guys just shrugged off his concerns. Then, in a moment of paranoia, he peered through the rearview mirror. Horrified by the sight of a police patrol car pulling up right behind him, his body flooded with terror and adrenaline.

"Holy shit, why now? Got dammit, why now?"

The guys inside were already running a few minutes late. The engine was running, but his nerves seemed to run higher. All he had to do was push the gas pedal and go. His heart was pounding as though it would jump through his chest. Suddenly, he noticed the unmistakable sound coming from the bank. A sound similar to a bolt of lightning that had hit the ground nearby. *Pow, pow, pow.* Three gunshots. The officer was already out of the car by this time. Hearing the gunshots, training and instinct forced the cop to run toward the gunfire just as his crew exited the bank. Chaos emanated from the entrance as bystanders ran for cover.

Time slowed, and he watched in shock as the officer fired his gun, taking out one crew member as he took a round to the chest. They both fell to the ground and died as their blood soaked the concrete, horrifying everyone. He could hear screams in the distance that terrified him when a second shot rang out, and another crew member went down, taken out by the cop's partner, who was using his patrol car as cover.

Seconds had passed when a fierce exchange of gunfire between the last member of his crew ended the firefight. One lucky shot to the neck that nicked the officer's carotid artery. This took out the remaining officer, leaving a smeared, bloody handprint on the top of the patrol car. He fell to the ground in slow motion, leaving a pool of blood on the street.

However, before his fall, he got off a round from his Model 39 service weapon, wounding the last man standing before falling to the ground. The last man was staggering, but still holding the bags of money. He opened the car door carefully, feeling a surge of pain from his wound. He swiftly threw the money bags in the back seat before getting into the running car waiting for him. Shocked by what he had just witnessed, Jessie turned the steering wheel somewhat to the left and floored the gas pedal, desperate to escape. As a wheelman, he knew time was precious and excellent driving was essential, but lousy luck could be a real problem.

Speeding away from the bank, the buildings seemed to fly by, but after a few blocks, he felt safe easing up on the gas to avoid attracting attention long enough to make it to the switch car. Once they arrived at their destination, sensing that moving him would make his condition worse, Jessie knew what he had to do, but he dared not say so out loud. He rushed after reaching the switch car parked in a secluded parking garage, hastily moving the money bags from the back seat of the car he was in to the ground near the switch car. Speed with precision was key, so he wiped any fingerprints he might have left on and in the getaway car.

Then, while taking care not to leave any new fingerprints, he leaned over and whispered in his partner's ear, "I'll be back for you." He said it knowing it was a lie, but it had to be done. Using negligible force, he closed the door and ran to the driver's side of the other car. In a flash, he opened it with a thin but strong wire and hook to get in. Then, he grabbed the bags of money as sweat rolled down his face and got into the switch car. Finally, taking a minute to calm his nerves, he hot-wired the ignition. As the engine roared, he firmly shifted the car into gear and drove off. On the ride home, one thought seemed to replay repeatedly in his head: *I had to leave him. I had to leave him, even if it meant leaving him to die.*

Paranoid and alone, he knew he couldn't go home right away. So he went to the one place he felt safe. A place where he could hide bags of money he now didn't have to split four ways. After hiding them there, he only told the mother of his son after arriving home. At that moment, he felt secure, with a sense of peace. In the clear...or so he thought.

Two weeks passed when three police officers showed up a uniformed officer and two detectives arrived at his house. One was white, a little overweight, with graying hair and a cigarette hanging from his mouth. The other detective was a young black man, a rare sight for that time and place. He didn't know they would tell him that his partner somehow survived. This was mainly due to a Good Samaritan who walked by. His surgery lasted hours, and the grueling questioning about how he got shot seemed to last longer.

It was only a matter of time before he would eventually crack under the pressure. After all, his attempts to lie failed. He had to talk. Especially when the police discovered the bullet removed from him originated from a police-issued gun. So, on a picturesque day, the detectives followed those breadcrumbs straight to Jessie after questioning his partner. Meanwhile, Jessie watched the officers walk up the driveway. Peaking through the window, nervous and terrified, he closed the curtain when they beat on the door, yelling loudly, "Jessie Bowman, police, open up." Feeling like he had no choice, he carefully opened the door. He slid the door chain latch to the left and unlocked it, letting them in. They walked in with a search warrant. He gave it to his girlfriend, who was standing in the living room with Jon Jon in her arms. For a moment, Detective Freeman got distracted by the gorgeous woman holding a squirming and crying one-year-old, scared by all the commotion surrounding him.

Detective Freeman regrouped, looking around the room, then turned his attention to the trophy with a car on it. Along with many pictures, he noticed a consistent theme, which mostly involved cars. Picking up one of them, he asked, "Mr. Bowman, is this you?"

"Yes, that's me and my dad at his garage when I was eleven or twelve."

Then he asked another question. "So, you grew up around cars?"

"Yes, I've worked on various types, but I spent most of my time driving them faster than I should."

His partner interrupted: "Mr. Bowman, we believe you were involved in a bank robbery, and we need you to come with us."

After reading him his rights, the police handcuffed him, causing discomfort and making him feel worse. The police officers shoved him into the back of the patrol car while his girlfriend cried and yelled. The officer and detective ignored her while searching the house, and Detective Freeman tried to console her. Jessie, sitting in the back of the car, knew they wouldn't find anything they could use against him, especially the money.

After his arrest, Jessie sat in a freezing interrogation room. Two detectives walked in. One seemed angry. The lead detective slammed a light-colored tan folder on the table. Then he slammed a yellow notepad down that had writing scribbled on it. "Do you know why you're here?"

"No, I've got no clue why I'm here."

"Your partner says you killed a cop, so you had better enlighten us about what happened."

Scared but not stupid, he used his one phone call to contact a lawyer, as demanded by his paranoia and girlfriend, Vanessa, after sleepless nights. When the lawyer arrived, all questions stopped. The lead detective was irate at facing a suspect who didn't seem intimidated by them. They realized they had to do a show and tell.

"Your partner fingered you as the shooter. We think he's lying because his story makes no damn sense. An eyewitness across the street saw the entire incident. The witness explicitly told us she couldn't see faces. According to her, the officer shot one of the bank heist men before he went down. Our witness claimed he entered the car on the passenger side before it drove away.

"We found your partner before he bled to death, sitting in the passenger seat of the getaway car. Who was driving? He was in no condition to drive. Also, the gun dropped at the scene had no fingerprints on it. Whoever shot the last cop wore gloves. So we don't know which one of you killed the last cop. We've got enough circumstantial evidence that you were at the crime scene."

"Officer, I need a few minutes with my client."

"First thing, if you lie to me, I can't help you. Do you understand me?!" Nodding his head to signal he understood, Jessie told the complete story, at least everything he could remember. Once he finished, his lawyer took a moment to think.

"Son, your criminal career is over. Your situation is awful and amounts to this: You're on a sinking ship. The outcome is death for one and imprisonment for the other. If you help ensure your partner gets the death penalty, it will go a long way to help you. You're both in a tough spot, so you need to do this. The only difference is the degree. I mention you because they need you to close their case; they need you to testify. The district attorney must eliminate the death penalty in exchange for your testimony. The district attorney will offer ten years for each cop. Plus, twelve years for the bank robbery. Which, based on your age, amounts to life in prison. If you follow the rules and you're not a problem, there's the possibility of negotiating to shave off some of your time, which is the play here, along with parole at your first hearing. Two cops are dead, and someone must pay. You may have just driven the car, but that still makes you an accessory to the deaths of those cops.

"If you want to see your son as a free man, we must get this right."

The lead detective, still angry, resumed questioning when the officers returned. He brought up a specific point. "Jessie... Can I call you

Jessie? We found your fingerprints at the location where you planned the job." Detective Freeman sat in the corner, listening intently.

Jesse's lawyer jumped in right away. "I need to speak with an assistant district attorney about a plea deal." He knew it wouldn't be a deal his client would like because officers were dead. But he had little leverage.

Assistant District Attorney Marcella, with her beautiful features, turned heads as she entered the room. She was confident, intelligent, and practical.

"Your case against my client is weak."

"My case against your client was weak until we found a fingerprint connecting him to this mess." She assessed his seriousness, then pulled a paper from her briefcase and laid it on the table. "Both men are on the *Titanic*, and I've only got a lifeboat for one."

After his lawyer reviewed it, he nodded, put his pen on the document as soon as Jessie signed it, and laid the pen back on the table. "Talk, tell the truth, and don't hold back," his lawyer urged, placing a hand on his shoulder.

Following his account of the tragic events, he gazed at Assistant District Attorney Marcella, his eyes conveying his sincerity. "I'm a driver only. I've never held a gun, let alone fired one to kill a cop."

His lawyer intervened. "Let's cut to the chase. My client was only the driver during this crime. He'll serve ten years per cop and twelve for the bank job, possibly getting parole at the first hearing. He must get time off for testifying."

"Why should I agree to this when they should both get the death penalty, and we should call it a day and go home?"

Then Detective Freeman spoke with the calmness and confidence of a man twice his age. "You should take this deal because if you call me to testify when I swear that oath, to tell the truth, nothing but the truth, based on the interview, I'll tell the jury I think he's honest. I'll have to tell them that his story matches the pictures in his house. Pictures of his dad's garage and him in a Sprint car race. Along with the many trophies on the mantel."

"Okay, if I agree to this deal, he must serve the sentences consecutively."

Jessie, leaning back in his chair with his head down, resigned himself to the prospect of spending nearly the rest of his life in prison. His attention turned to his son, who he knew he would never get to know, and his son would never know him. He was always told that a man was not supposed to cry, but at that moment, he just couldn't stop sobbing, saying the same thing repeatedly, "My son won't know me, my son won't know me," as he clenched his fist on the table in anger.

Then, once he regained control of his emotions, he looked directly at Assistant District Attorney Marcella. "I'll take the deal."

Detective Freeman, up to that point, was mute, but to everyone's surprise, he spoke up in a way that reassured Jessie he made the right decision. "I know you made the right call, given the circumstances. A young man without positive choices and too many negative influences can easily go astray. When I can, I'll try to check on your son to make sure the cycle ends with you."

"Do you promise?"

"Yeah, you have my word. I'll check on him and do what I can to make sure he stays on the straight and narrow." Granted, when Detective Freeman made that promise, he had ulterior motives: getting to know Jessie's girlfriend, Vanessa, better. However, it was a promise he intended to keep.

Time passed, and the days became years, turning what was a friendship into something more. Vanessa would eventually become Vanessa Freeman, but they both tried to be honest with Jon Jon, making it clear to him who his real father was.

They waited until he was old enough to explain his father's situation, but stressed their unwavering love and hopes for him. Eighteen years later, on an ordinary day, the phone rang while Jon was preparing to graduate from high school. He was in the kitchen with his mother, eating a ham sandwich. She stood there with the phone to her ear, but after a few minutes of listening, she felt faint. At that moment, a feather could have knocked her over, and she sat down and she started crying uncontrollably.

"Mom, what happened? What's upset you so much?" he asked, seeing tears rolling down her face. "What's happened to my dad?"

"They said his kidneys are failing, and he doesn't have much time. I shouldn't feel this way, but I can't help it. I had a kid with the man, and some of those feelings just don't go away!" Even though she was now a policeman's wife.

Visiting the prison from time to time in the last few years, something had changed, though at the time, he couldn't figure out what. Then he realized what it was. His dad was losing hope and moving slower. A few days after that call, his mom was sad but eventually returned to her usual self. Detective Freeman seemed disconnected from Jon's biological father because he was trying to fill the gap of being a father. The man who made little league baseball games despite a cop's schedule. Knowing their history, he wisely kept his distance, respecting her relationship with him.

The last picture he ever took remained in a frame on the mantel in the living room of the house he grew up in. In the photo, he held his diploma, his mom was there, and his dad looked sharp in his suit and tie. His other dad was there in a hospital bed as a free man. It was the oddest picture he could remember taking, and the one that meant the most. Twenty years from the time his dad went to prison.

In 1990, Jon Bowman completed his second year at C. S. University in Wilberforce, Ohio. In the township of Xenia, he attended a party usually held the weekend after final exams. It was the end of his second year in college. He figured he deserved to relax and enjoy himself, at least for a while. This party had plenty of food and, even better, plenty of beautiful women walking around. The party also had an exotic strain of marijuana, a fact the host, AJ, reminded him of when he walked in the door and slipped two already-rolled squares into his pocket. Walking into the grand oak-framed entrance, he noticed the theme of the party prominently displayed on a banner with flair on the door: *The Brown Sugar Bash*. The name may have needed some work, but it was alright, judging from the fantastic women there.

R&B music emanated from the speakers in the room's four corners. The sound, pitch, and vibe were perfect, not too loud or low, just enough to put everyone in the right mood. His best friend Jerry talked him into going to this party after exhausting all reasonable excuses he could come up with to stay home. Jerry, who was there from the first time he stepped on campus, was always his wingman. Michelle seemed to enjoy playing mind games and messing with his emotions. She appeared on the far side of the room, enticing him with her short red skirt, accentuating her curves. Their on-again, off-again relationship confused many, but everyone around them seemed to notice the chemistry.

Standing in the crowd of people at Alex's party, it was as if everyone else had disappeared, their voices faded to a mere whisper, and no one else was more important to him at that moment than Michelle. She was a woman of eminent beauty, with flowing black hair permed and styled as though she was vying for the cover of *Essence Magazine*. Her shapely figure always turned heads, while her confidence made her down-to-earth and approachable.

As he navigated through the crowd to get to Jerry and the two women standing next to him, he was struggling to come up with something to say to Michelle. Their relationship had begun during their first year at the university. He knew she was majoring in Business with a minor in Political Science. At the same time, she was open to law school. As he got closer, the words seemed to come to him; maybe the good lord was looking out for him.

"Hey, Jerry, I've got a question for you. How is it one of the nerdiest guys at this party happens to be standing next to two of the most beautiful women here?"

Jerry smiled a big grin before saying, "Dumb luck, I suppose." The two women smiled, approving of the compliment.

"Ladies, I only say *one* of the nerdiest guys at this party because I include myself as the second. I've never been the smoothest brother in the room, and the most stylish brother walking around has never been me." He knew in the back of his mind that a little self-deprecating humor hurt no one. He looked around the room at the crowd. "Most of the guys in here look like players in training."

Michelle was one of the first to speak. "Why should I believe you're not just like them, just another player in training?"

"I'm serious. Did you see that guy in black khakis and a blue shirt? That guy has talked to three women in the hour and a half since I've been here. Worst of all, he used the same line on all three: 'Girl, your feet must be tired because you've been running through my mind all night.'"

Michelle, Jerry, and the other woman beside them burst out laughing, shaking their heads, saying, "That's a damn shame."

"Coming up with smooth stuff that I don't believe to say to women is not my style, and something I've been terrible at. You must mix too many lies with the truth to be believable, while keeping all of the lies straight in your head to be smooth and effective. That's just a game I can't play well."

Studying him carefully, Michelle tried to decide whether she should believe him. Then she realized that Jerry and her friend seemed to conveniently disappear, sensing they needed to be alone. Smiling at Jon, she soon made her decision. "Let's take a walk."

As they both left the party and entered the hallway, the noise and music faded as they walked down the narrow walkway between the columns of meticulously spaced trees, one after another. A canopy of branches and leaves covered their path. Once they cleared the trees, the open, somewhat slanted field they entered offered a magnificent view of the moon and stars. They continued on, both of them enjoying the moment's serenity. They walked and talked for what seemed like an eternity, getting to know one another better. After almost an hour, they stood outside her apartment.

Once there, he kissed her like a gentleman. A quick, light peck on the cheek and then a swift turn to leave. However, in a moment of weakness, she grabbed his hand and stopped him. She wanted him to stay. She needed him to stay. He turned to face her, looking deep into her beautiful brown eyes. The warmth of the touch of his hand against the side of her face was intoxicating. All he wanted was to be with her. Their senses heightened with a flood of sexual excitement that filled the air. He caressed her and kissed her tenderly for a long time. Not wanting to let her go, he needed to keep her close. He moved his other hand between her waist and hips, pulling her closer. A flood of emotions overwhelmed them as every nerve in their bodies tingled like they were on fire. He wasn't sure if this was one night of fun or something else, but what he was sure of was he wanted something more.

She struggled to get the key into the door of her apartment. He steadied her hand until she found the keyhole and opened the door. After walking in, with a flip of a switch the lights turned on, allowing him a chance to look around when she hastily disappeared. Michelle's apartment reflected her: ordered, pleasant, and clean, unlike the chaotic mess that could describe his own.

When his attention turned to the Brown Sugar, the two marijuana joints , he forgot he had when he reached into his pocket. To the other Brown Sugar, Michelle he was waiting on. Then Michelle suddenly reappeared wearing nothing but a white-laced nightgown. It highlighted her curves, igniting a desire in him that only she could spark. Especially when she knew what she wanted and knew how to get it. He kissed her slowly, taking his time. He knew it was a special moment, and he didn't want to rush, so he took care to go slow to make love to her.

Chapter 2. Railroaded

He kissed her slowly, placing his hand on her thigh and caressing her, working his way up, raising the laced nightgown as he moved forward. Their excitement grew with every touch as she unbuttoned his shirt, taking it off. While gently pushing her hair to the side, continuing to caress her all over, he inhaled the enticing, sweet smell of her perfume before gently taking off her nightgown, exposing the curves of her body.

He stood there admiring the view, enjoying touching every inch of it and being stimulated by every sensation. She slowly unbuckled his pants, revealing just how excited he was. She smiled as she watched him rise to attention through his boxers. As their bodies came together, they seemed to merge. Sweat rolled down their faces as moans and groans of pleasure could be heard most of the night, until they both fell asleep from exhaustion.

The next day, the sun rose high in the sky. The birds seemed to chirp joyfully like they were singing to God. Singing like they somehow knew a secret that only they and God knew and would only reveal in time. Groggy and disoriented, Jon sat up in bed, unsure of his surroundings. Then it hit him: he wasn't in his apartment or bed.

Then, looking over at Michelle, he just couldn't help himself. He just sat there watching her sleep. She was so peaceful-looking, even with no makeup on. She was just naturally beautiful, he thought to himself. So, quietly getting out of bed while being careful not to wake her, he knew he needed to leave. He just couldn't do it without telling her how he felt. Something seemed to compel him to say he wanted to see her again in a note. Quietly closing the door to her room behind him, he sat down hastily at the dining room table to write a note, telling her how much he enjoyed spending time with her.

While struggling momentarily with what else to say, a flood of inspiration came to him that would've made Langston Hughes proud. This brief inspiration allowed him to tell her how he felt creatively. But he knew he had to show her too, so he slipped out, grabbed a flower from outside, and placed it beside the note. This was just the special touch he thought he needed. The whole point was to send her a unique signal. This was not one night of fun; he wanted it to be something special, something more. However, he wasn't sure if she felt the same way. He knew their on-again, off-again thing was getting old. He knew he needed to get serious with her or risk losing her once and for all.

The contradictions were stark and apparent after leaving Michelle's apartment and making the brief drive to his own. He had little to no furniture and entered college because of grades, financial aid, and scholarships alone. He almost didn't have enough to pay rent, let alone buy furniture. All because he saved some of his student loan money out of fear of graduating broke. Despite this fear, however, he knew one thing: how to survive. Looking in his refrigerator, it was a depressing sight. The only food there was a breakfast sandwich, a bottle of apple juice, a bag of grapes, and expired almond milk. Grabbing the breakfast sandwich, he put it in the microwave and waited two minutes for it to finish cooking.

Grabbing it, he sat on one of the few pieces of furniture in the room. At that moment, he could only think about his life until the vaporizer he bought months ago at a smoke shop with Jerry entered his mind. He blew on the breakfast sandwich to cool it down before taking a bite and searching for his vaporizer.

"I think it's time to become friends with Mr. White." Taking one of the marijuana squares out of his pocket, he slowly looked around the living room of his apartment. He couldn't help feeling a little depressed at the emptiness, thinking about how it almost didn't feel lived in. There was no furniture or flowers. No pictures on the walls or books on the shelves. Feeling overwhelmed with emotions at the direction his life was taking and the circumstances he found himself in, somehow he couldn't help but smile. He remained confident he could overcome any challenge life could throw at him.

Once his sandwich cooled, he quickly ate it and turned his attention to his vaporizer after cutting the filter and placing the dry herb in it. He allowed the heating element to work and the aroma to consume him. As the high gradually kicked in and his mind wandered, it reminded him of a time when he was a boy in church with his mother.

Sitting there alone with only his thoughts to keep him company seemed odd, peaceful, and satisfying. Then a bizarre internal conversation took an unexpected turn. An image flashed in front of him. "Dad, is that you? No, it can't be you. You're gone."

"It's me, son. I couldn't leave you knowing what I know about your future. I'm with you for a limited time to help you face an ordeal that won't be easy. You can only see me now because your mind is in an altered state because of the weed. When it wears off, I will disappear. I'll still be with you, but you won't see me unless you're asleep. I can't stay long, but remember, you can't take your own life, no matter what challenges you face. Suicide can never be an option." And then he vanished as quickly as he'd arrived.

Jon thought long and hard about the warning, the implications heavy on his mind, before finally dismissing it. He reasoned that since his parents and God gave him life, he had no right to take his own. He dismissed the thought as crazy and not worth wasting time thinking about. As the vapor filled his immediate surroundings, the effects of the Barry White grew more potent.

As his mind gradually wandered, he seemed to take a psychedelic ride to cloud nine. He couldn't help thinking to himself, *This is some excellent weed,* all the while contemplating the trip home. A powerful urge suddenly came over him to call his mom before leaving. Then, another ominous warning about the devastating events flashed before him.

Day became night and the effects of the drug wore off, while the side effects lingered on, putting him into a deep sleep. He woke up hours later, shocked by how much time had passed. Loud growls from his stomach scared him, as though a wild animal was staring at him, thinking he was dinner.

He realized he had skipped lunch entirely, and his stomach made all kinds of crazy sounds. He knew he needed to find something to eat to ensure the effects of the weed completely wore off. He walked across the street to the sub shop instead of driving to the nearby pizza shop, before returning to pack for the relatively short drive to Cleveland to see his mother.

It was an odd night because there were clouds in the sky. Early that morning, while listening to the radio, he remembered hearing something about the possibility of rain, but there was no guarantee it would. An ominous feeling came over him; something terrible was about to occur that he couldn't avoid, but only survive. Sitting there in that sub shop, it was like God said, "Whatever will be, will be," as a relentless downpour began.

He sat at that sub shop for what seemed like hours, watching the rain. It almost appeared that he might need a canoe to return to his apartment. He waited and hoped, then waited a few more minutes for the rain to stop until the clock reached 10 and the restaurant workers prepared to kick him out before locking the doors. He knew he had to leave now or risk not getting enough sleep to drive the following day to East Cleveland.

Dreading the likelihood of getting soaked, but knowing it was inevitable, he tried to mentally prepare himself before physically doing it. It was a mad dash across a two-lane road to get to his apartment. He looked both ways to avoid oncoming traffic while waiting briefly in the median before running again. Arriving on his doorstep, he was nearly out of breath and completely soaked from head to toe, so much so that his pants stuck to his body. To add insult to injury, it stopped raining the minute he put his key in the door. A puddle formed on the floor after standing there for just a few minutes, causing him to look up at the sky and scream, "Really, God? You couldn't stop all that rain a few minutes ago?"

As he packed for the trip, the rest of the night seemed to merge into the next day. He loaded a few bags and one suitcase into his car before falling asleep for a few more hours. Then he left with the one thing he loved greatly due to who gave it to him. It was a blue Malibu that used to belong to his mother, who got it because of a good deed performed by his dad while in prison. His dad served time as an accessory to a robbery that turned into a homicide. The messed-up thing about it was he wasn't even the trigger man. However, saving the life of a prison guard and another person proved not to be a high-enough price to buy his freedom.

The DA wouldn't shorten his life sentence because he was an accessory to taking the life of two cops and involved in a bank robbery. The district attorney reasoned that since he was still there and failed to intervene, preventing their deaths, his dad should remain in prison. The only reward for his good deed was to give the benefit to someone he cared about. And that's how his mother got that blue Malibu, and how he would eventually end up with it.

Driving down the road, the landscape became a green and brown blur, the trees rushing past in a dizzying spectacle of speed and motion. It was easy to get lost on those long drives, to get lost in thought. Especially when Stevie Wonder's "Superstition" blasts on his car stereo. He barely noticed the cop out of the corner of his eye in the rearview mirror. By then, he knew it was already too late to do anything. Suddenly, his heart beat faster as adrenaline flowed through his body.

At that exact moment, a phrase popped into his head. "If it's not on you, it's not yours." He instantly remembered the party from a few days back and what Alex had said...and the one remaining marijuana cigarette he still had in his pocket. It was like a voice was telling him, screaming at him, to get rid of it. Was it his guardian angel? He immediately took action, frantically reaching into his pocket and throwing it out the open passenger-side window, hoping it cleared the car enough to escape the officer's attention.

All the while, he was sweating heavily and getting more nervous by the minute as the sirens from the patrol car got closer. The red and blue lights could be seen in his rearview mirror. Beginning to pull to the side of the road, he tried to calm his nerves to avoid giving the officer a reason to be more suspicious. A vision of his mother entered his mind, and he started running through a checklist that she constantly drilled into him as soon as he started driving out of fear. He checked his seatbelt. He kept his license and registration on the dash so he wouldn't have to reach for it and risk getting shot. Then, he placed his hand firmly on the steering wheel to ensure no sudden moves would be made. Finally, and most importantly, he pulled into a well-lit gas station with security cameras. All this to prevent actions that could lead to his mother attending his funeral instead of him attending hers. This was her fear and the fear of all mothers of black men in America.

His goal was clear: Get the officer back into his patrol car and on his way as quickly as possible. What he didn't count on was meeting

Officer Anthony Donavon. Officer Donavon had two character flaws that made their chance meeting problematic.

The first was that he was a racist, and the second was that he was a dirty cop. He was destined to be racist because his father was. However, he didn't start out being a dirty cop—he got that way over time. He had quickly gained a reputation for the most drug arrests of any officer on the force. Most of those arrests came at the expense of black motorists during routine traffic stops. Some of those stops were justified, but most weren't. The drugs he planted on unsuspecting black drivers worsened as his greed and ability to get away with his crimes grew. It didn't matter what those drivers said because the blue wall protected him. Of the many arrests, most were questionable in ways that produced a paper trail. This eventually got the attention of the Justice Department, FBI, and Office of Civil Rights.

He slowed his patrol car, the tires hissing softly on the asphalt as he prepared to confront the driver, his heart pounding in his chest. The officer ran the plate, the familiar tap-tap-tap of his fingers on the keyboard a rhythmic counterpoint to the low hum of the police car's engine. Within minutes, he had his answer. As the red and blue lights from the patrol car continued to flash, the siren blared until he turned it off. Stepping out of his car and taking the short walk to the driver's side of the car, he knew he didn't have a lot of time.

Officer Donavon knew police procedure well. With a smirk, he had deliberately typed in an incorrect license plate number, replacing this plate number with one registered to a car he knew was stolen. He was careful to make sure the make and model were close enough to explain it later as an innocent mistake if asked. He also knew that if the car was reported stolen, he could approach the driver differently. Unbuttoning the strap on his gun holster, taking it out, and switching off the safety in one move without thinking, he positioned himself near the driver's side window at an angle, pointing his gun at the driver. He was breathing heavily but maintaining his control.

He was angry, yelling orders, because the driver didn't stop immediately. "Get out of the car, driver, get out of the car now!" His voice was loud and firm, but it cracked a little because he was always nervous, knowing stops could always go left quickly. "Driver, slowly step out of the car."

Jon felt a knot of dread tighten in his stomach as he assessed the situation, the heavy silence pressing down. This was a life-or-death moment, the potential for disaster looming large. He opened the door slowly and complied, asking, "What did I do wrong?" But he hadn't even finished speaking when Officer Donavon snapped his gun into its holster, ripped Jon from his car, and slammed him to the ground. The chilling weight of handcuffs was a final, suffocating measure as he lay there, stunned and subdued.

Knowing how long it took for the backup officer to arrive on the scene, Officer Donavon did a preliminary search of the car. Then he planted drugs he got from an officer in the vice unit who had a habit of not reporting all the drugs he seized. Waiting nearly five minutes for the backup officer to arrive, his action prompted a second, painstaking search of the vehicle. They found the drugs precisely placed between the cup holder and passenger seat, a location that was both easily accessible and well-hidden.

When finally allowed to stand up, Jon asked another question. "What's the problem, Officer?"

"Well, sir, it seems you're in a hurry. Where are you headed today?"

Jon strained to see the officer's name and badge number. "Officer, I'm going home to West Cleveland to see my mom."

While the officer looked at Jon's driver's license sitting on the car's dashboard, out of the corner of his eye, he observed something familiar on the floor in the back seat. Something he recognized; something he could use. A small box with a round tube sticking out of it. *A vaporizer*, he instantly thought. He knew it could be used for e-cigarettes, or it could be the type used for marijuana. Either way, it should be enough to give him probable cause to search the car, despite initially entering the wrong tag number.

"Sir, this road is routinely used by people transporting illegal drugs. So that's why I searched your car and why my supervisor will search it again when he arrives."

Jon wanted to refuse, but he was confident he had nothing to worry about. This was the moment when the situation got worse for him. His fists clenched as he was pulled from his car, the indignity of it and the injustice of the situation fueling his rage. He felt the officer's grip on his arm, a painful reminder of his powerlessness. Then, a weird, overwhelming urge to get out of the situation as quickly as possible fell on him. Ultimately, it didn't matter, because the officer searched the car anyway. In a cursory search, the officer only had enough time to plant marijuana and some pills. The two bottles filled with opioids would prove problematic.

Officer Donavon had to be careful not to stay too long after radioing for back-up. Everything seemed perfect. However, the more time that passed, the angrier Jon became. When the supervising officer arrived, Officer Donavon explained the details to him. He conducted a more thorough search of the car, where the drugs were eventually found. The supervising officer looked so mad, Jon thought his head would explode, to the point where the color in his face turned from pink to beet red. He was angry because this business—the drug business—was personal. He already lost one daughter to it and was at risk of losing another, the only one he had left. Jon was now off the ground and standing, looking at the supervising officer. "You drug dealers make me sick. You just want money so you can avoid getting a real job."

He could hardly contain his rage, and a respectful conversation turned into yelling and screaming when confronted with what they found in Jon's car. "It's degenerates like you who make it impossible for parents who love their kids to keep them safe!" the officer shrieked, his face contorted with rage, spittle flying from his lips.

Jon was tough, so he defiantly denied ownership. "You planted those pills, because I don't know where they came from. I don't know anyone who could supply me with them. Hell, I don't even know what the hell they are."

Officer Donavon, the man who instigated the whole mess in the first place, stood behind him, quietly and enthusiastically, but without showing his glee, anxiously waiting to arrest him. His plan worked almost perfectly. *Almost* perfect, because Officer Donavon had no clue an FBI surveillance team was nearby, watching his every move with cameras fitted with a telescopic lens capable of recording from a safe distance with impressive detail, along with well-concealed recording devices capturing Donavon's every word.

While Officer Donavon read him his rights, his supervisor suddenly interrupted him. "Sir, you've got the right to shut up, and I strongly recommend you do so. Screaming and arguing won't save you." Then he bent Jon down, but not enough to clear the car door, causing him to bump his head. Once in the back of his patrol car, he saw stars.

Officer Donavon looked over at him with a smirk. "That was for getting mouthy. Shut up, boy, or you'll get another one when we get to the station." Then he closed the door, and within minutes, they pulled off.

This ordeal would consume the next four years of his life. His mood was somber as he wondered what would happen next. He was also trying to figure out what, if anything, he could do to get out of the serious trouble he was now in. He needed to call his mother and, most importantly, reach a decent lawyer. The aim was to get off scot-free or reduce his jail time. Sitting in the back of that patrol car, it was as if his life flashed before his eyes. As though God pushed pause on the video of his life. The ride to the police station seemed like an eternity. However, for some strange reason, he was determined to survive and come out stronger on the other side. If his dad could lose the better part of his life for taking someone else's life, he had to be at least strong enough to endure his ordeal, and he was determined to survive it.

After arriving at the station, he knew he had to use the one call he could make to call his mother. Waiting in the cold, medium-sized cell with people he didn't know and many people he didn't want to know was unnerving. Standing there waiting for a man to finish and then a woman to use the phone, he overheard some weird conversations. Then an officer removed the handcuffs for a short time. The place was so depressing; even the officers seemed miserable. A genuinely awful process he wouldn't wish on anyone. Another officer signaled for him to come forward, and as he stood there, the officer at the desk asked, "Is this a local call or long-distance?"

"It's a local call."

"That's cool. You've got five minutes, so make it quick. Oh, and who are you calling?"

"My mom, Darlene Freeman."

"Okay, make it quick. Tell her where you are and what you're being held for."

He had dialed the number so many times before, but this time was different. As the phone rang, the familiar voice answered. The first phrase that entered his mind was, "Mom, I love you."

With a concerned frown, she immediately asked, "What's wrong?"

"How do you know something's wrong?"

"Because usually you ramble about everything that happened to you during the day when I first talk to you. You only say, 'Mom, I love you,' when something is wrong."

"Mom, you know me too well."

"That's just part of the job, son."

"Do you have a pen nearby?"

"Yes."

"Write everything I say. I got arrested in Mansfield, Richland County, Ohio. They're hitting me with opioid possession charges."

"Hold up, you don't know a thing about opioids."

"Mom, I know, and that's precisely what I tried to tell them. They won't let me talk long, so I've got to go, but remember: the Richland County Sheriff's Department." Then he hung up the phone.

As they booked him, he strained to read the paper describing the charge. The confirmation of the possession charges hit him like a physical blow, his heartbeat ringing in his ears.

He tried not to squint from the camera's flash during the mugshot. First, they took a picture of his left side, then the right side, facing forward, and within minutes, it was done. An overwhelming feeling came over him that summed up perfectly how he felt at that moment. Charged for nonsense, that phrase and sentiment came through in the mugshot. It was so clear that the woman taking it looked at him, then looked at his mugshot.

"Young man, you don't belong here, I can tell."

"Ma'am, I don't, and the suffocating weight of my predicament is like quicksand, threatening to consume me with each passing moment."

"Time is short, so tell me what happened—talk fast, I need the details!"

He didn't know this woman, but somehow he sensed he could trust her. His mother always told him that during his life, he would meet people God placed in his life to help at critical moments. They'd lend a hand, mostly small stuff, but sometimes bigger things. Being a momma's boy, he took her advice. This officer was a middle-aged black woman named Karen Johnson. She had to be maybe forty-five years old with a few graying hairs. She was one of the few officers of color he saw walking around for the brief time he was at the station.

Speaking softly, with a respectful tone, he said, "I'm being charged with nonsense. They found opioids in my car while I drove to West Cleveland to see my mom. I know about Mary Jane, but I don't know

Jack about opioids. Hell, I don't even know who to talk to or where to go to get the stuff."

"Young man, this is an important question: Who was the arresting officer?"

"Officer Anthony Donovan was my arresting officer."

"Oh God no, that racist son of a bitch was your arresting officer?" Her face sank. "Damn it." Looking at his name on the arrest report and then writing it down on a yellow sticky note along with the assigned booking number, she stuck it in her right pocket. She reached into another pocket and took out a business card with a lawyer's name.

The name on the card was Attorney John Merit JD. "He's a hardworking and fantastic lawyer, but I gotta be honest. This card comes with a warning. The chances of your success are slim, and likely, you will not win. This is a rotten system, not because he's a weak lawyer. The 'grand old white boy' system overrides impartial justice. Everyone knows each other, and many are close friends with the judge. Worst of all, they all have a low opinion of black people."

After that conversation, he felt more depressed than before talking to her. Despite the situation, he was determined to face whatever came because he had no choice. . He knew from the moment of his arrest and the days that followed that those events would shape his life in ways beyond his wildest nightmares.

Once they were done with him, they put him in a cell to wait for transport to the county lockup. However, the cell in question was already in use, and his path unexpectedly crossed with an unusual man who went by the name of Deon Soto. Deon was looking out from behind the bars of his cell; he appeared to be staring into space in deep thought. That is, until the officer showed up with Jon. As the officer opened the cell and put him in, Deon sat down on the bottom bunk. He was trying to figure out what kind of man he'd share a cell with. Then, he spoke words that stuck with Jon for a long time. "Young man, you don't belong here. You don't look like a criminal. Trust me, I know what criminals look like."

"Sir, what makes you think I don't belong here?"

"Well, what kind of student were you, and did you graduate?"

"How is whether I graduated from high school relevant to this conversation and whether I belong in this cell with you?"

Looking at him with a huge grin, Deon said, "Criminals don't usually use the word 'relevant' in a sentence. Your words are a dead giveaway, you're not one of us. Most criminals didn't pay attention in school to understand that word and how to use it properly."

After that statement, Jon could only lean against the wall with a smile. "You seem to know a lot about people. That's impressive! Did you figure that out from just a quick conversation?"

"No, it's a game I play to figure out who's a cop and who isn't."

"I spent two years in college, but grew up in the hood of East Cleveland. The only thing I'm guilty of is being tight with Mary Jane. I don't know what happened. All I know is I'm here because I was driving home to see my mom. A racist cop stopped me and found two prescription bottles of opioids in my car, which I didn't put there. I only know that one of the two officers involved in the traffic stop planted those pills."

Contacting John Merit, the lawyer recommended by Officer Johnson, the conversation didn't last long. In a short chat, he summarized the main points of his and Deon's cases, showing how they were alike. After weighing each case's specifics, Mr. Merit pondered their independent legal implications. His analysis determined that there did not appear to be any conflicts that could pose a problem with him representing both of them. There was also the fact that it was a slow couple of months for his legal practice, so he decided the two clients may be worth defending.

As he prepared for the legal fight of his life, Jon knew that time may slow down, but it never stopped for anyone. As the days spent in the county jail became weeks, and the weeks became months, his trial date approached with lightning speed. After taking a plea bargain, they moved Deon from his cold, concrete cell to the imposing structure of Redmond Prison.

Once they sentenced Deon and moved him to the stark, haunted prison, he shifted his focus to his pending trial. Inside the courtroom, all he could do was wait. The moment arrived; his case was finally called. The judge swiftly remanded him into custody. The decision weighed heavily on his shoulders. It seemed pretrial administrative affairs went by with lightning speed as he reflected on the entire process. Standing next to his lawyer, Mr. Merit, he entered a plea of not guilty.

The room wasn't large, but walking through those double doors. Enduring the intimidating presence of armed sheriff deputies serving as bailiffs. Men and women who hold the power to take a man into custody and deprive them of their freedom. As a defendant going through this experience. It created a sense of shock that he was here and a sense of fear of what could happen. All while simultaneously observing the interactions between the most intimidating individual, the judge.

As the trial began, the jury, a diverse group of twelve, took their seats, ready to listen. A key element of his trial was the prosecutor's questioning of Officer Donavon. He questioned him about the details supporting his probable cause. Then someone handed the prosecutor a document. After reading it, he immediately requested a sidebar and dropped the bomb, revealing fingerprints were found on the bottle of pills, but only Officer Donavon's were identifiable. The prosecutor immediately requested a narrower scope for cross-examination because the report could prejudice their case. Unfortunately, Judge Vaughan granted the request. Attempting to reduce the sting and explain away this detail, he said the officer may have accidentally touched them during the initial search. To further solidify the case, the prosecution highlighted the defendant's crisp and clear fingerprints on the vaporizer next to the two bottles, drawing attention to their proximity.

On cross-examination by Mr. Merit, despite his best effort to impeach the officer's testimony, his questioning wasn't enough to sway the jury. He tried to use this revelation to open the door to bringing up Officer Donovan's record on the force.

Judge Vaughan sensed the direction of this questioning and immediately signaled the two attorneys for a sidebar, urgently whispering instructions out of earshot of the jury and everyone else. Mr. Merit returned to the table, trying not to look dejected, but it was apparent.

Looking directly at Jon, he could only say, "I felt you were innocent of these charges, but now I have no doubt." After being hamstrung and undermined throughout the trial by the judge and the deputy district attorney, he had no plausible explanation for the drugs found in the car, a fact that further incriminated him. It gave the jury only two choices: Who do you believe, the officer or the defendant?

Chapter 3. Trial by Fire

Having minimal exposure to black individuals except through television, the all-white jury swiftly handed down a verdict of guilty. Convicted on two counts of drug charges and sentenced to 16 years in prison, giving him only the hope of one day seeing the blue Ohio sky as a free man in eight years based on behavior.

When something unusual happened during the trial's sentencing phase, a deputy United States attorney surprised everyone when he made his presence known and asked to address the court abruptly.

Agitated, the judge demanded clarification on the topic. "Your honor, I am Deputy US Attorney Michael Hill, and this is a sensitive matter I am not at liberty to reveal the details of. All I can do is file an amicus brief for the defense. The guidance provided to me by my supervisors on this matter deals with sentencing."

"What's your recommendation for this man?"

"I recommend a six-year sentence, with the possibility of only serving four years for behavior."

The judge slammed his gavel, finalizing the decision. It marked the beginning of Jon's arduous journey into the depths of Hell. The bailiff clamped the cuffs on his wrists and locked them tight. The jarring movement of the transport made his head spin as he was hauled away, the rough handling adding to his disorientation. Redmond Prison, a cold and isolated place, was where he began his six-year sentence. Despite his circumstances, he held onto the hope of serving only four years based on behavior, if he was lucky.

Feeling devastated by his conviction and isolated in his cell, he sought solace in his thoughts and the predictable routine of three meals a day. It was warm in his cell due to a weak air conditioning unit. He sat on his bunk with his head in his hands, looking down at the ground. Sheriff's Deputy Ronnie Jackson walked by and stopped. "Convict, stand up." With his hand, he signaled for him to come closer to the bars.

"Young man, I called you convict on purpose. As far as the state of Ohio is concerned, you're a convicted felon now. As a black man in the United States of America, life is about how well you deal with setbacks and challenges. This is a nightmare of a challenge for you, one I wouldn't wish on any young man. I've got a few contacts with bailiffs. They told me you don't belong here, and you don't belong in this situation, but it is what it is. I don't offer advice to every young man who shows up here. For the next two weeks, I'll share advice to help you survive in Old Big Red. Find an O. G. The right ones will help you survive. Be a student, listen, and apply what they tell you. You'll be at the county jail for two more weeks until you're moved because something happened at Redmond Prison today."

Nine o'clock Saturday, the day after Jon's conviction, it was a picture-perfect day, with clear blue sky as far as the eye could see and the sun shining high. However, as Warden Hudson approached the prison gates, he knew something wasn't right after hearing the unmistakable blare of sirens. After recognizing his car, the guards at the gate disregarded standard procedures and opened the gate without checking his ID. For them to do that, the warden knew something was seriously wrong.

"Guys, what's up? What do you know?"

"Sir, two inmates are missing and assumed on the loose. You'll have more answers by the time you get to your office."

Sure enough, he saw a flurry of activity in the hallways. Immediately after stepping into his office, the deputy warden for operations and his secretary walked in.

"Sir, two inmates, both convicted killers, used a medical issue with a sergeant and a distracted corrections officer as an opportunity to escape. They picked the perfect time to jump into a trash bin before the mechanical arm picked it up and dumped it into a waiting truck. The officer in the box was laser-focused on the shaking and convulsions of the sergeant. The corrections officer struggled to maintain control of the other inmates alone, allowing the two inmates to slip out. Since they were understaffed, when a lieutenant with another sergeant finally regained control and a count was done, they knew they had a problem."

"Who figured out how they got loose?"

"Watching the cameras, the corrections officer in the box reviewed the video and said something strange had happened. There is no video of them getting into that trash bin, but he's sure that's how they got out because it's the only way they could have."

"Well, how does he know for sure they're in there?"

"He's convinced they're inside, claiming he saw the Axeman, Chris Davis, in the video. Almost forty years of experience working at Redmond Prison tells him those poor bastards are dead, or they're going to die soon. The truck had been gone too long to have them come back, so I called Sheriff Bradshaw. He's sending deputies to the dump site to intercept it. We'll know something soon, and you'll get a call from him."

As time passed, Warden Hudson paced, trying to distract himself with other things, knowing the situation was out of his hands. After half an hour passed, the phone rang.

"Warden, I've got some convenient news for you and some tragic news for you."

"Tom, I appreciate your office helping with this. Let me hear it."

"Well, Warden, the convenient news is we found your missing inmates and they're in custody. The tragic news is they're both dead and a little thinner than they used to be. By thinner, I mean those poor bastards unintentionally found the worst way to die. The truck's compressor flattened the poor bastards like pancakes. When we opened the back door of that dump truck, a mangled-together mess of flesh and broken bone fell out of it. Then, a swarm of flies descended, which easily made this the worst thing I've seen in my entire career. It's a bloody mess out here, and the county coroner is coming soon.

"The cause of death is likely due to compression by the dump truck. A preliminary ID based on the pictures your deputy warden provided is impossible. Somebody planned this based on a 911-tip from the driver who was supposed to drive that truck. He was smart enough not to risk ending up as an inmate in a prison we pay him to haul trash out of. We've only made a preliminary ID based on the standard-issue prison orange they were both wearing. One of your inmates is missing an arm, likely severed on a sharp object near the body. You should try to get this classified as an in-custody death to avoid having to testify in front of ODRC."

Dealing with the ordeal of the trial took its toll on Jon, so much so that his eyes felt like weights were on them, forcing them closed. During the bus ride to Redmond, the heat caused him to fall into a deeper and more peaceful sleep with each passing moment. The stranger and more realistic his dream became, the more confused and disoriented he felt. He realized it might have been a dream, but it also may have been a premonition of the danger to come. In the dream, he was riding on a bus that lost its tire. It careened to the left off the side of the road, crashing through a guardrail and rolling to a stop in a nearby lake.

Shocked by what happened and disoriented, instead of water, a flood of blood like a tsunami rushed in. Briefly panicking until controlling his fear enough to keep his wits about him, he struggled to overcome the dismay and sheer horror of what he saw and felt. Then he realized the other inmates on the bus with him were dead.

Their faces were pale and haggard, and their clothes seemed worn, partially decomposing, with their bones exposed. Despite outward appearances of being alive, their inner essence felt lifeless and devoid of energy. He recognized this was a dream, but he was smart enough to know it symbolized the death and danger he was heading into. It was a clear warning that he would be wise to prepare himself for.

He tried to calm his nerves when the bus got so cold that he could see his breath as it left his mouth. As the condensation accumulated, it fogged up the windows next to him. To add to the strangeness and creepiness of the whole affair, a woman appeared in front of him. She looked at him for a while, staring before asking, "What is your name?"

"My name is Jon."

"Jon, my name is Helen Catherine Bauer. I was born in 1909 and died in 1950." Just as she uttered that statement, a hole appeared in her head which looked terrifyingly like a gunshot wound. The gaping hole, along with a corresponding exit wound, allowed him to see through her head to the seat behind her. He decided to listen to what she had to say, even if it was an odd conversation with a ghost.

"Young man, you don't belong where you're going. I know this because I'm the wife of the former warden. Obey the rules of Redmond, the written and unwritten ones.

"Rule number one: The Axeman of Redmond can only take souls stained by the blood of others.

"Rule number two: The ladies of Redmond deserve respect and will not tolerate disrespect.

"Rule number three: Redmond is a spiritual beacon to ghosts. It attracts them and strengthens them.

"Rule number four: Stay strong, show no weakness while striving to overcome all fear.

"Rule number five: When confronted with a life-or-death situation behind the walls, the law of the jungle applies. You either kill them, or they will surely kill you.

"Obey these rules and the additional ones you'll learn when you arrive. Do this, and you may survive the inmates during the day and the restless spirits who roam the prison halls at night; you may just live long enough to see your release date. I wish you well, Jon, and good luck, because you'll need it."

With that, she faded and then disappeared.

He woke up from the strangest dream he'd ever had to the nightmare that was now his life. Any average person would have a reason to go back to sleep. However, he knew he was always better off facing his problems. So as the bus pulled up to the Redmond Prison's reception intake area, he took a long look around. It was a modern facility, even though nothing was unique about the new prison compared to the old.

The Redmond Reformatory cast an enormous shadow on the entire area. Even though the old building was close to the new one, soil and a spiritual link connecting them were the key to understanding both. While this connection was essential, the intake process revealed the most crucial evidence. All those who went through it received a medical evaluation to determine if there was a need for medication and to identify any conditions preventing an inmate from remaining at the facility.

During this process, inmates have gone crazy, swearing ghosts were standing next to them, naked. Another inmate freaked out, screaming that an inmate was getting shanked in the shower's corner. For Jon, it was the most embarrassing part of the intake process. Stripped down to his birthday suit and searched to identify any attempt to smuggle contraband into the facility. After enduring that process, the weird part occurred. It was then that he knew he was in a strange place. He thought he saw someone standing next to him, only to turn his head for a moment and then back, and the person was gone.

Guards handed him prison-issued clothes along with other new arrivals. The speed of the process was outstanding, efficient, and terrible. Then they were all taken to a room with desks and a single book in front of each chair, the Holy Bible with a black cover and gold letters on it, and told to sit down. After ten to fifteen minutes, some members of the group got restless. A man with dark, gradually graying hair walked into the room. Three to five minutes passed without a word, as the man deliberately took his time to get a sense of the room. Then he finally spoke.

"Gentlemen, I'm going to give it to you straight. Most of you belong here, and if you're being honest with yourself, you know this. A small few of you don't belong here, and you know who you are. However, what makes all of you the same is that for now, this prison will be the home none of you ever wanted. Oh, by the way, my name is Michael MacPherson, Bishop MacPherson to you, and I recommend the book in front of you becomes your new best friend. Why? Because this will be the weirdest place you will ever spend time in. And if you say, 'Bishop, this is a state facility, isn't there separation of church and state?' I'll answer that like this: The church, your religious beliefs, and the state are separate, embodied in the warden and this prison. We will not force religion on you here. However, that term, as you know it, doesn't mean jack here. That's why I said I *recommend* the book become your new best friend. There may come a time when the Holy Bible saves your life.

Gentlemen, I told you I would give it to you straight. Well, here it is. Redmond Prison is a haunted place in every definition of the word haunted."

The room grew silent. Then, after hearing a few giggles and many men busting out laughing, Bishop MacPherson repeated his warning.

"Gentlemen, heed my warning, because some of you won't live long enough to reach your release dates or see the blue sky outside this prison."

Jon studied the body language, tone, and firmness of the man standing before him and took the warning to heart with a wait-and-see approach. *What the hell am I in for in this place?* As Bishop MacPherson left, a guard reappeared and ordered them to get up and walk a line in an orderly fashion, as though they were in kindergarten. Then the guards separated them from the group and took them to another prison area that few inmates ever saw: the warden's office.

The warden of Redmond Prison, Allen Hudson, was a quirky guy. This was a man responsible for a prison with a capacity of 2,523 inmates—the actual count fluctuated somewhat, higher or lower at any time. And the prison also had the unusual reputation of being haunted.

The guard escorting them explained that Warden Hudson did not meet with all the new arrivals, only the select few deemed special cases. And this group were among those outstanding cases, placed in the easy-to-deal-with category of inmates. Sitting in the secretary's office leading to his office was nothing special; there were a lot of pictures to look at that revealed some of the history of the original prison and elements of the new one. Some of the men went in and didn't stay long; others stayed for almost half an hour.

The waiting room had two portraits of Civil War colonels—Colonel Daniel French on one wall, Colonel Marcus Spiegel on the other. The gold label read *120th Ohio Infantry Regiment 1862*. Fascinated by the history, despite his circumstances for being there, Jon couldn't help touching it. The moment he did, it gave him an odd and painful shock, causing him to flap his hand in pain, which attracted the attention of the warden's secretary.

"Young man, what's your name?"

"Jon Bowman, Mrs. Wilson." He got her name from the nameplate on her desk.

Upon entering, Jon observed pictures of the warden's family and a younger version of him with Labrador retrievers as a child. This was along with the enormous black and white portrait of a former warden standing near the entrance of the old Reformatory with two dogs, a German shepherd and a Doberman pinscher. The picture gave him the creeps; it felt like the man in it was looking at him. Despite being positioned behind the warden's desk and a little to the left, it was inescapable to anyone walking into the office.

The warden reviewed an open file with two pictures as he entered the room. "Jon Bowman, your booking picture suggests you're out of place. My gut tells me you don't belong here. People here usually have long criminal histories. Your file has no criminal history. Where in the hell did you get two prescription-sized bottles of Roxy from in the first place?" Jon looked confused, with no clue what the warden was talking about. "Young man, I'll be clearer. Where in the hell did you get two prescription-sized bottles of Oxy? Opioids? There's an epidemic of overdoses in this state with that stuff."

Jon responded in the only way he could: he told the truth. "Sir, this is a nightmare I'm going through, and I'm just trying to figure out how to survive. I'll say the same thing I told my lawyer and the court in the court records and filings. I know about Mary Jane, but I don't know jack about opioids. How they found their way into my possession may be due to a suspect traffic cop. I don't belong here, but I'm determined to serve the time I've got to do without this destroying the rest of my life."

"Mr. Bowman, in your file, there's something unusual. There's a friend of the court filing by a deputy US attorney on your behalf. This isn't normal; it suggests a criminal investigation they couldn't disclose then. The traffic cop you mentioned might be under investigation. Don't forget the phrase 'the fruit of the poisonous tree.' The DA must review any cases touched by a corrupt cop. From now on, until you're released, you will be called Inmate 70594. Stay strong, stay on the right side of the rules of this institution. Stay alive, find older inmates who will give you advice for surviving this place, and heed my advice as well as theirs. Also, there is no shame in listening to and heeding the advice of Bishop MacPherson. This place has spirits roaming the halls, despite the giggles and laughs you may have heard before you got to me."

With that said, the conversation ended with a quick signal to the guard for one inmate to be ushered out and another to be ushered in.

Assigned to Unit 2, cell block C, house number fifty-two, Jon walked with a pile of linen, a pillow, and a small box with legal documents, along with other personal effects, through an open corridor. He was a little nervous walking through the cell blocks, as screams echoed throughout. Inmates screamed, "Fresh fish, fresh fish!" from behind bars to a raucous volume. Determined to show no fear, he reacted with a stone face, reaching deep into his anger, pain, and outright hatred of Officer Donavon and the judge who made this stay possible. Other inmates walking behind him made the mistake of showing fear and emotion where all could see. One made the worst mistake of crying like a baby, like a little bitch.

The other inmates seemed to take mental note of which new arrivals showed emotion and, even worse, fear. Jon saw that they showed these poor souls not an ounce of sympathy or mercy. Here, he learned his first lesson. The first rule behind the walls is to show no fear because fear equals weakness.

Upon arriving at his cell, he discovered he was very fortunate because he had no one else in it with him. Another welcome surprise was his neighbor, a kindred spirit and familiar face.

"Deon Soto, good to see you, old man. Jon looked at his hair with a slight smile.

"I know, it was a different color at the county jail the last time you saw me. Been concealing it for years while trying to fight a losing war with my hairline. That's combined with nightmares and a freak diagnosis of stage one diabetes." Deon motioned him to come a little closer, then whispered near his ear, "Do exactly what you are doing now. Show no fear, no emotion, and above all, don't shed a tear or make a sound for the rest of the night. If you survive your first night on the inside, we'll talk in the chow hall. Tomorrow begins your prison education. Get some rest, you're going to need it."

Deon motioned for him to keep walking as a man behind him said, "Hey, man, quit holding up the show."

Jon turned and faced forward while looking at the number above his cell, C fifty-two. *So, this will be home for a couple of years.* He went inside. If being in prison and deprived of his freedom hadn't dawned on him before, it sure as hell did when the cell door clanged shut and the lights flickered off.

The following day, as the sun rose, the guards assembled for the morning count that would become a part of Jon's new daily routine. They positioned themselves to eyeball each inmate and hear each one during roll call to ensure all were present and accounted for. Jon observed that any system, large or small, must be consistent, efficient, effective, and absolutely work. In a single file line that made him have flashbacks to elementary school, they headed toward the chow hall for breakfast. After some confusion, he caught a glimpse of Deon and, with a head nod, followed him to the table where they took their seats.

A man somewhat older than Deon named Freddie C. P. Castile was the O.G. of their group. His name, C. P., was in honor of Charlie Parker, a well-known jazz musician, a man who his parents had high esteem for because he helped create the mood that made it possible for him to be conceived. The elder man was the first to speak, looking at his tray with confusion. "Hey, guys, what the hell is this? It's supposed to be food, but it may take a police crime lab to verify it. So, Deon, who's this young man you've got hanging out with us this morning?"

"Well, this young man I met after I retired from a life of crime."

"Deon, how can you claim you retired from a life of crime?"

"Easy. If you end up in prison and you're not likely to get out before you die, then as far as I'm concerned, you retired from a life of crime."

Freddie smiled. "Young man, that's why we keep him around."

"Anyway, he caught a case for opioid possession. He's here and doesn't belong here because some a-hole cop planted pills on him to get rid of them. Then he got sentenced to prison time despite it being a first offense by a judge to get kickbacks to meet the prison capacity quota. Freddie, this young man needs a prison education if he's going to survive this place."

"Why have you taken an interest in him?"

"At the time, he needed a friend and guide to help him deal with this screwed-up system, and I needed a contact on the outside. The contact is a lawyer, so he can't do anything illegal."

"Young man, try to get your lawyer to bring you some nicotine patches. You may not smoke, but it's a commodity that serves as currency in here."

Jon nodded, agreeing to the arrangement.

Freddie then looked directly at Jon. "Listen carefully to everything I'm about to say. These are the rules that have helped me survive this place. You can call them Freddie's Prison Rules to live by.

"Rule number one: Respect other inmates' property.

"Rule number two: Don't get involved with a gang.

"Rule number three: Don't do drugs in here. They dull the senses and slow reaction time.

"Rule number four: Don't gamble. Owing too much on the outside is not good, but it's worse in here.

"Rule number five, my most important rule of all: Don't succumb to the love that I'm even afraid to name."

"The what?!"

"Do not succumb to the love that I dare not name."

After looking confused, someone eventually asked Jon, "What is your favorite movie?"

Responding fast, he said, "*Star Wars* is my favorite movie."

Nodding their heads in agreement, everyone at the table smiled. Then Deon told him to turn his head to the left while concealing who or what he was looking at. Once he saw the gay inmate twisting while walking like a woman to attract attention, he instantly realized what they were talking about. Shaking his head slowly, his reaction was hilarious, repeating the same thing over and over again. "Oh hell no, oh hell no, that's not me. I love women, and if I can survive this place, I want to get back to being with women."

Freddie responded by saying, "Good, very good. Padawan, do not succumb to the dark side. Stay strong in the Force."

Everyone at the table busted out laughing, almost to the point of tears.

"Rule number six: Do not talk to the guards.

"Rule number seven: Stay busy and focused on positive things.

"Rule number eight: Get God in your life.

"Rule number nine: The ghosts of Redmond can only hurt you if you give them the power to do so. Here, they can only hurt you through your fear."

#

Freddie's prison rules to live by became seared into his brain and applied over the next three months until committed to memory. During this time, he observed noticeable changes in his friend Deon that he couldn't ignore. His diabetes, combined with other health issues, was causing him serious health complications that weakened his ability to survive. Jon tried to help in small ways when possible. However, in prison, inmates seize on any perceived weakness, and then other inmates would pounce in a shark-like feeding frenzy.

This came to a head one morning when he noticed Deon was excessively sweating, even though it wasn't hot or even warm.

Freddie asked, "Hey, Deon, you alright?" As the group elder, he somehow compelled the others to be honest.

Even though he wanted to lie, Deon couldn't. "No, no, I'm not." He held his head in pain from a throbbing headache and dizziness. "I think my blood pressure is higher than it should be, and my sugar is low. I'm seeing things that aren't there, but they seem so real."

"Tell us what you're seeing."

"There's a man with a gray suit standing in front of what looks like a castle with two dogs. A Doberman pinscher on one side and a German shepard on the other. They're just looking at me, staring. The man doesn't say a word as drool drips from the dogs' mouths." Deon could hear a low-pitched growl that got louder. What really stood out was the weird sound the dogs were making, a growl that seemed to echo as though the dogs had been dead a long time.

Freddie looked at him for a few minutes, noticing that he looked unsteady in his seat, to the point of almost falling out of it. Jon offered help with his balance. "You need to go to the infirmary." Freddie looked over at Kenneth Eastman, a man everyone respected because he was doing 25 years on a wrap he maintained he never committed, and the evidence suggested he maybe didn't commit.

Kenny motioned for the guard. As the guard walked over, Freddie asked Deon another question. "Deon, when you first arrived, did you go to Warden Hudson's office?"

"No, I went to Deputy Warden Sheldon Porter's office."

When the guys heard this, they all bowed in sadness. They knew something he didn't realize: he was being tormented by ghosts.

After Deon left, Jon immediately asked, What do you know that you're not saying?"

"Young man, did you talk to Warden Hudson when you first arrived?"

"Yes, I did. The conversation was mainly about my record. We talked about the fact that I had no criminal history and how his gut feeling told him I might not belong here. That was along with what he probably told all inmates to do, which was to follow the rules."

"This is important. What do you remember about the warden's office? What stood out?"

"Well, what stood out to me was that giant picture of the former warden standing next to a Doberman pinscher and a German shepherd. I only noticed because I love dogs.

"However, now that I think about it, I remember another picture. A picture of a younger version of the warden standing next to a Labrador retriever."

Freddie said, "This is bad," and the others nodded in agreement. "Use the organ between your ears and your critical thinking skills you developed in college. Warden Hudson loves dogs too, so much so that he instituted a program to allow inmates to train seeing-eye dogs for the blind. You haven't been here long enough to know that. He's a good man trying to do a tough job in a state that doesn't want to spend money on rehabilitation. That's the one rehabilitation program he could get money out of the legislature to fund. Hell, how could any politician be against blind people? I say that to say this: There is no way in hell Warden Hudson would meet with an inmate convicted of dog fighting. That's why Deon met with the deputy warden instead. I may prove to be a prophet, but I think ghosts will torture our friend until he suffers an unfortunate premature death."

Chapter 4. Fresh Fish

The next day, most of the guys were curious to see if Deon had returned from the infirmary. When they saw him leave his cell, they were visibly relieved, but that relief was short-lived once they looked closer. Deon seemed nervous, fidgeting. Worst of all, his heart was racing like it was about to jump out of his chest. Jon was right there, trying to look straight ahead while waiting for his name. However, Deon was looking down toward the left instead of facing forward. As the senior guard called names, he failed to hear or notice Deon's words until it was too late.

"They're going to get me, they're going to get me!" Deon screamed. As the count stopped, most of the guys on the block looked to see what he was talking about. They looked at him, then in the direction of his gaze, only to see nothing but the wall. However, what he was seeing was a ghost. Either that or a very real-looking hallucination of a man with a Doberman pinscher and a German shepard growling at him. In total terror and fear, Deon broke the line, violating the warning given to all inmates. Such an offense would ordinarily result in time in the hole. However, at that moment, Deon didn't seem to care, because he was running for his life, sweating profusely until his shirt was soaked. It was like time slowed down, like he was running in slow motion as guys on the line, upon realizing what was happening, turned to stop him, only a step too slow.

Deon ran out of real estate, clipping the guard railing while look-ing back at whatever he thought was chasing him. He flipped off the balcony, amounting to a three-story drop, where he landed hard awk-wardly, breaking a rib. However, we would learn later that the worst damage he suffered was to his internal organs.

To the shock of everyone, he survived the fall. Upon hearing the reports of how high the fall was, the infirmary immediately had an ambulance on standby to rush him to the nearby hospital. There, they discovered the extent of the internal damage. The broken rib bruised his heart and punctured his lungs, causing him to bleed in-ternally. Upon arriving at the hospital, the medical team prepped him for surgery. The doctors tried to make him as comfortable as possi-ble while notifying his mother he likely would not survive the night. Upon hearing this, she took a moment to cry, then wiped the tears from her face and entered Deon's room with the appearance of every-thing being normal. Like the strong woman she was, she stayed by his side to the very end.

When word got back to the guys that Deon had passed away, it was as if dark clouds of grief and sadness descended on the table. His loss was profound, and no one felt it more than Jon. Deon had helped him at a critical time. Maybe he was afraid of what the nightmares re-vealed. He may have had premonitions about his death that he knew he couldn't avoid. Maybe by helping Jon, he would find salvation. By saving his life, Deon thought he could save his own soul. In the end, who knows the reason? All he knew was the man and his impact.

Jon never cried when he lost his father, who died a few months af-ter gaining his freedom. He'd never gotten the chance to know him or have a relationship with him. He never cried when those assholes convicted him of a crime he never committed. However, at that mo-ment, his future was uncertain. How would he survive in Redmond without his mentor? His future was the most unknown it had ever been. Feeling like he was under a fog of uncertainty, he took a sheet of paper and wrote to his mother, begging her not to visit him in the hole he now found himself in. He needed to stay mentally tough and physically strong to survive, and he knew he couldn't do that if he saw her. He also knew the toll visiting his father in prison took on her, dealing with severe depression afterward. That night, after lights out, Jon sat alone in his cell and quietly cried until he ran out of tears.

The following day at breakfast, everyone was unusually silent. Losing Deon shook the guys. No one had realized the comic relief he brought to start each day, along with the funny phrases that would be stuck in everybody's head all day, making life bearable in this place.

Freddie, as usual, was the first to speak. "I have no one to play chess with now. Whatever the man's sins, hopefully he's in a better place and at peace."

"Freddie, you play chess?" Jon asked.

"Yes, I do. What about you?"

"I played it a little with my grandpa a long time ago. He told me it was a thinking man's game and encouraged me to learn it."

"Well, well." Freddie leaned forward and smiled. "Young man, your grandfather was an intelligent man, and he's right. It is a thinking man's game. From now on, you and I will play three chess games, the best of two. Simultaneously, you will receive continuing education. Deon had asked me to look out for you for as long as possible if anything terrible happened to him."

When Freddie made a statement, it carried respect from all the guys. Everyone would honor his word. "Men, this young man is now my chess partner. As a result, he's now our responsibility, because I need a chess partner, and he needs friends to help him survive. Sometimes I've helped you, and you've helped me. Share what you've learned about this place to help him survive in memory of Deon. Because we were the only friends Deon had, I'm going to ask Bishop

MacPherson if we can have something for him. Maybe it will get us out of our cells for a few hours."

All the guys nodded in agreement. Then Jon reminded everyone it was fresh fish day, when new arrivals would appear. Everyone wondered what new characters would show up on the block.

Listening to guards gossiping about a new guy, they got their answer. A man who was just convicted of murder; he was guilty of domestic violence against his wife for years, then finally grew tired of her and killed her, stabbing her with an eight-inch chef's knife with a somewhat serrated blade. The inconsiderate bastard left her in a pool of blood on their kitchen floor. The cops arrested him at a nearby bar, drinking a beer with her blood still on his clothes. When the police asked him why he killed her, he answered, "It's cheaper to kill her than divorce her." The depressing part was what led to his wife's demise: the argument they had wasn't about him having an affair with a woman, but with a man, a fact that didn't go over well with the women on the jury. So, in the last week of April, Devin Patrick became Inmate 60540 after a jury convicted him of murder and domestic violence with only ten minutes of deliberation.

Devin was aware of his impending conviction. Unbeknown to him, however, was what the ladies of Redmond had planned for him. Their punishment would be creative, much worse than anything he dished out. They regularly devised innovative methods of torture for inmates who had blood on their hands and souls. These ladies of Redmond Prison had less tolerance for disrespect in life, and zero tolerance for it in death. So, to no one's surprise, the oddest thing happened in a segregated unit of Redmond while Devin was alone in a cell. Blurred figures appeared, figures initially that only Devin could see. The ghosts of Dovie Dean, Cassidy Holloway, Phoebe Wise, and Carrie Glattke. Usually, the world of the dead couldn't affect the world of the living, but there were exceptions.

As the figures surrounding him came into focus, what he saw terrified him. Four women, deathly pale with dirty brunette hair, stood around him. Their demeanor left no doubt in his mind that they weren't friendly, and within minutes, they started going in on him. One ghost hit him in the eye with enough power to stun him. He stood there, temporarily paralyzed, as if weights were holding his feet to the ground. He was helpless, forced to take what they were dishing out. Another ghost socked him in the gut, knocking the wind out of him. He keeled over in pain when a third ghost scratched his face, drawing blood. The fourth ghost scratched him on the arm, also drawing blood. Then they all punched him repeatedly for nearly half an hour.

The guards assigned to this unit had to do a welfare check every hour, primarily for documentation purposes to ensure inmates didn't commit suicide. A recently hired guard, after making his rounds, eyeballed each inmate. He stopped to peek through the small window of Devin's cell, and for nearly an hour, he watched in astonishment the crazy scene playing out before hastily radioing control. "Sue, Sue, are you seeing this?"

Susan was one of the few women working in Redmond Prison. She responded as calm as a pond on a clear sunny day and as relaxed as an ice cube. "Do not enter that cell. Observe, but do not respond until the beating appears over with. You can take him to the infirmary *only* when the beating is finished. You're new here, so you don't know why we do things the way we do. The inmate you're guarding? No one beat him up. I've got no video in this control room that shows anyone entering his cell beating him up. There's a form titled *Beat Up by Nobody* to fill out." The radio grew silent for a few moments. "The inmate you're looking at deserves what he's getting. I'll need your statement for that form before your shift ends."

"Ten-four."

The best description of Devin would be that he was a lifelong member of the Slap-a-Ho Tribe. His grandfather was an abuser of women. His father was an abuser of women. Devin, however, was different. He was much worse. He had the unique character flaw of being an abuser of women and men. This made him an equal-opportunity piece of crap that was despised by the homicide detectives working his wife's case, as well as both attorneys handling his trial. The prosecutor and his defense lawyer, when they discovered he was abusing his wife *and* his gay lover... Well, if Devin somehow got trapped in a building that was on fire, both attorneys would sing joyfully, "The roof, the roof, the roof is on fire. We don't need no water. Let the motherfucker burn."

Before he arrived at Redmond, Devin received premonitions that his stay would be unusual, warnings that he simply ignored. He then received premonitions in the form of dreams while asleep in jail. On the bus ride to prison after his conviction, one memorable dream started serenely enough. The closer he got to Redmond Prison, the stronger the power of the spirits trapped and concentrated there became. These dreams may have started peacefully, but they didn't end that way. In time, his dreams would turn into nightmares.

It was as if someone pressed a rewind button in his brain, and his life rewound to when he killed his wife. He watched helplessly as the lifeforce drained from her body along with her blood onto the kitchen floor. It started like all the previous arguments, but with one difference: a brief fit of rage that seemed to accumulate over time until released in an uncontrolled burst. He grabbed a nearby butcher knife in what seemed like an out-of-body experience. He watched helplessly as the knife seemed to merge with his wife's stomach.

It was a tragic and unnecessary loss of life over an argument about coming home late. An argument where a woman suspected infidelity even if she didn't know for sure. She caught him in bed with another man six months before her demise, but she tried hard to forgive and understand. As a result, she knew her husband was an unfaithful dog.

It was a terrible situation, and what made matters worse was that he was violent. However, for some reason she just couldn't take the next step and leave.

He was exhausted from the inmate intake process and the sit-and-wait time wasted before arriving at his assigned cell. He sat on his bunk, realizing he had a cell alone. So, on the first night Devin spent in prison at the Redmond Prison, he took the experience in. Falling asleep, he would soon have an unwanted visitor. A slender, rather petite woman with brunette hair, a classy style, and a muted demeanor that he recognized. Sensing it was a dream, he rushed to the corner of his cell, still on the bed in fear, until she spoke.

"My name is Helen, and this will be your only warning. The ladies of Redmond Prison know who you are. We know your heart and find it vile and devoid of compassion. You mistreated and murdered your wife and mistreated your gay lover. You won't leave this place alive." Then she repeated her warning, this time screaming with an eerie echo, "You will not leave this place alive! You will die here!"

An average person would've responded with a profound sense of fear. However, in Devin, there was only fear of what she could do to him. He woke up from his dream covered in sweat and looked around to confirm what he already knew: he was alone. He put the warning out of his mind with no sense of right or wrong, as is the way of sociopaths. The days became weeks and months until the warning faded from his memory, allowing him to revert to past habits.

Getting adjusted to life behind the walls, along with being deprived of access to the company of women, after denying his true feelings for years, he was now free to indulge in the love he denied himself. He met Javier during a brief conversation near the showers after he overheard two other inmates discussing how they would pass him around like a plaything. He felt compelled to warn him not to go in there alone, sensing he wasn't as strong as he needed to be to survive behind the walls. In this young man, he found a prime target to be turned. Inmate 50456, Javier Rodriguez, became the primary target of his focus and affection. Devin was a predator, and Javier was his prey.

Javier's questioning of his sexuality months before his conviction of grand theft and evading arrest made him a confused and vulnerable young man in a place filled with predators. This made it clear to prison officials that they had to grant him protected status, just like the other inmates of a similar persuasion. This further made him a target of attention. Seeing Javier's vulnerability, Devin offered something he needed: protection. That got him in the door, and as time passed, their relationship developed and flourished. But like the snake he was, Devin would eventually shed the false skin he was wearing, and Javier would see his true nature.

Meanwhile, Jon was receiving a rather thorough prison education from Freddie during their daily chess games. On this occasion, Freddie perched on the top row of the bleacher with an unobstructed 360-degree view of the rec yard, a fact that was not lost on either of them. The guys on both sides still flanked him, adding additional protection. He asked a profound question while sitting there. "Who do you see when you wake up and look in the mirror? I know you see a man. But what kind of man is the question? I see a black man in the mirror. You see those Skinheads over there? Behind these walls, never side with Skinheads against the brothers.

"Suppose you were on the outside and took the side of a hate group against the black community. You'd be a traitor, your name dragged through the mud, and you'd be denounced as anything but a child of God. The whispers would follow you like shadows. Treat them like they're oil and you're water. We just don't mix."

Jon nodded, signaling he understood, and the game went on.

Devin walked by, hastily following Javier until he caught up with him, and they started talking. The conversation seemed cordial initially, but it soon turned as raised voices carried within earshot of the chess game. No one knew what the conversation was about. However, it got Kenny's attention, and he seemed suspiciously interested in the soap opera that was playing out before his eyes.

He sat up when Devin punched Javier in the face, leaving a visible bruise. After Devin walked away, Javier stood there, somewhat shocked about what happened and confused about how to deal with it. Observing this play out before his eyes, Kenny, now standing up, broke one of the unwritten prison rules: Mind your own business. Something buried deep in his past compelled him to say something, possibly the years of child abuse at the hands of his father as well as the years of watching domestic violence against his mother until he was old enough to threaten to kill his father, forcing him to leave.

"Hey man, you alright?"

Reluctantly, and after a few minutes, the answer came. "Yes, I'm alright." Then Javier walked away as though nothing happened.

This same soap opera played out in the same spot on two different occasions. Kenny took a particular interest during the third incident. Devin hit Javier harder than ever as the anger built up inside of him reached its climax, and he could no longer contain it. Javier took such a beating that it eventually got the attention of the other guys, disrupting the daily chess game.

The general rule in prison was to mind your business and avoid other inmates' affairs. That usually served the inmate who abides by this rule well. Kenny just couldn't let it go, so he waited until Devin walked away and motioned for Javier to come closer. It was the most emotional any of the guys had ever seen Kenny get. His patience must have run out, because he ripped into Javier.

"What in the hell are you doing letting him treat you like that? It's not my place to get in your business, but you have a big problem. I've seen his kind before. He's from the Slap-A-Ho Tribe. If you don't figure out a better way to deal with him, he's going to kill you."

Javier tried to defend Devin, raising the point that he would always come back later and apologize, saying how sorry he was. Kenny, in a flash, shot down that response.

"That's how all abusers attempt to get back in the graces of the people they abuse. But the treatment never seems to stop until someone's dead, usually the person being abused. My old man was just like him. He used to beat my mother. For years, I used to watch her cry. I saw her bruises. And I watched, waiting and praying for the day when I was big enough to take him. Do you know how messed up it is to think about killing your father? Smelling the alcohol on him and simultaneously watching him hit the woman who brought you into the world before saying enough is enough, I'm now big enough to take him. Do you know how messed up it is to beat your father to within an inch of his life? Threatening to kill him if he ever lays a hand on your mother again? My friend, that's the messed-up thing about domestic violence. Not wanting to see your father leave, but knowing he has to go to save your mother's life, while praying to God you become nothing like him."

The guys sat there speechless, just looking at Kenny. "What in the hell are these arguments about anyway?"

"I overheard a conversation between Devin and someone else I don't know about a way to smuggle drugs into the prison."

"How?"

"They'll get guys to swallow balloons and see if they can corrupt prison staff while using new tech drones too, but mainly as a distraction."

"Drones won't work because the range doesn't reach far enough yet; someone has tried it already. And the guards in the towers are excellent shots. They'll easily shoot them down."

"That's what I tried to tell Devin. He told me it would work and told me to mind my business. My celly thinks he's dangerous and warned me not to talk about his plans, and he also warned me he might try to hurt me."

Meanwhile, in the second cell near the corner of C-block, a white-haired fifty-year-old man named Eric Hays sat on his bunk contemplating the direction of his life. He was suffering from severe depression while wavering in deciding whether to end his life when a chill filled the air, the cell turned cold, and the ghost of Ester Foster appeared.

Esther was a black woman who had spent time at Redmond. It seemed she had a bit of a temper, which led to her killing someone and getting sent to Redmond, only to make the same mistake and take another life while incarcerated. This resulted in her being hanged. Even though she died, her death proved only to be the beginning of her punishment. Ester's soul was ripped from her body and condemned to haunt the cold, echoing halls of Redmond Prison, forever trapped within its stone walls, searching for an inmate weak in spirit whose soul she could steal.

She found her mark in Eric Hays, an older man convicted of a white-collar crime. His fraud involved a Ponzi scam to inflate the stock price of what he knew to be a worthless company, only to dump it at the best time for him and at the worst time for his shareholders. Shareholders who, it turned out, could not afford the loss, resulting in the suicides of three people who lost their life savings. He sat on that bunk with a rope made out of the linen from his bed sheets wondering whether he should take his own life. Sheets that he should not have had for the very risk of taking such a drastic step. After thinking of his family, he stepped away from the ledge. He knew he deserved to be where he was because he hurt people. So, after staring at the rope tied into knots in sections to ensure it would be strong enough to hold his weight, he rolled it up, stuffed it under his mattress, then lay back down and fell asleep.

Ester's plan changed when the Axeman appeared. He was a ghost other ghosts feared, and once she saw him, she disappeared. While

Eric was asleep, the Axeman appeared and laid his axe on the ground with the handle leaning against the foot of the bed. Suddenly, in a flash, he possessed Eric's body, using it like a puppet and taking unconscious control over it. He forced him to sit up and remove the rope from underneath his mattress. Then, like a rag doll, he carefully threw the rope around the mounted pole connecting the two beds, putting it around his neck. Simultaneously, he sat awkwardly on his cell's bottom bunk bed to support his weight, until sliding off, supported by nothing.

The Axeman wasn't sure if the rope or the mount would support his weight, but ultimately it didn't matter. He had only one goal: to take Eric's soul. The Axeman needed tons of energy to take over someone, so he'd only leave when they were almost dead. Weak and trembling, Eric awoke to the chafing rope and struggled in vain to free himself. His face turned increasingly red with every minute as sweat soaked his t-shirt until the rope effectively choked his carotid arteries, slowing the blood flow to his brain, starving the oxygen and the life out of him until he was very much dead, eventually allowing the weight of his body to break his neck.

The Axeman was there when his soul left his body, salivating over the chance to absorb it. Even though other inmates walked past Eric's lifeless body, no one seemed to notice what happened. Not until Devin walked around the corner and noticed something odd out of the corner of his eye. Then, a black woman stood in front of him, deathly pale. She just glared at him, not saying a word until she pointed to the left and uttered a phrase that terrified him: "You're next." She disappeared moments later.

Devin looked into the cell, horrified by what he saw, and screams for dear life until a guard showed up, shoved him aside, and promptly ordered to move along. The guard was careful not to enter the cell, leaning against the nearby wall. Devin's cell was two cells down next to Eric's, so he pointed the other guards in the right direction while somewhat bending forward, trying not to throw up and feeling the nausea well up inside of him.

When a man's in prison, he'd do almost anything to waste time. It's just the way of things. The morning after Eric Hays took his life—or rather, when the Axeman made him take his life—the rumor mill ran rampant about the unusual circumstances of his death. Jon, Freddie, and the guys stood outside their cell with the men of C-block. The men were nervous as well as curious. Nervous about why Eric died and interested in learning how he died. Simultaneously, many guys consciously avoided Devin like the plague out of fear that they might suffer the same fate, mainly because many of the guys were a little superstitious. It seemed living in a haunted prison would do that to a man.

Everyone went to the cafeteria to get breakfast when the daily count ended. While in the kitchen, trustees—inmates trusted with the job of preparing the food for the inmates—scurried under pressure to get food out on time. Generally, they were under the close supervision of the guards, unless they were distracted by their daily routine. Something strange happened when someone improperly stored a chemical solution near a whole pan of powdered eggs. Dovie Dean appeared. Dovie, when among the land of the living, made the cold-blooded decision to poison her husband for failing to fulfill his husbandly duties. Later, she would face conviction and spend time at Redmond until authorities executed her by the electric chair. She haunted inmates who failed to meet her standards of character. Through sheer force of will, Dovie knocked over the bottle of chemical cleaning solution improperly stored on a shelf above a food prep area.

The container was half-full, and after emptying, it fell conveniently to the floor and rolled out of sight. When an inmate reappeared, he cooked the contaminated eggs, placed them in a foil pan, and took them to the line to serve. Meanwhile, the guys went to their seats with their breakfast trays.

"What do you know? What did you find out about how Eric died?" One guy answered he knew Devin found his body hanging from the bed frame. Everyone quietly stared at Devin as he walked by with a giant scoop of contaminated eggs. Guys hastily switched tables when he sat down, isolating him intentionally. Devin looked around, and with a raised voice and a forceful tone, he said, "You guys act like I killed him. I only found him." Javier showed up and quietly explained to him that living in a haunted prison makes guys paranoid that they could be next. He also encouraged him to calm down as attention returned to their meals and conversations.

Chapter 5. Consecrated by Blood

A few minutes passed, and the contaminated eggs slowly made their way to the digestive systems of the inmates who consumed them. The effects of the poisoned eggs manifested into symptoms of massive nausea. Groans from inmates spread, and guys keeled over in pain and discomfort throughout the cafeteria. The guards had to alert their supervisors in the control room, warning them that a mass food-poisoning event was in progress. After recommending a limited lockdown for treatment, the guards investigated, alerting medical teams to prepare to triage the victims.

Meanwhile, information filtered into the warden's office. "Hey, didn't we install surveillance cameras down there to eliminate blind spots only a month ago?"

Calvin responded promptly, "Yes, we did."

The warden immediately ordered senior guards to pull video of the kitchen surveillance recordings. After reviewing the footage, he leaned back in his chair, shocked by what he saw, a supernatural element that he just couldn't explain.

The video revealed the bottle of chemical cleaning solution spilling onto the pan of powdered eggs below. Surprisingly, nothing was in the room, no human contact, which confused Warden Hudson. *How is that possible?* He continued watching the video along with Calvin, the senior guard. They saw the bottle fall to the floor and roll underneath the prep table. Warden Hudson nudged Calvin on the leg. Thinking the same thing, Calvin immediately said, "I'm on it," and went to the kitchen to confirm where the bottle had ended up, retrieve it, and label it as evidence for documentation.

While Calvin was gone, Warden Hudson observed something unusual in the image he'd almost missed. Slowing the video down almost to a frame-by-frame rate and freezing it precisely at the right moment allowed him to see it, and it terrified him. It was the image of a familiar woman who should not have been there: Dovie Dean. He saw her in the image, enough to almost touch her. Worst of all, she eerily stared back at him momentarily, taunting him so much that the lights flickered on and off, similar to when the electric chair was in use. It was a not-so-subtle sign from her that made her presence felt. It also reminded him of an earlier time in his career that he hated, having to oversee executions. At that moment, the overwhelming feeling bubbling up inside him was fear, which eventually compelled him to turn off the video.

Jon, Freddie, and the guys narrowly escaped the food poisoning incident. Other inmates were less fortunate and still recovering from the effects of the ordeal. This would be the first mass food-poisoning incident while Jon was at Redmond, but it would prove not to be the last. As Jon continued playing his daily chess games, Freddie mentioned something that caused his ears to perk up. "You should get a job to waste time."

"What kind of job could I do here?" he wondered.

Freddie was always thinking a few moves ahead, and his madness always had a purpose. "You've spent time in college, you can work in the prison garden."

This piqued Jon's interest. "Wait, this prison has a garden?"

"Yes, and with your skills, you're the perfect man to work in it. Also, while there, you can help improve the food by growing herbs and other things. Just don't let anyone talk you into growing Mary Jane, because if the guards find out, you'll get years added to your sentence."

When the sun was a bright orange in the sky and close to setting, everyone knew that meant it was time to eat dinner. Lunch always seemed to fly by, so no one counted lunch as a meal because it usually involved some type of sandwich with less time to eat it.

Freddie pointed out something that caught Jon's attention as everyone gathered to line up for the chow hall. "Hey, Jon." He tapped him on the shoulder. "You see that rainbow tattoo on Devin's leg?"

"Yeah."

"Do you know what it means?"

"No."

"It means he's gay."

"Wait, that's what that means?"

Freddie smiled with a huge grin. "Yep. Welcome to your fifth, or is it your sixth, prison education lesson. It doesn't matter, but know the signs. Avoid getting too close unless that's what you're into."

The subject changed when Devin elbowed Javier with enough force to cause him to keel over in pain. Jon shook his head, disgusted. "Didn't he learn anything from getting food poisoning?"

Freddie responded, "It doesn't look like it. Hey, Freddie's rule number fifteen is to treat others how you want to be treated. Because karma can be a temperamental bitch who may love you one day and destroy you the next."

"Hey, Freddie, how do I get a job in the prison garden?"

"You should ask Bishop MacPherson to talk to the greenhouse director. He'll be happy to see you because Alonzo, the current director, has been there for years and is struggling with incompetence. He's clueless about farming and couldn't care less about learning, even though it's his job."

"Well, how did he get the job in the first place?"

"It seems he knew somebody who owed somebody a favor in the governor's office. They recommended the former warden hire him if he wanted job security, no questions asked, and then leave him alone, no matter how bad at his job he was."

"What's he trying to grow?"

"He's growing wheat, corn, oranges, and cabbage."

"Hold on, why is he even trying to grow oranges in Ohio?"

Freddie responded with a confused look. "I don't know."

"Doesn't he realize if it gets cold, those oranges might burst? If he's growing fruit, he should stick to local stuff, like apples or strawberries. This place needs this, and the inmates would love it. If we grow some of our produce at the prison, we could save money and not have to buy from a distributor."

"You need to be there doing that work, young man. Helping grow things we may benefit from has the potential to make life on the inside bearable."

So, after the request to Bishop MacPherson was submitted and promptly forgotten for a few days, the usual anxieties of the day-to-day seemed to fade. A guard approached the table during dinner, a rare event, mainly to avoid being seen as too friendly. When the guard approached, all conversation stopped in anticipation of what was about to be said.

"Is anyone at this table named Bowman, Inmate 70594?" This was routine for how the guards addressed inmates to keep things professional. Jon promptly signaled he was the man he was looking for.

"Are you Bowman?"

"Yes, sir."

The guard then handed him a white envelope and said that after breakfast tomorrow, he would report to the prison garden for work assignment. "The letter inside this envelope is your pass to get to the garden and the permissions needed to work there. Someone advised me that most of your daily routine will not change. With this pass and work assignment comes a level of trust. Don't do something stupid to cause us to question it. Is that understood?"

"Yes, sir."

Before walking away, the guard took a few minutes to look at him. "Is your name Jon Bowman, convicted on a bogus opioid charge by Judge Kavanaugh?"

"Yes, I am."

"My brother is a bailiff in his courtroom. He told me if I came across you to look out for you because you don't belong here. Judge Kavanaugh and the arresting officer in your case are two racist a-holes who shouldn't have their jobs. My advice to you is to stay strong and listen to your elders." Then he turned and walked away. The guard's authoritative tone confirmed Jon's background in that statement, leaving no doubt in anyone's mind, while simultaneously encouraging the relationship he needed to maintain with the inmates at the table. The guard's statement did not escape the attention of Freddie or his entourage of inmates.

Following what had become his daily routine had made him feel as though he was sleepwalking through life. But this day was new, and he looked forward to the one event that was changing. He went through various locks, guards, searches, and checks before finally arriving at his destination. Once there, he looked around, taking a quick inventory of what the land was producing and who was helping grow on it. When he met the gaze of Alonzo, the director of the prison garden, he approached him. The first words out of his mouth were, "Who in the hell are you?" After handing him his envelope containing his credentials with his last name and inmate number, he saw a familiar face: Devin, from the Slap-A-Ho Tribe.

He also observed an inmate using the bathroom near one of the nearby orange trees, which caused him to wonder where the actual bathrooms were. After getting his letter back, he noticed something that would prove significant later on. He saw a sprinkling of white-brownish dots on the ground that, upon closer inspection, were mushrooms. Once the formalities were out of the way, a question had to be asked.

"So, what's my job now that I'm here?"

He soon got his answer when someone shoved a hoe in his hand. "Start digging," Alonzo said, then advised he was one of the few non-violent trustees allowed to use this tool. "Don't hand it to anyone else in here. Bring it back to me or a guard when you finish two rows. Don't forget to till the soil before planting."

Standing next to another inmate, he asked what they were growing.

"Cabbage, I think."

The hours passed, and the sun set in the sky, turning it a magnificent shade of orange with clouds sprinkled in the evening Ohio sky.

When it was time to call it a day, they washed up hastily before dinner. The line leading to the chow hall seemed like it went on forever, and it always seemed like he was at the very end of it. Working in the prison garden was hard work. As time passed and his curiosity overwhelmed him, he wondered what was being served for dinner. He tried not to complain, happy to gain some semblance of joy out of the terrible experience that was his life. The more the sweat rolled down his face, the hungrier he became. Finding a new way to waste time gave him newfound hope behind the walls. He was determined never to lose hope, to survive.

The next day, they repeated the same routine. After observing the same inmate relieving himself on the same nearby orange tree as the day before, Jon noticed Devin kneeling for a few moments, then stuffing something into a small plastic bag underneath his shirt. He looked down at the ground, realizing that the spot where some of the mushrooms had been was now mostly green grass. He wanted to mind his business, wavering on whether to say something or remain silent. But his conscience got to him, and he wanted to do the right thing, so he spoke up.

"Hey, Devin, I don't know you well, but you're known by reputation on the block. Did you get some of those mushrooms?"

"Yes," he snapped back with an attitude that caused Jon to reconsider whether his intervention was wise.

"I only mention them because another guy was here—"

He was rudely cut off before he could even get the words out by Devin, demanding that he mind his own business.

"But, Devin, that spot where those mushrooms were—"

Devin interrupted again, screaming at him to mind his business.

He threw up his hands while looking up at the sky. *God, I tried. I guess that stupid S.O.B. doesn't want to know that someone watered those mushrooms in the most disgusting way possible. Well, that's on him. He doesn't even know if they're poisonous.*

Soon after, to his surprise, a spirit appeared before him with a ghoulish smile and a worse demeanor: Anna Marie Hahn, a former resident of the old Redmond Prison, whose favorite method of killing was by poisoning her victims. She appeared for only eight minutes, but she delivered an unmistakable warning.

"The vile man you know as Devin belongs to us, the ladies of Redmond! He will never leave this place. You can't help him, and you can't save him, so don't waste time trying. He's destined to die here. That's his fate!" The statement was followed by a dire warning. "Do not interfere in this matter, or we will come after you. You don't belong here, so we've got no problem with you. Go in peace, and focus on staying alive."

Since Jon could not warn him about the danger he was in, he watched helplessly as Devin became the victim of one tragic event after another. He was powerless to intervene and unable to convince him to change his ways.

Meanwhile, Javier showed up with fresh evidence of abuse at Devin's hands—bruises he couldn't conceal easily, ones they could not ignore. They all followed the same routine as usual for dinner, lining up and waiting to be served. But this night was different; word spread like wildfire that spaghetti with meatballs and a salad was being served. Devin didn't seem to be phased by the excitement.

When Jon finally got to the front of the line and got his food, with his tray in hand, he had to be the one to ask. "What's the special occasion?"

One of the guys on the serving line said something that shocked everyone. "Man, a jailhouse lawyer sued the state about the conditions in this prison. He wrote that the conditions in the documents filed were unconstitutional. He mentioned in the brief that we're not getting enough to eat." The trustee in the serving line grinned. "The clever bastard won."

"Hey, where did you learn that word?"

"The prison library. In this place, I've got nothing better to do than work here and read."

Offering a word of encouragement, Jon said the best thing he could have, "Hey, brother, keep reading, keep learning, and never stop until you die."

Making his way to their table, the guys assembled, taking their seats in their usual spots. The place was relatively silent for the first time since Jon had been there. Everyone was busy stuffing their faces, so few conversations were happening. Out of the corner of his eye, Jon saw Javier and Devin walk by. He noticed that after Devin took his seat, he took out the small bag of mushrooms, the ones from the garden that he had smuggled out. Maybe he'd had inside information about what was going to be served.

Taking out his mushrooms and breaking them into pieces, he gave a few to Javier. Being greedy, he kept most of them for himself and spread them over his spaghetti. He devoured his meal with a zeal that was a sight to behold until those mushrooms unleashed a wave of nausea and violent cramps, his insides a battlefield of toxins. Javier winced, but the pain was less intense. The guards watched, their faces frozen in indecision. All the while, the symptoms grew more severe.

The other inmates continued to eat even though the two suffered from some unknown issue. A decent meal in Redmond didn't come around often, and they shouldn't waste it. Jon may have been powerless to prevent their suffering, but he could still relieve it, even if he felt no sympathy for Devin.

He waved for one of the guards to come over but told the guys around the table exactly what he would say beforehand, getting permission to do so. Almost whispering, he told the guard to let the medical staff know that they ate wild mushrooms from the prison garden. Describing them as light brown and likely native to Ohio, he recommended the treatment, small doses of atropine.

Close to lights out, Javier returned to C-block, escorted by a guard. Because of his condition, the guard allowed him to visit one inmate on the way to his cell: Jon.

Jon looked out from behind the bars of his cell as the two men approached. He recognized Javier, but the guard in the crisp, dark uniform was a stranger.

"Jon, I'm happy to see you."

"While I'm glad you're walking around, you appear unsteady."

"I wouldn't be standing at all if it weren't for you. I wanted to thank you for that. Those mushrooms have landed Devin in the hospital. It seems they were poisonous. They damaged his kidneys, which were already weak because of that food poisoning incident. Now he's on death's doorstep."

"Well, how bad is he?"

"He's close to meeting God, and we both know if that happens, he'll find himself in the hottest part of Hell."

FBI Field Office in Cleveland, Ohio

Special Agent Ron Coleman sat impatiently in the office of Supervising Agent in charge Mike Evans, waiting to be chewed out for a case that went sideways. Even though the Office of Professional Responsibility cleared him, stipulating that it all went wrong in ways that were beyond his control, the events of that day left a permanent scar in his memory. It was a cascade of tragic events, all based on one terrible decision. At the time, it felt like he was deep in a hole, with water flowing up to his waist and more continuing to come. It all went wrong when the target of his investigation did something idiotic.

Pointing a loaded semi-automatic rifle at local law enforcement officers is like asking to die. Especially when he's standing next to his wife and two daughters. This resulted in a young rookie squeezing off a round, which set in motion a domino effect that was hard to stop once started, at least in time to prevent tragedy from unfolding. *Why in the hell would someone need fifteen semi-automatic rifles along with other handguns in the first place?* He wondered how anyone could be dumb enough to threaten a federal judge on television. A move that directly led to the death of his wife and kids right in front of him. Constantly replaying those images in his mind made him think he might have PTSD. He remembered screaming like a crazy man to cease fire, but to his horror, it was already too late.

When Mike walked in, he had a stone-faced expression. Entering the room with a light blue folder with a seal on it, he laid it on his desk and slumped down in the leather-covered executive chair. He leaned back, then handed Ron his new assignment. "Ron, you have my sympathies." That phrase stuck in his mind. He thumbed through it, scanning the documents after looking at the picture, trying to figure out why it looked so familiar.

"So what's up with Redmond Prison, Mike?"

Mike told him to keep reading, repeating his previous statement. "You have my sympathy for your years of dedicated service to this organization. Ron, you're in the doghouse with the bosses upstairs. Your new assignment will be to investigate strange deaths at Redmond Prison. You deserve a better assignment with your years on the job, skill, and ability. I know this is beneath you, but you're still here and you still have a job. Even though what happened wasn't your fault, the whole mess just looks extremely bad for the Bureau. As a result, the director had to spend enormous amounts of time on the hill explaining the horrible optics of this incident to the politicians as well as the public and why it happened in the first place. It's been determined that it's better for the Bureau and you if no one sees your face on television for a while. That's why I'm giving you this assignment. Try to keep your head up and your brain focused on the job and why you do it every day."

After leaving the office of the supervising special agent in charge and making his way to his car, he wondered what strange deaths were happening there. Preparing to go to Redmond Prison took time because he had to remember exactly where it was. He had to review more odd reports on Redmond and try to wrap his brain around the strange details surrounding the deaths. The excessively high numbers of deaths that occurred there within the last year piqued his interest. Meanwhile, State Rep. Kimberlee Townsend also went to Redmond to investigate the strange incidents.

Special Agent Coleman arrived a few minutes ahead of Rep. Townsend and made his presence known by identifying himself while showing his FBI ID. He was distracted upon catching a glimpse of Rep. Townsend and wondering who this extraordinary, beautiful woman was standing behind him. Remembering why he was there, he asked the guard to see the warden or deputy warden. Rep.

Townsend then made her presence known, stating that she also needed to see the warden.

A conversation developed about why an FBI agent would be at Redmond asking to see the warden instead of an inmate.

"Well, when people die on the street under questionable circumstances, you call a homicide detective. When an inmate dies in a state corrections institution, we take it seriously. Especially if part of your funding comes from the federal government, since a few of our inmates are here. An FBI agent shows up asking questions. To make a long story short, I'm here because too many inmates are turning up dead for unusual reasons. When that happens, it attracts the attention of someone at the Bureau who monitors those details."

After being escorted by a guard to the warden's office and exchanging credentials, Ron, the no-nonsense agent, proceeded with the business he was there for. "Warden, I'm here because there have been too many inmate deaths under mysterious circumstances, including a federal inmate who was about to give testimony."

The warden smiled and told the truth. "Here, we believe in giving information to inmates straight. This applies to you as well. There are ghosts in this prison."

Ron and Rep. Townsend looked at each other with a smirk.

"You're kidding."

"Nope. I'm not only not kidding you, but I have video evidence of a recent food poisoning incident to back up what I'm saying."

They watched the video and were shocked by how the chemical somehow turned over with no apparent human intervention. The video of the contaminated pan of powdered eggs caused Ron to be inclined to believe the warden. This evidence eventually proved that he likely wasn't doing anything nefarious, but further investigation was needed. State Rep. Townsend advised that she was there for the same reason, being honest with him. "The State Corrections Oversight Committee didn't officially sanction this visit. This is my fact-finding visit."

"So, neither one of you is here to interview an inmate for a specific case?"

"No, we are here to talk to a few inmates. Maybe look at reports of individual deaths and speak to staff related to those cases."

The warden then called his secretary in and ordered her to draft a letter, advising all the staff to cooperate with Agent Coleman and Rep. Townsend. He recommended that the agent also serve as a personal bodyguard to Rep. Townsend along with a prison guard, to provide an escort and protection for them as well.

Meanwhile, Devin's condition was getting worse by the day. The poison caused severe damage to his vital organs. The short-term prognosis was surgery to remove one kidney, along with a recommendation for a transplant for the other. However, since he was in prison, they knew he was a terrible candidate even to be considered for placement on the transplant list. The only option was to make him as comfortable as possible by moving him to a wing with older inmates or those with severe medical ailments. The guards only allowed him back into the general population for a few weeks until a spot opened in another facility.

Another set of events simultaneously unfolded in B-block. Tyrone Bennett, Inmate 506768, was putting the finishing touches on a letter to a pen pal, a woman another inmate had befriended over a few months, who Tyrone didn't realize had had a mental health break that would set into motion a shocking chain of events that would go down in Ohio's history. Tyrone Bennett, known as "the Word," was known as a talented writer throughout Redmond. He wrote outstanding letters to women on the outside who were lonely.

Some women already had relationships with inmates before their arrest and conviction, while others developed behind bars. Tyrone possessed the unique talent of persuading these women to say things they wouldn't tell their best friends. Things that would shame their parents and embarrass their pastors. Actions they thought were beyond their wildest intentions or imaginations, they put in these letters.

Tyrone was writing to Laura Swain, a troubled woman dealing with mental health issues and a difficult divorce, when the most devastating event of all occurred. She lost custody of her two children. The stress from this caused her to have a psychotic break, which allowed another inmate to manipulate her into helping him attempt an escape. The woman tricked a pilot into taking her on a sightseeing tour, then forced him to land at the prison at gunpoint. Shaun, the inmate Tyrone was writing the letters for, and two other inmates scrambled aboard.

Laura opened a bag with two long rifles, a handgun, and bullets. The escaping inmates, knowing they had little time, loaded them in and buckled their seatbelts. Then they opened fire on two of the towers, taking out the guards. This improved their odds, but not by much. Cassidy screamed at the pilot while pointing a gun at his head, "Get us out of here now, got damn it!"

As fast as he could, the pilot maneuvered the helicopter into a steady ascent. Then they leveled off to avoid giving the tower guards enough time to fire on them. They moved forward, away from Redmond with speed and precision. The remaining guards, temporarily in shock over the unfolding event, regained their senses and opened fire. But it was too late to hit the fuel tank or engines, either of which would have prevented the helicopter from taking off. In the chaos, inmates were running in all directions to avoid the gunfire. Sirens blared, and the prison immediately went into lockdown.

Chapter 6. Rules to Live By

During all the chaos, even as the sirens sounded, cooler heads eventually prevailed. Word reached Warden Hudson. As the phone on his desk rang, he felt a sense of urgency to answer it. It was Emerald City, a nickname the guards gave to the prison control center because of its importance to the entire facility. The central security center controlled inmate movement, locks, and various security cameras throughout.

The warden's two guests patiently waited to find out what was happening. The warden's reaction to what he was being told was priceless. "Oh shit, you've got to be kidding me. You've got to be kidding me! How bad is it?"

Special Agent Coleman and Rep. Townsend looked at the television monitor as the warden switched camera angles. It showed a closed-circuit feed from the security cameras in the yard. "Are you fucking kidding me? Is that what I think it is?" The monitor showed a helicopter, its blades a blur, descending smoothly before a brief touchdown, then rising again and disappearing into the distance.

"Oh, this shit is worse than bad."

Soon after, the sirens sounded. This facility went into lockdown. The senior guard rushed in within minutes, struggling to catch his breath. "Sir, after sounding the alarm and getting brief reports from the affected areas, as I can best tell you, you still control this prison. The worst news is three inmates we know for sure got on that helicopter and are now classified as escaped and in the wind. One inmate is down and likely dead. We've got the yard contained but not secure because we lost two guys in two towers. The chow hall was providing lunch to, I think, A-block of C-wing, basically a bunch of predators and the most violent offenders housed here. They're contained, but chaos broke out when the helicopter landed. The inmates overwhelmed the guards, injuring one. We're sending in reinforcements to secure the area. We should have things settled down for you with some time to work. After a count, we'll identify the escaped prisoners and see who is missing and unaccounted for."

"Calvin, if you need anything, just let me know."

"Yes, sir." The senior guard left, knowing that once he positively identified the escaped prisoners, it became the warden's headache to notify law enforcement for a manhunt.

Ron realized he could make the manhunt more effective by offering federal help through a partnership that the FAA had with the Bureau, a partnership that tracked civil aviation traffic. "Warden, we could get a fix on where the helicopter is and where it's likely to go by requesting a position fix from an FBI or law enforcement agent, especially since the aircraft is being used during the commission of a crime. The prison break could give the Bureau jurisdiction due to the likelihood that the fugitives pose a risk of crossing state lines."

True to his word, the senior corrections officer got things settled down after conducting a thorough count. He promptly passed along information about the missing inmates, identifying them by their names, numbers, and criminal history. Special Agent Ron Coleman provided the aircraft ID number and position tracking information, along with all known information about the inmates, allowing law enforcement to isolate the escapees where they could corner and apprehend them. Unfortunately, not before they killed their accomplice, wounded the pilot, and abandoned the helicopter. A sad end to a troubled woman's life; they killed her because they knew they couldn't run with her and successfully escape.

Meanwhile, at the press conference the warden had to give, he explained to the public the shocking events that occurred. Ron stood behind the county sheriff, trying to avoid the spotlight, but Warden Hudson encouraged him to say a few words after revealing his role. "Agent Ron Colman of the FBI was remarkable in helping coordinate the effort to track down the helicopter." Rep. Townsend asked to be left out of the press conference to prevent the press from discovering she was ever there.

After all the drama was over, Ron went back to FBI Branch Headquarters. Mike and several fellow agents greeted him with huge grins. Mike was the first to speak. "Got damn, man, I thought I told you to keep a low profile. How did you get stuck in the middle of a prison break? A prison break where a helicopter, of all things, was used to aid in the escape! It's an incident that will no doubt go down in Ohio History! Please explain to me how that is possible! Maybe God is having fun with me and laughing at my expense." Everyone standing around busted out laughing.

"Okay, Ron, we're going to try this again. When you go back, try to keep a low profile...because you've got to go back."

Smiling at his boss, he replied, "I'll try, sir."

Mike put his hand on Ron's shoulder and gave him a word of encouragement. "Thanks for making the Bureau and me look good. Keep it up".

Meanwhile, the sky over Old Big Red darkened as gray clouds drifted overhead, and a deluge of rain poured down. Sporadic lightning appeared in the sky, causing the birds to disappear and the leaves on the nearby trees to tremble. At that very moment, The Axeman's spirit appeared in Redmond's darkened halls, casting a shadow over every inch of space he occupied. He was the personification of evil, but not just because he committed a crime in the land of the living. It was what he said the day he died, and the deal he made with the Devil after his death.

A group of thirty men had assembled to hang him for a crime he didn't commit, and out of anger, he cursed God. The mob gave him only three minutes to pray before hanging him and throwing his lifeless body off a nearby bridge, murdered after being falsely accused of using an axe to kill a woman who rebuffed his affections. When he appeared, animals had the sense to leave, and inmates had the unfortunate habit of dying.

Up to this point at Redmond, Jon had avoided confrontations and fights. At least until Robert Jackson, Inmate 80456, showed up. He was known as Rob for short. Jon's problem with him came a few days after his arrival. Rob went both ways and took an interest in him, an interest Jon wanted no part of. To make matters worse, he refused to take no for an answer. After sitting at the table with the guys, the conversation turned to the prison break as well as the sad end to Devin.

The discussion, however, stopped when Rob rudely interrupted the conversation, addressing Jon only. "I've seen you around and I'd like to be your friend."

Jon's intuition kicked in. "I've already got friends, and they have no interest in being that type of friend you have in mind."

Rob then put his hand on Jon's shoulder, squeezing it, causing discomfort and pain, while leaning over and saying, "No one tells me no, and those who do soon regret it. Things don't usually turn out well for those who tell me no."

After he left, Kenny was the first to speak. "Young man, that looks like a problem you'll have to deal with." Freddie remained unusually silent, letting Kenny deal with the problem. When he did speak, he supported Kenny's observation of the situation with well-reasoned analysis, saying what everyone else felt. "The man disrespected us at our table by trying to proposition one of the members of our entourage, which is a problem that has to be dealt with." The only questions on their minds now were on what Jon was made of and if he was up to this challenge.

Kenny offered his view of the two men. In doing so, he said something profound based on his lived experience. "I believe there are three types of people in this world. The first is a bragger who talks loudly about how big and bad they are. The second is a follower, a sheep, someone who will follow and is not interested in leading anyone anywhere. The third type of person you have to watch, because they are silent. Their goal is to be the wallpaper on the wall. They're the ones you must watch because they aspire to be left alone. A trait that makes them dangerous and highly unpredictable."

Another group member said, "Based on what I've heard, he's in here because he raped a woman. The bastard left her to die, but fortunately for her, someone found her before she did. Rob's a bragger who talks loud about how big and bad he is, and to a point, he may be able to back it up. Or at least intimidate others into backing down and giving him what he wants. An old-fashioned American butt-whipping may be what's needed here. Jon must be the guy who teaches him that no means no, something his old man should have taught him.

"Rob may have a slight advantage in size, but Jon has long arms and can box his way to a win. He might not need to win a one-on-one fight; a draw could be enough. So long as he's not double-teamed. Jon also looks like the type who just aspires to be left alone. A young man raised never to start a fight, but also not to run away if someone starts a fight with him. He just needs to do a few push-ups to ensure that when he throws a punch, there's power behind it and it's not a love tap. Again, he doesn't even have to win. So long as he does enough damage to force Rob to think long and hard about whether it's worth the effort and pain of trying him again."

Alvin asked whether he needed a shank. Jon risked being double-teamed. He knew that the guys couldn't be with him at all times. He also understood the risk of being caught with a shank meant solitary confinement for a week or more, especially if it was used in a fight and hurt another inmate.

Kenny, Freddie, and the guys were going over plans and contingencies for dealing with Rob while other developments occurred. Most recreation took place in the yard, as did most fights. A beef had started with the Skinheads and the Cholos over an issue that didn't even take place inside the prison. It all started over a drug deal that went bad when members of a Mexican cartel were supplying significant weight to a Skinhead gang. The deal was discovered by the DEA, resulting in many arrests as well as the death of a significant regional Mexican cartel leader.

When those arrested arrived at Redmond, they shared details of what happened, including the fact that it was due to a weak link on the Skinhead gang's side, a snitch that the DEA flipped for information on key players involved. They wrapped up the entire crew with information that compromised their regional drug trafficking network and money supply. As a result, gang members on the inside wouldn't receive money credited to their books to buy items at the prison commissary. Once this information surfaced, many Latino inmates became enraged.

The inmate-to-inmate interactions generated sparks all over the place that lit the fuse of racial dynamics within Redmond, eventually leading to the explosion of the Redmond Civil War. Dynamics in the yard were ominous in day-to-day interactions. The layout was typical of most prisons of its day. When you combined the design with human behavior, it painted a horrific picture. Black inmates concentrated near the basketball court in the center. Along with the Latinos, they concentrated near the main building and one of the towers to do push-ups and other exercises. This put them in an excellent position to be first in line to eat lunch or dinner. The two groups agreed on little, but one issue they did agree on. They wanted the Skinheads to be where they and the guards could see them. So they pushed them close to the edge of the yard. Since the black and Latino inmates combined outnumbered them, they didn't seem to have a problem with this arrangement.

Meanwhile, back at CS University, one hundred and twenty-seven miles away, Michelle Kimbell had been calling Jon for two months with no response. That was until she ran into Jerry on campus. When he told her about the entire ordeal he was going through, she immediately wanted to see him, but he advised against it due to who her father was.

"You can't see him because your dad is a state representative for part of Dayton in District 39. The optics make that a terrible idea."

"Well, what should I do?"

"Be patient and wait for him, because he's doing time on a bogus charge."

What she did not tell Jerry was why she needed to see him. The night she and Jon spent together, they had a little too much fun, and she was having morning sickness a few weeks before she realized she missed her period.

The arrival of the Axeman on the anniversary of his death every year signaled the beginning of a killing spree that left the county coroner with plenty of work. Christopher Davis set off a period of terror and widespread fear none of the inmates or staff could fully prepare for. Christopher's victim would be Roberto Cortés, Inmate 830948, convicted on three counts of murder and only spared the death penalty because he owned up to the murders. He had many tattoos, but the three teardrops signaled to all that he had taken three lives.

While mopping the floors near what he thought was one of the few blind spots of the Redmond security camera network, Roberto saw a flash that he couldn't make out or explain. He rolled the mop bucket into the corner to keep it in one spot and left the mop in it with the handle sticking out to keep it stationary. Noticing something out of the corner of his eye, he turned to the door, then stopped and walked a few feet away from the mop bucket. An image of a man faded in and out of existence until it fully came into view.

The axe he carried was heavy and wet, and water ran down his arms as he walked. A purple welt encircled his neck. He had pale black skin like he was two hundred years old and dead. He was a towering figure, standing nearly seven feet, and muscular in build. He seemed to eclipse the light, causing it to dim around him, which was unnatural and evil.

Christopher Davis appeared in front of Roberto. Without saying a word, he somehow tapped into the power of the concentrated spirits trapped in Redmond. Temporarily frozen, Roberto struggled frantically to move, but all attempts failed. He felt like a fly stuck in a web, frantically trying to break free, as he was lifted five feet off the ground by some unknown force. Shaking in sheer terror while dangling in the air, he wet himself, and it dripped down his leg to the floor below. Suddenly, a force threw him across the room into the corner, and the mop impaled him. Roberto stood there, leaning against the wall in shock, the mop handle sticking out of his chest. Blood soaked his orange prison-issue jumpsuit. His eyes slowly became fixed on the last image he would see. The Axeman had another victim and wasted no time absorbing his soul, gaining renewed strength from it, before he turned to walk away.

When the guards found him, the unwelcome sight they faced horrified them. In Redmond, guards talk, and you best believe an inmate is somewhere listening. Despite the echo of the corridors and the silence during lights out, inmate-to-inmate stories and rumors spread. Through a low-key campaign by the guys to learn more about what happened, they eventually figured it out.

Attention turned to finding out who else might have had problems with Rob. A eureka moment occurred when Jon became friends with Devin's replacement in the prison garden. Inmate 604323, Andre Scott, was a short-timer who wanted to do his time while anxiously awaiting release. Jon discovered Rob had propositioned Andre. This made Jon think about all those chess games he played with Freddie, games that forced him to think strategically. With a smile, he thought of a phrase he'd heard long ago. *The enemy of my enemy is my friend.* When Andre looked at him with a smile, he knew he likely had an ally in case someone double-teamed him in the yard. He also knew he now had an ally to double-team Rob in the yard to deal with their mutual problem.

The guys in Freddie's entourage were advisers on surviving in prison, but that was all. Jon knew they were older, and he likely shouldn't depend on them in a fight. They did not say it, but the general rule was to leave the old-timers alone out of respect. Plus, getting beaten up by older inmates was embarrassing and risky. That young guy would be the butt of jokes until he was free or dead. As the wheels in his mind started turning, Jon thought about the position that they were both in. They were determined to fight rather than suffer the risk of losing their manhood. Any dispute resolution they felt would be a waste of time and so, not an option.

As more time passed, and Mexican cartel members inside Redmond were unable to buy things they wanted from the prison commissary, they became angrier. Tension grew by the day to a level that even the guards noticed and worried that the place was a volcano waiting to blow. Warden Hudson tried to relieve the pressure once he was told of the tension. His goal was simple in execution and involved trying to prevent the spark that could trigger a confrontation, which he knew could lead to a riot. He was sure a confrontation would likely occur in the yard. So, he strategically placed guards and equipment around the yard in advance, all close enough to reduce the reaction time for his guards.

The ghost of Christopher Davis began a bloody melee at 10 o'clock after breakfast, seeking a host to possess and manipulate, feeding and gaining strength from the hate he could feel building in the Latino inmates toward the Skinheads while simultaneously tapping into the souls trapped in Redmond. He came across the perfect host: Diego Mejia, Inmate 805686. He was a leader among the Latinos, as well as the most violent and notorious drug dealer in Redmond before his arrest and conviction. The Axeman, after possessing Diego's body, realized he also had a shank on him just as a Skinhead leader, escorted by two of his comrades, passed by on their way to use the phone. Evil spirits worked in the shadows to manipulate the living in this gathering as the perfect opportunity to start a war.

The Axeman used Diego as the perpetrator of a shocking crime that would spark and trigger the Redmond Civil War. He took the shank out and carefully concealed it until it was too late for his prey to defend against. The Skinheads got closer and closer until they were nearly touching. Despite being stabbed with a shank, Steven Conner remained alive, if only for a few minutes, carrying his liver and intestines in his hands before falling to the ground. This astonishingly gruesome sight temporarily froze the men escorting, and the Axeman wasted no time in stabbing one of them in the neck, slicing through the carotid artery and causing a gush of blood to flow to the ground.

The Axeman used near-superhuman strength to choke the last man to death. He accomplished all of this using the body of Diego as a host. From a distance, the other Skinheads carefully watched this scene play out, temporarily shocked by what they saw until they came to their senses and took action. Sensing that something was going wrong and knowing that just one spark was enough to trigger something terrible, they reacted in a way that was predictable and obvious. As fights broke out everywhere, the guards temporarily had no choice but to retreat.

Seeing the two forces converge, the black inmates realized they were squarely in the middle. The two sides nearly surrounded them on the basketball court. Instinctively, they moved to evade the smashup. As most of the black inmates watched the melee unfold, many of them wished they had a hot dog along with a cold one to throw back. They knew they had front-row seats to a brawl of epic proportions that many had not seen since being outside watching a pay-per-view fight on TV.

The older and more calculating black inmates saw the brawl as an opportunity to settle scores and disputes. Freddie and Kenny watched the whole melee go down and observed the guards hastily retreating. Kenny looked at Jon, saying to him with a sense of calm and clarity that almost seemed like an order, "Young man, now would be an excellent time to deal with our problem."

Understanding Kenny instinctively, he tapped Andre, who was sitting nearby, on the shoulder. Even though Andre wasn't quite a member of the entourage, he reminded the guys of Jon when he arrived, so they let him hang around until they found an obvious reason to let him stay. They both walked to the basketball court. It took a while, but they eventually found Rob and beat him as if he owed them money. Four hours later, the guards showed up in force. However, not until after ten inmates had died, and over twenty more were wounded.

Even though the press questioned Warden Hudson's judgment, the guards never did, due to their appreciation of him for not unnecessarily putting their lives at risk. They were careful to tell the politicians exactly what they needed and wanted to hear to leave Warden Hudson alone over that question.

When the Axeman finally left Diego's body, it was like he was waking from a deep sleep. Disoriented and clueless about what had happened, he did not know his role in the horrific events he set in motion. When the guards arrived in force, the field resembled a war that had been waged for hours instead of minutes. A river of blood flowed during the melee, and inmates lay bleeding, in pain, or dead all over the yard. The guards found Diego standing in the yard, covered in blood, confused about how long he was there and why he was holding a shank that he didn't remember having, let alone what he used it for.

He didn't remember the warning shots the guards fired to warn the inmates to stop fighting. He didn't remember them issuing orders to cease all hostilities and to lie on the ground, putting their hands on their heads while interlocking their fingers. The gap in his memory he simply had no explanation for. So, when they took Diego to an interrogation room inside the prison, Special Agent Ron Coleman walked in and stared at him. Then he played the video from the closed-circuit security cameras in the yard.

"What in the hell was going through your mind when you killed those three men? I mean, you just snuffed out their lives for nothing. In doing so, you destroyed a federal drug case. Man hours, wiretaps, and stakeouts, all for almost nothing. The state is going to charge you with murder, and it doesn't supersede a federal drug case. However, the deputy US attorney is mad because of all the time and expense of trying to build a criminal case against you, and this complicates things. Then, to see it go up in smoke, watching you on video commit an asinine murder against three nobodies in what amounts to a slam dunk murder case...

"I saw a ghost."

"You saw a what?"

"I saw a flash that I can't explain. It caused me to blank out. I don't know what happened. I know ghosts haunt this place, and I've got to get transferred. Agent Coleman, if I plead guilty to the drug charges, will the deputy US attorney have me moved to serve my sentence somewhere else? Please, please, help me get out of here! I'll plead guilty to the federal charges, but you must get me out of here. I'll serve the federal charges first if you get me out of here."

"Well, because we charged you first, if you plead guilty, now we have more leverage regarding what happens to you. I'm not a lawyer, but I know there is no statute of limitations on murder, so they can charge you whenever they want to on the state level. Pleading guilty to the drug charges may be better for you if you want out of Redmond. You should know it may mean a life sentence. Dying years later may be better than dying sooner here in some terrible and unspeakable way."

Chapter 7. No Power

Warden Hudson arrived at work early the next day after what amounted to a civil war inside his prison. He sat alone in his office with the lights off, trying to think about the unique problem he was now facing. He wondered to himself how to lower the tension. After a sudden burst of inspiration, he gathered the leaders from both groups. He announced a price reduction at the prison commissary, contingent on the two sides squashing their beef and resolving their differences.

Bishop MacPherson also helped Latino inmates since many of them were devout members of the Catholic faith. He offered to find new supporters outside the prison who would put money on the books of inmates willing to take rehabilitation courses. In exchange for peace, inmates could participate voluntarily in rehabilitation programs within the prison. This plan had the possibility of benefiting all parties involved. Since some of these inmates would return to society, the focus changed to preparing them for life outside prison. He considered this solution to be the perfect answer to his unusual dilemma. The only question was, would it work?

Also, finding more paid work for the inmates would help them pass the time. This would allow them to earn money they could use in the commissary. This plan would force him to contact the governor's office for permission to contact corporations for work his prisoners could do while simultaneously requiring him to call in favors that he knew would eventually come due—political favors that would give him additional options, along with resources he could incorporate into his tools to maintain positive control of Redmond.

In the meantime, the Axeman wandered Redmond's darkened halls, causing chaos everywhere he went. He possessed the body of one inmate, compelling him to run into a wall repeatedly. The inmate was taken by a guard to the infirmary bloody and bruised, suffering from a mild concussion and with no memory of why he did it. This incident confused and freaked out the infirmary staff to no end.

Jon's life went on, which meant sticking to a routine that refused to end. It started with the morning count, then breakfast, the noon count, then lunch, and finally dinner, with the day nearing the end with the last count. While waiting two hours for lights out, only to start the entire process again the next day. Along with interactions with other inmates and individual work assignments, this was life on the inside. All inmates followed this routine. You made it work, or you lost your mind. That was the cold, hard truth of it.

Warden Hudson made many efforts to put the events of the Redmond Civil War behind him. The inmates were afraid but calculating, always thinking of a person to use or a thing to get that might give them an edge. Some of his programs and policies worked to plant the seeds of a lasting peace, measures that relieved the tension. Although periodic setbacks caused individual disputes to flare up, nothing major happened. However, as soon as things seemed to calm down, another problem appeared when the phone rang...

"Warden, I'm Ryan Foster from the Ohio Emergency Management Agency. I don't know if you've been paying attention to the weather lately due to that crazy escape attempt and even crazier civil war. I'm calling you because we're looking at what meteorologists call a polar vortex. It's a weather event that will pull enormous amounts of cold air from the poles. It's headed straight for us, bringing along freezing conditions."

"Well, how bad are you expecting this weather to get?"

"Twenty degrees below zero."

"Damn, that's polar bears and penguins cold."

"Yeah. Just calling to warn you."

"Ryan, I appreciate the call. If it's not one thing, it's something a lot worse. We'll get ready. Thanks again for the heads up."

"Before you go, Warden, what's your backup generator system look like? Also, will we need to evacuate some of your inmates? What does your food situation look like?"

"Based on my current information, I can report that we don't need to evacuate most prisoners. There's an exception with death row. They may need to be evacuated due to that wing's older and unreliable generators."

"Warden, I'm allowed to speak for the governor on that matter. The answer is no, and not only no, but hell no. They stay exactly where they are."

"It sounds like the governor doesn't want to risk a bunch of death row inmates using this storm as an opportunity to escape. So I guess they stay put?"

"Warden, that's precisely what you should conclude."

"Understood. The answer to your other question is we're below this prison's maximum capacity. Let me be crystal clear: Now would be the wrong time to transport inmates from other state prisons. Also, we just received our scheduled delivery of cold storage food. We expect to receive dry storage food tomorrow. How much time do we have?"

"Meteorologists forecast this severe weather might impact us in about two days."

"Okay, last thing, our backup power generation system is old but works. We serviced and tested the generators four months ago. The ones on death row are much older and unreliable. If we lose them, we'll have problems. There's also a potential fire risk if we lose power and depend too much on those generators for an extended period. Temperatures in that wing without heat will fall fast due to limited insulation. The contractor did too good of a job keeping construction costs down while maximizing the inclusion of reinforced steel to prevent escapes. Those inmates won't stand a chance if we lose power and those generators fail."

"What about replacement generators?"

"On short notice, and with no funds, impossible. The legislature rejected a request for funds for this equipment six years ago under the previous warden. I resubmitted the request last year, and they firmly turned me down, citing tax cuts and the overwhelming need for taxpayer relief."

"Sounds to me, Warden, like you covered your ass well."

"Well, Ryan, I minored in political science, which helps me a little in this job."

As the countdown began until the cold front moved in, guards and staff worked to get ready. They worked aggressively, making preparations and distributing blankets to all inmates. Guards and additional staff were told to stay on rotation for a week or two to maintain security and continuity. The closer the storm got, the more the temperatures dropped. Once Ohio experienced the full impact of the storm, the only thing Warden Hudson could do was to pray.

A blanket of snow descended across the state. Traffic on the roads disappeared. Schools, stores, and office buildings all over closed. Police presence even retreated temporarily to their stations. Officers hoped and prayed that even the criminals would find a hole and crawl into it until the weather improved.

Then, two days into the freeze, Redmond Prison lost power, and all hell broke loose. The warden's worst fear became a reality at midnight, leading to the third day. The boilers shut down, causing a loss of power and, with that, a loss of heat. Backup generators kicked in, providing most of the prison with power. D-wing lost power, and backup generators were fluctuating. Sparks flew everywhere, and a single spark landed in the worst place—a leaking diesel fuel line. It caught fire, small at first, but it eventually grew, causing the entire room to be engulfed in flames before anyone could get to it, let alone think about how to put it out.

Even though the senior guard was well-trained, there were limits to what he could do. He was aware of a toxic fume issue and a command-and-control issue. He understood that losing power meant losing communication, and he ordered his guards to leave because he was concerned about the risk of them being stuck without computer access for locks and lacking heat and food. Not to mention the risk of the locks freezing shut, trapping his guards in that wing for an unknown time.

Unbeknownst to the guards, the ghosts of Redmond played a role in the fire that caused the power outage. One ghost in particular, the Axeman, somehow triggered the initial sparks, setting in motion the series of tragic events. The temperature in death row continued to plummet. The inmates trapped inside knew, on some level, they were going to die, especially when they started seeing ghosts marching through the block. Spirits wearing Union military uniforms from the Civil War. All the while, the Axeman watched with a ghoulish smile as the men in D-block slowly froze to death.

The senior guard of D-wing only had minutes to decide, but he knew it was a decision he would have to live with for the rest of his life. Once he ordered them to leave, he was determined to stand by it. Memories of better times flashed into his head. This caused him to think about the men he ordered to go who had families, men who had his back and who he had gotten to know well over the years. There was John Thompson, who had 20 years on the job and had to make sure he lived to walk his daughter down the aisle. There was also Matthew White, who had to make it out to be a father to his twin boys. The guards were part of his extended family, a family he refused to lose.

The inmates assigned to D-wing were the worst of the worst. It was death row for a reason, and because these men were on it, they were expendable. He couldn't securely move the inmates anywhere else in the prison. Following the warden's order, which came directly from the governor, left him with no choice and no options. Since the call had to be made, he made it. His men would go, and the inmates would stay.

After the guards left, time passed and bone-chilling cold set in. D-wing looked like the hall of an ice palace. As hours passed, the remaining inmates endured freezing temperatures with only blankets and their body heat for warmth. Heat became a declining commodity, and once it was lost, it was impossible to get back. The scene was depressing as well as tragic. The inmates appeared like human popsicles standing inside their cells. Their faces turned pale and bluish, with blank stares looking out from behind the bars of their cells. They just stood there with terrified expressions on their faces. Knowing they were going to die, they gradually lost all hope. They tried to face their fate with some ounce of dignity, but in the end, they only felt resentment.

When the power returned, the warden saw the tragic scene. He immediately called the Ohio Attorney General's office to explain the circumstances and the decisions made surrounding it. He knew there would be lawsuits, not necessarily from the families of the inmates who lost their lives but from the civil rights lawyers suing on their behalf.

Within minutes of the inmates reaching death's doorstep, Frank Hanger appeared. Frank was a former guard who an inmate murdered, and once his spirit appeared, it meant a death sentence to Hell.

The inmates in death row stood shivering and freezing, icicles hanging off their faces. Frank fazed in and out of view. When their bodies died and their spirits released, Frank was able to be seen clearly as a powerful force handcuffing them in unbreakable chains, not physical, but supernatural. Chains that, despite their best effort, they couldn't break.

When a flame appeared, it began on the floor and gradually outlined a door. The handles appeared in the form of snakes, along with a keyhole. Frank grabbed a set of keys hanging from his waist, opening a door that was on fire but never seemed to burn up. The door opened to the most hellish place the inmates could ever imagine. A place filled with moans of suffering and pain. Through the door, they saw and heard those who had died over the centuries, tortured by devilish-looking creatures and screaming in pain. Souls begging for mercy but receiving—and deserving—none, engulfed in flames but not burning up. Each inmate who froze to death on D-wing struggled to break free of the force dragging them ever closer to that door. Fear set in as they squirmed in their futile efforts, dragged, kicking and screaming, through the gates of Hell, their souls facing an eternity of torture, screams, and misery.

There's a saying: God knows all and sees all, but the Devil knows sin. In the case of the inmates of D-wing, the Devil knew their sins and dragged them to the desolation of Hell. While among the living, God may have shown compassion and mercy, but in Hell, the demons didn't care. It was worse than the prison they left behind. They found themselves in a lonely place filled with flowing lava, as though they were in the bowels of an active volcano. Steam vents appeared periodically, releasing sulfur dioxide into the air, causing many of them to wish they were dead, only to realize they already were.

After the freeze, Redmond Prison eventually returned to normal. The problem was, what's normal for Redmond Prison was pretty weird for everywhere else. The inmates, after spending what seemed like an eternity in their cells, eating meals, exercising, and sleeping, were getting irritable. The ones who didn't have cabin fever had something worse: rage. When their cell doors finally opened, no one hesitated to come out for the routine count before breakfast. The men of C-block made their way to the chow hall. Despite the odd attempt at normalcy, there was a weird feeling that they were not alone.

Something extremely odd happened as they got their trays from the inmates serving breakfast and sat down. Some invisible force mysteriously snatched their trays from where they were sitting in front of them, raising them off the table for a few moments, supported by nothing. Then, to the shock and dismay of all, something then flung their food across the room, splattering it on the wall.

Meanwhile, miles away, at the office of Doctor Vanessa White, a gynecologist in Dayton, Ohio, Michelle Kimbell sat at a medical table, looking up at the ceiling, afraid that her doctor would come in and confirm what she already knew. *How will I tell my parents? They'll be upset because I didn't finish school first.* All kinds of crazy thoughts entered her mind.

When Doctor White walked in, she looked at her with a smile, only to ask the pointed question she feared the most. A question she dreaded, but one that also revealed the results of the tests she ran. "So, who is the father?" All Michelle could do was lower her head as tears ran down her face like water falling from a briskly flowing river.

Being the excellent doctor that she was, Doctor White took off her stethoscope and became somewhat of a psychologist. Holding Michelle's chin, she gently nudged her head. She comforted and listened to her, finally providing solid medical advice. "I have known you since you were a curious little girl. I've been your doctor for a long time. Hold your head up and think your way through your current short-term problem as well as the implications of your condition on your life in the long term. When was the last time you saw your parents?"

"I saw them during spring break. Knowing Dad, he's at the capital, likely on the state house floor, giving a speech."

"You should see him first and tell him."

"Why should I tell my dad first?"

"Because when he finds out his first grandson is on the way, he may be less likely to get mad at you for not finishing school."

"I'm having a boy?"

"Yes, you're having a boy based on the blood test. I'll know for sure in another two weeks with an ultrasound. Compared to many young women in your position, you're in much better shape. Finishing college is at least two years away for you. You're about ten weeks along with a bit of a baby bump that will grow. A little stress now is okay. However, there should be no stress from now on. Your mother will be the problem, so you need to tell your dad first so he can help you break the news to her."

"Okay, that makes sense."

"Also, I'm putting you on a regimen of prenatal care vitamins and a list of what you should eat, as well as what you should absolutely stay away from, which includes alcohol."

As she listened to the advice Doctor White provided, she felt more at ease. Her tears eventually stopped flowing.

That's when she explained she was oddly not upset about who the father of her child was. She was primarily worried about the circumstances of his situation along with how to break the pregnancy to her parents, and that the father was a good man who was dealing with a legal problem that caused him to go to prison. That amounted to serving a chef-prepared New York strip steak with steamed vegetables and red potatoes on the lid of a garbage can.

"Yeah, that poses a problem. It won't be the best presentation if you carry this child to term. By the way, I strongly recommend that you do this. They may not be happy with you once you tell them, but may feel differently later. You should tell them that your doctor says if they don't accept this child now, they may not get another grandchild later on because there's a risk of complications that may prevent you from having another one. By the way, what's the name of the father?"

"His name is Jon Bowman."

Doctor White promptly wrote the name down to avoid forgetting it. She knew she might not get a second chance to persuade Michelle to open up and tell her again.

After thanking Doctor White for all her help and good medical care, it was time for Michelle to leave to prepare for the next day's short drive to the capital.

The following day, Michelle embarked on the hour and thirty-minute drive to Columbus, Ohio, to have what she thought would be a challenging conversation with her father. She had no clue how it would turn out. After driving for nearly thirty minutes, it occurred to her she was going a little too fast for someone in her condition. That's when it sunk in that she would be a mother soon and should be extra careful. Her lead foot would have to be restrained. Taking three breaks for gas and rest, she eventually arrived in Columbus.

After taking a few minutes to organize her thoughts, she could hear her dad's voice in her head. *Consider what you want to say, then make your case clearly and well-thought out. Doing so makes the argument more persuasive and, more importantly, more effective.* She walked into the capitol building and went to where the offices were. She scanned the House directory until she found her dad's. She made her way to it and was greeted by his secretary.

"Wow, girl, you've grown up! My goodness."

"Hey, is my dad in his office? I need some time with him."

"Yes, he's in there. I'll clear his schedule a little for you."

"Thanks."

She walked down the hall, smiling at the members of his office staff, many of whom she didn't recognize. Arriving at the big door at the end of the hall, she firmly knocked before a voice inside said, "Come in."

"Daddy, you're working too much as always, but I love you anyway."

When her dad realized who it was that came to see him, a huge smile came over his face. He opened his arms wide to hug her. "How's my girl? Tell me how you're doing. You also need to call your mother. She misses you and struggles to figure out what to do with her time since you've been gone."

"Dad, I'll call her, but I need your help to talk to her. You always told me to come to you if I had a problem. You told me you would help me deal with it. And you said if you couldn't help me deal with the issue, you would find someone who could."

Sitting up in his chair with his firm baritone voice, he shook his head and smiled. "It's a damn shame my daughter is using my own words against me."

"Dad, your words are coming back to bite you. I'm pregnant."

After being shocked into speechlessness, within a few moments the words came to him. "Michelle, you're my daughter, and nothing will change that. The timing of this could have been better, but I'm not mad at you. My condition for not being angry at you depends on whether you let this stop you from finishing what you've started. You must finish school, that I insist on. I love you, and I always will. You will always be daddy's girl, even though you're now a young woman. Also, I thank God you made it through high school every day without this happening. I'm incredibly grateful that this didn't happen in your first year of college. So let me reassure you I'm not mad at you. I need to know who the father is and when I will meet him. Is he the type likely to stay in the picture once he's told? Your mother, however, is going to be a problem."

"Dad, what if I tell her I'm having a boy?"

"Wait, she told you what you're having? You've already seen Doctor White, and she says I'm getting a grandson?"

"Yup, that's why she told me to tell you first. She's an excellent doctor."

When he heard that, he immediately got out of his chair and kissed her on the forehead. "I will do anything to help you break this to your mom."

"Thanks, Dad, but you should know there's a problem with the father that I need help with."

"Who's the father?"

"He was a student at my school, but I recently found out he was going home to see his mother after final exams. His friend told me that the police arrested him, and the court convicted him on a bogus charge."

"I'll need his name to look into his case, or to get someone who can look into his case so you can find out what happened."

"His name is Jon Bowman, and he was a junior at my school, earning a degree in agriculture and social work."

Scribbling the name on a piece of paper, he took a moment to correct the spelling. "We should have a family dinner where we can tell your mother together if we're going to drop this bomb on her tonight. We should order food from her favorite restaurant so she doesn't have to cook as we wrestle with the best way to reveal the arrival of the newest member of the family."

A strange feeling came over them as they talked. Something wasn't right, but they couldn't quite grasp it. That's when the meeting eventually broke up, and Michelle went home to the house she grew up in to see her mother.

Unbeknownst to them, the matriarch of their family was in a doctor's office receiving the worst news a doctor could tell a woman under his care. Mrs. Victoria Kimbell received a breast cancer diagnosis. Despite the doctor's best efforts, he couldn't comfort her. She remained inconsolable, but he assured her they caught the cancer early and that current treatments were incredibly effective.

"Mrs. Kimbell, your prospects of making a full recovery are excellent."

She still didn't take the news well.

"Your recovery depends on you being strong and staying strong through the chemotherapy treatments."

He explained that his experience has been those who have survived cancer were people who had something to live for.

Chapter 8. Solitary Confinement

After making the drive home from the doctor's office, Mrs. Kimbell arrived home to an empty house, and after looking around, she felt extremely depressed. Suddenly, the doorbell rang, surprising her. The serene melody of the doorbell, which repeated with each press, reached her ears in her bedroom. Getting up to answer it, she had an overwhelming feeling of having no interest in entertaining guests...until she looked at the monitor linked to the security camera outside and realized who it was. Standing there was a woman in the doorway with a big smile waving at her.

Recognizing her daughter, she immediately opened the door, feeling overwhelming joy and happiness. Seeing Michelle standing there beaming at her was a sight she really needed at that moment.

"I don't know what brought this surprise visit, but I'm happy you're here."

She hugged her. The emotion of the situation overwhelmed her as tears flowed down her face in a manner that she just couldn't stop.

"Mom, why are you crying?"

As she looked at her daughter, a terrifying thought crossed her mind. *Will I live to see her get married?* As the tears continued down her face, words blurted out of her mouth in what felt like an out-of-body experience: "Michelle, I have breast cancer."

"Mom, what do you mean you've got cancer?"

"Well, I told my doctor about a lump that I found during a self-exam, and he referred me to an oncologist. The oncologist ran some tests, and after a biopsy was done, the next thing I knew, I was sitting in his cold sterile office getting this terrible news. It's been a tough day for me, and I just got here not long before you did. So I'm going to get some rest before dinner. It's been a tiring and depressing day for me."

"Okay, but, Mom, is there anything I can do for you?"

"Yes, you can stay with me and have dinner with me. I can't be in this house alone."

"I'll stay with you, Mom, but what about Dad?"

"You'll have to be the one to tell him. I'm too upset right now."

After waiting until her mother fell asleep, Michelle called her dad. She was cautious not to talk loud enough to be heard by her mother or to wake her. When he answered the phone, she told him, "Dad, you must come home."

"Did you slip and tell your mother without me?"

"No, Dad, we've got to deal with another serious problem."

Before she could say another word, her dad interrupted her. "I already know about your mother's medical condition. Her oncologist sent his report to her primary care doctor. Usually, doctors aren't supposed to reveal the details of a person's medical record. She only told me because she leads a medical association that owes me many favors, primarily for supporting and helping pass key pieces of legislation over the years. So, she told me about her condition and advised me to do anything we could to help her stay strong. I'll be home for dinner around seven-thirty. I've already sent an emergency medical absence request to the house speaker. Please, don't tell your mother anything about your condition until I arrive. Her primary care doctor said to me on the phone she must have something to live for to survive the grueling chemotherapy treatments."

"Okay, Dad, I won't say a word, and I've already told her I would stay with her instead of driving back."

"Perfect, I'll see you soon. I ordered the food, and it will arrive shortly before eight o'clock."

Michelle prepared the table after the delivery driver showed up with all of her mother's favorites. Preparing the round table brought back memories of discussions about the day's current events. They would discuss school, Sunday school, news, and politics. Even though her dad was born and raised in Ohio, her mother was a Southern belle who enjoyed her Southern dishes. Simultaneously, she was careful to watch and maintain her shapely figure.

Taking out the food containers, Michelle could tell what was inside without opening them. Aromas of smothered pork chops with gravy and sautéed onions with collard greens, along with mashed potatoes with the best cornbread she had ever tasted. Capping it all off with peach cobbler from the only place in the black community that could do Southern food justice.

Just as she finished setting the table, the door opened. Her dad, having perfect timing, stood there looking at the table, then smiled at her.

"Michelle, the table looks perfect."

The table looked like it could have been on the cover of a magazine, with everything perfectly arranged. The dishes and silverware were in picture-perfect positions.

The smells all seemed to complement each other in ways that called to her mother, waking her from her pain-induced sleep. Walking out of her room, she saw her daughter standing beside a table with a magnificent spread and her husband looking at her. Without saying a word, she went to him, and he held her in a way that comforted her as she cried. He cuddled her while kissing her, whispering in her ear,

"Your doctor told me. Cry until you feel better, cry until you run out of tears."

That moment lasted nearly twenty minutes until she grew tired of crying and standing. When she finally sat down, they said grace, thanking God for their meal while also asking Him to heal the most important member of their family. They ate and talked, talked and ate, until the food was nearly gone.

Her dad sensed it was the right time and signaled to Michelle that it was the time to drop the bomb. Then he stood up dramatically, looked directly at his wife, and gave the best speech of his life to an audience of two.

"You are the love of my life. I love you, and I need you. It's painful to think of my life without you in it. Today, you were told you have cancer. No one told you today you're going to die from it. In the coming months, going through chemotherapy treatments, you will not go through this alone. We will go through this with you. If you lose your hair, I'll cut off all of mine. If I have to go with you to shop for hats or wigs, I promise I'll try my best, even if I've avoided shopping with you, mainly because of that childhood incident with my aunts when they shopped for hours and forgot to get lunch."

Michelle smiled but motioned to her dad to ensure he didn't get off topic.

"Which brings me to the second love of my life. Our daughter. You must be here to see her get married. That's combined with ensuring you're here to see your grandson, who will show up in a few months."

When the room went silent, her mother looked at him, then stared at her daughter. "Wait, what grandson? I have a grandson showing up in a few months?"

"Yes, Mom, you do. I know this is sooner than you wanted. It kind of just happened."

"So who's the guy?"

"Explaining his situation isn't easy, but he's in the picture. Dad's helping me with a legal situation he's dealing with."

"Okay, so when did you find out?"

"Doctor White told me yesterday."

"Well, what about school?"

"Dad insisted I finish school and made me promise I would."

"That's my girl. I will accept this child, but you must finish what you've started, which I also insist on."

"I promise, Mom, I will finish."

Standing up and leaning over to give her a big hug, Victoria said, "You're my only daughter, and I will always love you. We'll have to lean on each other in the next few months. In the next few months, we will both have to be strong."

Meanwhile, Jon was sitting in a conference room at Redmond for reasons he had no clue about when a tall, middle-aged man walked into the room with a rather attractive woman.

"Young man… Can I call you young man?"

"Sure, that seems to be what all the older guys here call me, except the guards."

"Warden Hudson told me a little about how you ended up here. I've got to say, it's piqued my interest and curiosity. Where in the hell did you get two prescription-sized bottles of opioids?"

"That's the same thing Warden Hudson asked me. So, who are you?"

"My name is Agent Ron Coleman of the FBI. I should warn you, I'll be asking you some odd questions."

Jon responded with a smooth but honest comment that Warden Hudson expected from him based on his character. It's why he had arranged the interview in the first place. "Agent Coleman, it would've been interesting to meet someone like you in my past life as a college student. Although, given my current situation, I shouldn't be talking to you."

"Why shouldn't you be talking to me?"

"Because I'm no snitch. I don't even have anyone or anything to snitch about anyway. However, you could leave the room while I talk to this beautiful woman you're with. It's been a while since I've seen a fine woman like her. I'm honestly more interested in talking to her than talking to you." He changed the direction of the conversation and ignored Agent Coleman. "So, what's your name?"

State Rep. Kimberlee Townsend was content letting Agent Coleman take the lead, but she felt compelled to keep Jon talking. "Mr. Bowman, I'm glad to meet you. My name is Kimberlee Townsend, and I'm a state representative. We're both here to ask an unusual question. Is this prison haunted? If so, what can you tell us about the mysterious deaths that have taken place here? We'd appreciate any information you can give us. Have you witnessed any strange events or goings-on here that you can't explain, especially involving the death of an inmate?"

Looking back at Agent Coleman, Jon said, "We'll be here a while. Before we get started, is it a crime to lie to an agent?"

"Yes, it is. Think of this interview as a trial. You can't lie in court to a judge, and you can't lie to me. I can't do my job if I'm not getting the honest story."

"When I was first convicted, I had this weird dream influenced by a ghost named Helen. She warned me of what I was in for at Redmond. If you've done your homework on the history of this prison, you know she's been dead for a long time. Then there was my friend and mentor, Deon Soto, who died from a fall off a three-story tier because he thought dogs were chasing him. The problem was, those dogs belonged to the former warden, all of whom had been dead for decades."

"What else can you tell us?"

"Then there was the ghost I saw before an inmate named Devin ate poisoned mushrooms. The ghost told me not to interfere or warn him because the women of Redmond wanted him to die here. He was from the Slap-A-Ho Tribe, so no one felt any loss or sympathy for him or shed a tear when he died."

A guard opened the door, signaling they needed to wrap things up for the day. Agent Coleman asked his last question. "Jon, I've got one more question for you. Who should I talk to next?"

"You should talk to Freddie Castile so long as you don't ask him about any inmate currently in here unless it relates to the ghosts or spirits in here. He may help you. I'll talk to him for you, but he's a guy you'll want to talk to because he's been in here for over fifteen years. He also had five or ten years at the old Redmond before it closed, so he's a walking archive of all kinds of creepy stories."

The next day, Warden Hudson arranged for Agent Coleman and Rep. Townsend to interview Freddie. Neither of them would be prepared for the bone-chilling and blood-curdling stories he would recount.

"So, Agent Coleman, the guards told me you're doing interviews. None of them would say to me what the interview was about. Jon, a young man we're helping to survive in this crazy prison, told me you're asking about ghosts and spirits and other strange things that may explain the high numbers of inmate deaths."

"Freddie... Can I call you Freddie?"

"Yes."

"Your friend Jon was being honest with you, if that's what he told you."

"Agent Coleman, I've been in prison going on twenty-five years of my life for a stupid mistake. A wrong place, wrong time kind of mistake. I was an accessory to a robbery-homicide that led to a young cashier's death. I didn't pull the trigger, but I didn't stop my friend from pulling the trigger either. My first year in Redmond was at the old Redmond Reformatory before it closed in 1990. Then they moved us to the new Redmond Prison nearby. I worked the prison laundry during a time in my life when I had more hair and more color in it. It was a different time and a different generation.

"I remember the laundry was hot because they were still fixing the bugs in the prison power plant and air-conditioning system. I remember that year because a few of the guys who helped me survive those early years were worried and terrified of the ghost following them. The fear was so pervasive, you could cut it with a knife. I specifically remember them hoping the ghosts or spirits they knew of at the old Redmond stayed there. We soon realized that the ghosts followed us to the new facility. We figured a prison without inmates was just a building, and maybe the ghosts there made the same calculation. Old-timers remembered shoveling tons of dirt from the old Redmond. They needed to elevate and level the foundation of the new Redmond Prison. We think it created a connection that was impossible to ignore.

"The old-timers knew they were right when inmates started dying for unexplained reasons. We were certain when an inmate did something out of character. Shortly after they completed the new Redmond Prison, a man grabbed another inmate by the collar and bent him over a hot commercial ironing press machine. Then, to everyone's astonishment, he pulled the hot press down on his head, squeezing it like a grape. We tried to stop him, but he seemed to get some extra power from somewhere. When he was questioned a few days later, he said he blacked out. We watched in horror as the blood squeezed out of the guy's head along with brain matter in a way that just stayed with you. That scene, it stays with you. It's got to be the worst way to die, and probably the most painful. They damn near had to scoop up his head with a shovel. And all the while, blood squirted out of his decapitated body all over the place.

"We later found out the man who died abused children. Child abuse is one of the worst offenses to be imprisoned for. If found out by the other inmates, it would have caused him to be tormented and tortured. It seemed the guards and the warden intentionally kept his criminal offense a secret to protect him from the other inmates. We believed then, and I still believe now, that they could keep secrets from us, but they couldn't keep secrets from the ghosts of Redmond."

Agent Coleman continued interviewing Freddie and some of the other guys about the weird experiences they had, while in a building nearby, Jon sat shivering in a visitor waiting room to see his lawyer for the first time since his conviction.

Sitting at a round table in the secure family room of the prison was a weird experience. He saw children talking to their fathers. In one group in particular, an older child sat crouched on the floor in the corner, angry and crying. His mother tried desperately to explain why his father couldn't come home with them. As he looked into the eyes of the man in question, he noticed the contours of his face, the wrinkles that come with the stress of a hard life, as well as the gray hair that comes with age. He could see at that moment that a piece of the man died inside. His heart broke looking at his son as he struggled to hold his emotions together, knowing he could never be the father his son deserved.

As this scene played out, Jon's lawyer, Mr. Merit, walked in with two cartons of nicotine patches and documents to appeal his conviction on the grounds of mistakes in his trial and other factors. Standing there looking at him for a few moments, he smiled.

"I'm glad to see you alive and well, young man. So what's this place like on the inside?"

"It can be bizarre at times, but I'm surviving. Some older guys are helping me."

"Can I bring you anything else, like books or anything you're legally allowed to have here?"

"Can you bring me some science fiction books?"

"Sure, what do you like to read?"

"It doesn't matter what it is, I'll read it. Also, anything that involves traveling through the galaxy in a cool-looking spaceship, fighting wars, and meeting aliens. I would appreciate it. In here, a man will do damn near anything to waste time."

As the conversation went on, another inmate walked by, acting like a woman even though he was a man. This caused Mr. Merit to ask, "What in the hell was that?"

"That's what happens when you're a man on the inside and you're not strong in your manhood."

Mr. Merit smiled and said the funniest thing he could have said. "Padawan, stay strong in the Force. Do not succumb to the love that I shall not name."

Jon couldn't help himself. He burst out laughing, attracting the attention of people and inmates nearby and generating stern looks from the guards.

"What's so funny?"

"Mr. Merit, that's the same thing the O.G.s in here told me."

"Oh, so you are alright."

As the conversation moved on to more important matters, Jon asked, "What's the deal with that U.S. attorney filing a friend of the court brief on my behalf?"

"There is no word on that yet, but it caught my attention when it happened, and as soon as I know, you will know too."

After the weird interviews with Agent Coleman ended, Jon was content going back to his routine, talking with the guys and exercising while maintaining a job in the prison garden. However, Robert Jackson was simmering in his rage and anger toward Jon. His ego wouldn't let him get over the beatdown he took at Jon's hands. Scheming and biding his time, he waited patiently for the perfect opportunity to take his revenge.

A small window of time appeared, creating an opportunity that he seized on. In a carefully choreographed process, a line of men was being walked in one direction. Simultaneously, another line of men was walking in the opposite direction. The process was usually smooth, but problems frequently occurred when human beings were involved, and sometimes stuff happened. Jon was walking in one line and Rob made eye contact, and once it registered in his mind who he was looking at, a massive brawl ensued. Guys were throwing punches left and right. To his surprise, Jon was holding his own. It seemed push-ups and gardening paid off.

Rob threw a punch that connected with his chest, taking the wind out of him momentarily. He recovered as his heart raced, and adrenaline gave him a momentary burst of energy and power he didn't know he had. He threw a jab, then a hook. This combination stunned Rob and caused his friends to come to his aid. Double-teamed and taking a beating from all sides, Jon narrowly stayed on his feet. Suddenly, an unfortunate jab caught him in the eye, blurring his vision.

Knowing he was now at a severe disadvantage, he made a high-risk, huge-reward move. He hastily stooped in a crouch low enough to reach the shank he had concealed in his shoe for just this situation. He grabbed it in a flash, then, like a retracted coiled spring, released to a standing position, head-butting one of his attackers with enough power momentarily to freeze another at the right moment. Like a rattlesnake with his tail warning any attacker, he held his shank in his hand, warning attackers to leave him alone. It worked, but the guards soon regained control of the area and caught him with the shank before he could safely hide or dispose of it.

After dropping the shank, he was promptly taken into custody to meet with the prison guard responsible for inmate punishment. He knew the outcome after walking to his office and seeing a mountain of folders stacked on his desk. There was no way he was walking out without spending time in solitary confinement. The supervising guard walked into the room and asked for his name, and when he provided it, the man moved files out of the way, shuffling through a stack that started with the letter B.

"Bowman?"

"Yes, that's me."

After confirming his inmate number, the guard was reassured that he had the right man. "So, Mr. Bowman, this report says guards caught you red-handed with a shank."

"Yes, sir."

"However, after reviewing a video of the incident, what we learned creates a problem for us. Number one, you didn't start the fight. Number two, they double-teamed you through the whole thing. Third, upon encountering the guards, you immediately dropped the shank. That's combined with only using the shank to defend yourself and not attacking anyone unless provoked. The circumstances of the incident explain everything, but the rules are clear and provide no flexibility. I have to send you to solitary. The shank itself is contraband, which carries a punishment of four weeks in the hole. However, I will not classify this as a significant offense that could harm your overall record here. We'll classify it as something else, but you must accept and serve some time in solitary as punishment."

He was escorted to the segregated cell and, while looking inside, he was shoved in. There was absolutely nothing impressive about it. It amounted to a walk-in closet with a relatively narrow, lean-looking bed and a toilet in the corner. A poorly lit room due to no windows or natural light, and the one light automatically turned off at a set time. This left him isolated, in the dark, and *almost* all alone. This was Redmond Prison—no inmate was utterly alone, no matter where they were. There was always an unwelcome spirit willing and able to keep an inmate company. Whether it was to torment or torture them, it made no difference, because here, prisoners always had time, and the ghosts always found a way.

Chapter 9. Stabbed for No Reason

Two days into his punishment, Jon was trying to figure out how to tell the passage of time in order to maintain hope and keep his sanity, when he got advice from an unusual source. On the third night of his stay in solitary, a spirit appeared, refusing to give his name. The spirit appeared somewhat transparent, in an old, dingy-looking prison uniform with what appeared to be a bloodstain.

"How long have you been in here?"

"I've been in here, I think, for three days. How long have you been in here?"

"I don't know. I know I've been here for so long, but I don't remember when I got here or how much time has passed. All I know is that they locked me in here with another man, but then he left. No matter how much or how loudly I screamed, no one seemed to hear me. The guards never offered to let me out."

The spirit walked through a wall and disappeared, only to return the next day at roughly the same time. This spirit did, however, provide some jewels of advice. He said to observe the shift changes and the guards who bring food to figure out the time of day.

After a few nights of these conversations, a guard opened the cell and ordered Jon out while handcuffing him to a nearby chair. Standing in the doorway of the empty cell, he looked back, asking who he was talking to.

"I was talking to nobody."

The guard looked confused, then released him from the handcuffs and placed him back in the cell. He locked the door, then offered some advice of his own. "Young man, don't lose your mind in here. It's happened before."

The next night, the spirit appeared just as he had the night before. This time, Jon asked a probing question. "The other man they locked you in with, was he mean to you?"

The ghost looked directly at him. "Yes, he was extremely mean to me. He terrified me in ways that the guards refused to listen or do anything about. Why do you ask?"

"I think the man you got stuck in the cell with killed you."

Anger and rage grew in the ghost, eventually reaching a level that had to be released. The lights flickered and the walls began to shake, and a chilly breeze radiated outward in the cell and throughout the hallway. There was a split-second vision of a man stuffed underneath the bed. His limbs appeared broken and deformed, and his body was in an unnatural position. Two men may have entered that dark hole that was solitary confinement that day, but only one would leave. The other was trapped in a perpetual life sentence that took his life and deprived him of peace after his death.

Meanwhile, strange things were occurring all across Redmond. Sometimes the inmates as well as the guards looked around in a daze, confused by the unusual events. Walking the prison halls, the guards sometimes experienced the strange smell of a woman's perfume or cold chills in areas that should have been warmer. This was along with the strange sense that they were being watched, not by anyone living, but by the many spirits of Redmond.

Random acts of violence all over the prison, many involving stabbings with shanks, caused Jon to be released a week early from solitary confinement. Inmates flooded the prison infirmary for chest wounds along with other lacerations, bruises, and defensive wounds. Prison staff and administrators were struggling to manage the problem, scratching their heads trying to figure out the reason behind the rash of stabbings. It seemed that some of the ghosts of Redmond were possessing inmates and reliving how they stabbed other inmates while serving their sentences. The staff only realized the similarities after reviewing files from the prison archives and records office.

Pleasantly surprised to be removed from solitary confinement and put back into the general population early, Jon noticed the strange events going on around him. Unexplained stabbings for no apparent reason triggered his curiosity. It was as if inmates were sleepwalking through the heinous acts they were committing. When a man he didn't know got brutally stabbed with a switchblade in front of him, it caused everyone to wonder. *How the hell did he get the blade into prison in the first place, let alone be insane enough to use it? Worse still, what could cause a man to be depraved enough to slice another inmate's face from ear to ear, disfiguring him in a way that would later cause him to take his own life?* This stayed with Jon, causing him to have nightmares until it eventually faded from his memory over time.

He was happy to see familiar faces after returning to his cell for the first time in three weeks. He gradually got up to speed on what he had missed. The guys told him that a defense lawyer from a prestigious law firm had taken an interest in Kenny's case. Freddie said the lawyer even got a DNA test done on some of the evidence, which revealed shocking details: misconduct by the assistant district attorney which, at a minimum, could trigger a retrial.

"That sounds like exciting and excellent news. So, Freddie, what else have I missed stuck in the hole?"

"Well, I'm up for parole, and because of my age, as well as the fact that I pose a low risk of re-offending, my lawyer said they might release me or move me to a safer block. Maybe even a facility for old geezers like me. Young man, you may have to prepare to deal with life on the inside without leaning on us."

Jon lowered his head with a deep sense of sadness and unease. Freddie then reminded him why they were friends.

"Young man, hold your head up. I'm not going anywhere yet. Be strong and stay strong. Never forget, you're not the young man I saw when you first arrived. You're much more rigid and resilient now. You've been through and seen a lot and you're still here."

Following the conversation, the men returned to their cells to prepare for lights out when something bizarre and terrible happened. In a freak accident, the automated electric cell doors were triggered to close. The guards frantically scrambled to fix the computer system after being temporarily locked out, preventing them from stopping them from closing electronically.

The guard assigned to the control room frantically attempted manually to prevent the doors from closing. He was sweating profusely, getting more nervous by the minute as all his efforts failed. In the end, he ran out of time. His worst mistake was not warning the inmates before the five-minute sensor triggered. Once it did, the motors turned on, closing the cell doors on all tiers. The result of the heavy cell doors closing without warning meant pandemonium. Inmates standing partially in the doorways of their cells socializing had no clue what was about to happen.

Limbs that these inmates had become intimately attached to were lost due to amputation. There wasn't time to get to a hospital capable of reattaching them, and even then, how could they figure out which finger, arm, or leg belonged to whom. Body parts were horrifically sprawled across the floors of all tiers. Severed fingers rolled down to the floors below. A river of blood flowed down the walls, forming pools on the floor. Shrieks of pain echoed throughout the halls.

While the guards struggled to deal with the chaos caused by the prison door malfunction, another tragic event was occurring elsewhere. An inmate, acting on a crazy story he heard, would try something that would end his life. Standing before the mirror after taking a shower, he took a few minutes to wipe himself off and cleared the condensation from the mirror. Then he said the name of a spirit he would have been better off leaving alone, a name he'd heard during a conversation in the yard. "Christopher Davis, Christopher Davis, Christopher Davis." He nervously waited, only to lose interest after time passed and nothing happened.

Looking away for only a second, something told him to look back. Staring back at him wasn't his image in the mirror, but something morphing into someone he didn't recognize. When he looked closer, the image staring back terrified him. He saw a tall, pale man, not muscle-bound, but strong enough to hold an axe. His noticeable short, nappy black and gray hair combined with his bloodshot eyes was a terrifying image. His pale, charcoal-gray skin gave the impression of a demon-possessed man. Worst of all, his face was decomposing as though submerged in a lake, chained to a rock for many years. Fear and panic grew inside the inmate just looking at this figure.

They stared at each other for a while, then Christopher suddenly made his move. Using his axe through some supernatural force, he somehow paralyzed the inmate. Then he threw his axe at a horizontal angle through the mirror, stabbing him in the forehead. Using the sheer power of thought, he compelled it to return to him. Blood splattered on the mirror, sink, and floor below. The power of the blow struck with so much force that it nearly split his head in two, leaving the poor soul in a state of shock. He rocked back, then slid down to the floor, where he died as the blood drained from his body, diluted by the water and mist of the showers. When his soul left his body, Christopher absorbed it through the mirror, smiled, then disappeared.

Miles away in Columbus, Victoria and Michelle spent their time together watching Michelle's belly grow with the new life inside and monitoring the tumor shrinking in Victoria's breast. They always started their day at Michelle's mother's doctor's office, then at her doctor's office, and ending with a light lunch. Light, as they shared the view that breakfast was a waste of time because the nausea from their conditions would cause them to throw up everything they ate anyway. Michelle gained more weight from the new life growing inside of her, while the chemo weakened her mother, but put her on a path to recovery. They both remained mentally strong.

As the hours passed by, the days flew by too. Michelle became more anxious as she got closer to her due date. The better her mother felt, the more she bought baby furniture and clothes. While her dad was sitting at his desk in his office, he tried to think about how to honor his promise to his daughter. His chief of staff, Darnell Jackson, walked in.

"Sir, the Ways and Means Committee has approved the language of your line item. The entire house will eventually vote on a bill that includes that language."

"Good, I have another matter for you to work on that needs special attention. Do you know anyone in the Attorney General's Bureau of Criminal Identification and Investigation office? I need you to look into the case of a young man named Jon Bowman."

"Sir, I know a guy, my sister's husband, who works for that office. He could help look into the young man's case. They have jurisdiction over it if it's a state case, and he can find out about it."

Leaning back in his chair, the state representative said, "Perfect, because this matter is of special importance to me. It involves my daughter."

"Sir, how sensitive is this?"

"It involves my grandson. That's how sensitive."

"Oh, I understand, sir. Congratulations. We must handle this discreetly and carefully until we know the full details of the case to minimize any political damage to you, while ensuring that no public harm or embarrassment comes to your daughter."

"Darnell, that's precisely how I need this handled."

"Sir, I'll get on this right away."

Darnell walked out of the room and immediately called his brother-in-law.

"Derick, how are you doing?"

"Well, well, I haven't heard your voice in a while."

"Avoiding you was a given after that loss by the Buckeyes to Michigan. The three-pointer near the end of the fourth quarter was brutal, and I was a little depressed after that, but I'm alright now. I'm calling you because I need your help on a sensitive matter. Do you have a pen nearby?"

"Yes, I've got one."

"I need you to look into the case of a young man named Jon Bowman. Also, I haven't forgotten about that small wager on that basketball game. Dinner on me, for you and my sister at her favorite restaurant."

The next day, Derick arrived at the Ohio BCI office, and after clearing all the security procedures to get into the building, he arrived at his desk. He sat in the chair while stuffing his lunch bag and standard-issue gun in a secure drawer. He stared at the screen of his computer with the space shuttle screen saver. Glancing at the clock, he watched as the long hand struck twelve and the small hand moved to nine. It was time to get down to business. He took the paper with the name he had written the day before from his shirt pocket. Moving the mouse around to wake the computer up automatically switched off the screensaver and revealed a user ID and password screen.

He navigated through the relevant software programs to access the criminal records of all individuals convicted in the state, typing the name *Jon Bowman* to narrow down the search results. The file appeared in PDF format within a few moments. Carefully and methodically, he read while stopping periodically to take notes. After a few hours, he stopped to eat lunch. He took time to analyze and think about what he had read, eventually reaching the point where he had to make the call. Dialing Darnell's number, he worried about how to explain what he had learned. However, the words seemed to flow when Darnell answered the phone.

"Hey Darnell, this is Derick. We need to talk. Do you have some time?"

"Sure. Is this about that name I dropped on you?"

"Yes, it is."

"Well, how bad is it?"

"The situation isn't good, considering how they unfairly accused this young man. I need to see you about this in person."

"Okay, that will also allow me to get that gift card for you so you can use it for my sister's favorite restaurant."

They met at Darnell's office in the Ohio House office building within a few hours. He greeted him, and they both sat down and discussed the details of the file.

"Derick, happy to see you, but this must be serious if you want to meet in person. Is it that serious?"

"Darnell, it is that serious. This case is an example of how the black community is losing too many young brothers and sisters over nonsense. To start with, police arrested this young man after catching him in possession of two prescription-sized bottles of Oxy along with two or three joints of marijuana. The marijuana I buy, that many opioid pills I don't. Especially when you consider the fact that black men don't usually have access to those types of drugs or anyone who could supply them. This arrest makes me suspicious because this young man had no criminal history and it occurred during a routine traffic stop by an officer. Based on internal affairs records, this officer has a suspicious number of arrests, which is unusual for this area.

"The record established by his lawyer states he was on his way home from Central State University. The lawyer provided corroboration evidence introduced at trial. There's also no statement or confession here, which means he was smart enough to keep his mouth shut and listen to his lawyer. He was also smart enough to avoid trouble before eighteen. It's been my experience that a person is less likely to get in trouble after eighteen. This young man had the added motivation of having a father convicted of being an accomplice in a bank robbery. A bank robbery where not one, but two cops died."

Then, with a smile, he dropped a shocking detail on him. "Darnell, one of the officers who arrested his father married his mother and raised him."

"What? Oh, my God, are you serious?"

"I'm dead serious. That's in the record too. He died last year. If you can spare the time, you must talk to his mother. You need to speak with the attorney in this case. You also need to reach out to someone on the Correctional Institution Inspection Committee to find a member who knows the warden of Redmond Prison. Mainly to let him know that this young man may have a friend in high places. You might not think it'll make a big difference, but prison staff try not to mistreat inmates who might be innocent and have friends in high places out of fear that the press would make a story out of it. Last, but most important of all, a deputy US attorney filed a friend of the court letter on behalf of this young man."

Hearing this caused Darnell to sit up in his chair in shock. "Derick, are you serious?"

"Darnell, I'm dead serious. He recommended a downward departure during sentencing. This is not normal, and there's a supplement in the criminal record file by Internal Affairs about the arresting officer. Perhaps the feds had to let him get charged and convicted to show harm had been done, knowing they could rectify the situation later."

While Darnell listened, the synapses in his brain started firing. He started thinking about how to use the information he was getting, making political calculations while thinking about who else to talk to and what favors may need to be called in. The room went silent as Derick wrapped up his briefing.

"Derick, I think this is above my pay grade. I need you to repeat everything you told me to my boss, State Rep. Kimbell."

Darnell left the room for a moment, only to return a few minutes later with Rep. Kimbell. When the formalities and handshakes were out of the way, Darnell advised Derick not to get nervous, just to repeat everything he had just told him. Derick ended the briefing with a statement that stuck with both men.

"Sir, I haven't met many politicians in person because my position encouraged me to be non-political. However, I spend a lot of time with young people who are growing up in circumstances that are not the best. Trying to keep them from going down the wrong path is a second job I don't mind doing. Sir, you represent the black community in the statehouse. I have family in your district who voted for you. I also know members of the black community who you don't even represent who would call you before they call their representative. I say all of this because we're losing too many young brothers and sisters to the criminal justice system for stupid reasons, and it must stop."

Rep. Kimbell's senior secretary interrupted the meeting. "Sir, I'm sorry to interrupt you. Your wife's doctor called."

"Do I need to talk to him, or should I just call him back later?"

"No, he just told me to tell you that things look good. She's not clear yet, but her prognosis looks good."

He leaned back in his chair with a huge smile. "Darnell, do we know anyone on the House Committee on Correctional Institution Inspections?"

After a moment of confused silence, Kimbell's secretary spoke up. "I know someone."

"Who do you know?"

"I know State Rep. Kimberlee Townsend's secretary."

"Well, how well do you know her secretary?"

"I know her incredibly well; she's my little sister."

"Really?!"

"Yes, I'm the one who recommended her to Rep. Townsend's chief of staff for her job."

"Okay, what do you know about Rep. Townsend?"

"She was recently at Redmond Prison, mostly asking questions about the weird stories."

"Really?! Was it official or unofficial?"

"It was an unofficial fact-finding endeavor to find out about unexplained inmate deaths. The committee did not sanction her visit."

"What did she learn?"

"She learned that Redmond Prison is the weirdest, most haunted, craziest place to do time."

"Do you know how well she knows the warden of Redmond?"

"She knew him well enough to convince him to keep her name out of the press during that crazy prison break. When that mentally ill woman lost her mind and forced a helicopter pilot to aid the escape."

The three men in the room responded in unison with the same statement.

"Holy shit, are you fucking kidding me? She was there during that incident? We watched that craziness on television."

Rep. Kimbell looked directly at her. "Pat, I need you to arrange a meeting with her right now."

Walking out of the room to make the call to her sister, she was a little curious as to why the men in the room were so interested in Rep. Townsend's relationship with the warden of Redmond. Her experience during her relatively long career as a secretary taught her not to ask too many questions. It was her major priority to get things done, which also required her to keep secrets, only revealing them when necessary, ensuring the smooth operation of her office.

Sitting at her desk, she placed the call and waited for the familiar voice of her sister to answer the phone.

"Hey, Janet, what's going on over there?"

"Not a lot."

"What's your boss doing?"

"She's in her office eating a salad while going through a mountain of prison oversight reports."

"Where's her chief of staff?"

"She's at her desk looking at polling data, campaign finance reports, and the members' district demographic data. She seems a little worried."

"I need you to do something for me."

"What can I do for you?"

"I need both of them in State Rep. Kimbell's office right now."

"Wait, Rep Kimbell, the Democratic ranking member of the House Judiciary Committee?"

"Yes, and you should know they were interested in Redmond Prison, so I had to tell them quite a bit about what you told me. However, I don't think you're in any trouble. I feel her knowledge of Redmond may be of benefit to her. So try to get them here now."

"Okay, I'll work on it."

After an hour had passed, the call came. "Pat, they're on their way."

"Good."

She prepared the larger conference room while everyone assembled and took their seats. Rep. Kimbell was the first to speak. Looking at and speaking directly to Rep. Townsend's chief of staff, a woman who doubled as her campaign manager, he asked, "What are you afraid of?" However, before she could answer, he answered for her. "You're worried that because the conservatives redrew the district lines of Rep. Townsend's district, the slight change in the demographics complicates your boss's re-election calculation, which presents a problem for you. Specifically, more African Americans that you're not used to dealing with. You're also worried about possibly a primary challenge from the left. You know she's a savvy politician. However, she's inexperienced in dealing with this problem. And you don't want to look for another job, especially after having managed your first successful campaign. Am I right?"

"Sir, you're on the money."

Then he looked at Rep. Townsend and smiled. "I hear you've been having some rather interesting adventures at Redmond Prison. Adventures involving a helicopter."

She smiled. "Oh, so you've heard about that?"

"Ms. Townsend, that shocked the hell out of us when we learned about it. Let's get to the reason I called you here. What do you know about the warden of Redmond?"

"I know he's a decent man doing the best job he can, trying to run the craziest prison in the state. Why do you ask?"

"I need his help to ensure the safety and well-being of one of his inmates."

"Who's the inmate?"

Derick handed her the folder he was holding. When she saw the name on it, Jon Bowman, she went mute and leaned back in her chair. "I know this young man."

Everyone in the room went silent and listened with extreme interest.

"Please explain what you mean when you say you know him."

"Warden Hudson arranged for me and an FBI agent to interview a few of the inmates concerning the strange deaths there. He was one of those inmates."

"What was your impression of the young man?"

"My gut screamed that he was out of place and didn't belong there, primarily due to his intelligence and the words he was using. His determination to survive a place he knew he didn't belong in was how he carried himself. He was also trying to flirt with me, even though he was in prison. The funny part of the interview was that he did an excellent job of it."

Everyone in the room laughed a little. Rep. Kimbell then encouraged her to continue reading.

"Okay, it says here he spent some time in college, along with a brief detail about his father being incarcerated as an accessory to a homicide. Despite the previous detail, this was Mr. Bowman's first offense, no priors. The report states that police found two prescription-sized bottles of Oxy and some marijuana on him during a routine traffic stop. It stipulates in a supplement that the arresting officer has a questionable reputation, which is documented by internal affairs. Who was his supplier? Did the prosecutor even offer a deal to find out? If not, then they knew this young man didn't have a supplier because the officer planted the drugs. It may mean the judge and prosecutor were in on railroading this young man and many others.

"Okay, this makes no sense. The marijuana, I get, but the opioids? No way. As a former prosecutor and defense attorney, I believe this report contradicts logic, which makes me suspicious of this arrest."

"That's the reaction I was looking for," said Rep. Kimbell. "This young man spent some time at Central State University. While there, he had a relationship with my daughter. He doesn't know it, but he's my grandson's father, who will arrive soon. I need assurances that this young man will live to see his release date. To see if he will be the father I hope he's willing to be to my grandson."

Chapter 10. Political Ramifications

During the meeting in Rep. Kimbell's office, Darnell remained silent. Once the meeting ended, he went to Rep. Townsend for a private conversation. "Miss Townsend, can I talk to you for a minute?"

"Sure."

"There's one detail you mentioned everyone paid no attention to. What was an FBI agent doing at Redmond Prison? What was the agent's name?"

"His name is Agent Ron Coleman. He was there for the same reason that I was: unexplained inmate deaths. Someone at the Bureau who keeps track of those statistics noticed the high numbers and sent him to investigate. Why do you ask?"

"Miss Townsend, I've become a collector of people in this business of politics. My goal has been to build a Rolodex of contacts, an array of names and phone numbers. It makes my job easy if I can call people when I have a problem that I need help with on my employer's behalf. That can be a valuable commodity. Miss Townsend, I recommend you develop a relationship and maintain contact with Agent Coleman. Also, I have something else I need to discuss with you. If for any reason you find yourself back at Redmond, please don't tell Jon about his son before he's released. We need to speak with him directly to see his reaction and allow him to decide if he will be a part of this child's life."

"I understand and respect that position. I won't say a word or mention it." She then left to go back to her office.

A month later, at the FBI field office in Cleveland, Ohio, a phone call ended with the US attorney of Ohio advising the special agent in charge that indictments were coming against targets of major investigations into the Ohio legislature and criminal justice system. As the news spread throughout the organization and reached Agent Coleman, he didn't care. He couldn't focus, primarily because he couldn't get one person out of his mind: State Rep. Townsend.

Ignoring the flurry of activity in the office and following orders, he and a few agents walked into a briefing room. Their boss walked in a few minutes later, slamming the door behind him. He then played a shocking video of what should have been a routine traffic stop. It involved Officer Anthony Donovan planting drugs on a young man he knew by the name of Jon Bowman. Agent Coleman sat watching the video, astonished at what he was seeing. He accidentally blurted out for all to hear, "Holy shit, that son of a bitch?"

Upon hearing the name, he immediately sat up in his chair and demanded they replay the video. He restarted it from the beginning and began paying closer attention. When they played another of the same officer at a different traffic stop, the supporting videos revealed high-quality surveillance of Officer Donovan's terrible conduct. Conduct that disgusted Coleman and made him mad in ways he tried to conceal. He knew that was why members of the black community didn't trust law enforcement.

His boss stood up as the presentation ended, and as someone turned on the lights, he asked the most challenging question he could have of those who served under him: "Who would like to volunteer to arrest this officer and take him into custody? Considering our video evidence, the US attorney will not likely allow him to surrender himself. This officer will have to suffer the indignity of being walked out of his station in handcuffs. There's also interest in pressuring him to roll over on other targets. A deal may be on the table only if he reveals other criminal behavior he knows about involving other officers throughout the Ohio criminal justice system, especially if it's related to private prisons."

Looking around the room, no one raised their hand. Coleman understood the reasons and sentiment of being a career member of law enforcement. No one aspired to be the guy on television arresting a fellow member of law enforcement and walking them out in handcuffs. Against his better judgment, a voice in his head screamed at him to stand up. As he slowly did, he could feel the eyes of his fellow agents sear into him. The room fell so silent you could hear a pin drop. His boss was shocked.

"Why are you willing to do this?"

"I'm doing this because of you. You asked me to go to the Redmond Prison to investigate strange, unexplained inmate deaths. Warden Hudson arranged for me to interview a few inmates and staff. The young man in that video, Mr. Bowman, was one of those inmates. While there, he and other inmates and staff told me that Redmond is the weirdest, craziest, and most haunted prison in Ohio. Well, for the short time I spent with that young man, my gut was telling me he didn't belong there. The video evidence makes it clear to me that a miscarriage of justice has occurred, and we must correct it. Sir, I'll do this job for you that nobody else wants to do, but I need a copy of that video."

Hearing his explanation and reasoning for his decision, even if they didn't quite buy the part involving spirits and ghosts, they accepted his explanation. The meeting ended with his boss ordering a technical support agent to provide him with a copy of the video he requested. However, the video came with a condition: he couldn't reveal it to the public or use it before the trial of Officer Donovan. His boss clarified he had to wait until the deputy US attorney trying the case entered the video into evidence. At a minimum, he could show it in a judge's chambers to get a new trial in another matter. After Donovan accepted a deal, the case against him would go to trial or another resolution.

After returning to his desk, he thought about what he had learned from the video. Suddenly it hit him, as his mind wandered to a woman he just couldn't seem to get out of his head. He got the courage to call her. Navigating through the automated Ohio state legislative switchboard to get to her secretary, he patiently waited until he finally got to a human.

"State Rep. Kimberlee Townsend's office, how can I help you?"

"Hello, my name is Agent Ron Coleman of the FBI. Can I talk to Rep. Townsend? She's not in any trouble. You can tell her I'm the tall, handsome man she met at Redmond Prison." *Hopefully I left a good enough impression for her to remember me.*

Her secretary hastily placed him on hold to relay his message.

"Who is it?" Rep. Townsend asked, speaking through the microphone on the inter-office system on her phone while looking up from the papers she was reading.

"He said his name was Agent Ron Coleman of the FBI."

She tried to calm her nerves to avoid revealing that she had an unusual feeling about him or any sign that he had left an impression on her.

"Hello? What brings on this unexpected call from you?"

"Since I met you, you've been stuck in my head day and night. I've been having problems concentrating on my work."

"That sounds like something you should see a doctor about. So, Agent Coleman, why do you want to get me out of your head?"

"That's my problem. I don't. I think you're an extraordinary woman, and I want to get to know you better. I was hoping you would go out to dinner with me."

"Now why should I do that?"

"Because I've recently come across some information about that young man that was trying to flirt with you. Information that you may find interesting."

"It's funny that you brought up that young man, because I recently found out some information about him as well. It seems he has some friends in high places he doesn't know about. Those friends have made it clear I should maintain contact with you and maintain a relationship with you. A professional one, of course."

He knew he was not interested in pursuing only a professional relationship with her. Playing it off, he was careful to signal agreement. In his mind, however, he grew more determined to pursue something else. "So, where do you want to go for dinner?"

"Somewhere that has seafood, that's also healthy."

"I know a place that serves excellent blackened catfish but also has some fantastic grilled salmon."

Hours later, he arrived at her door with a rose and a sense of unease about how the night would go. Pushing the doorbell nervously, he waited for her to open the door. When she did, he stood there amazed. She came out in a blue dress that highlighted her figure without being too revealing. Her stunning appearance left him speechless. While she looked at him in his casual dress suit, he looked at her up and down without saying a word. She thought to herself, *Yep, that's the reaction I was looking for.*

He didn't know what to say. He regained his bearings and complimented her shoes, not because he was sure it was the best thing he could have said, but because he knew it took time to coordinate the dress she had on, the shoes she was wearing, and the purse she was carrying. All in a well-thought-out effort to make her ensemble work.

After arriving at the restaurant and taking their seats, the conversation began. Being a skilled FBI agent, it wasn't easy turning off his inquisitive mind. It kept forcing him to ask probing questions.

"So, what do you know that you feel comfortable sharing?"

"I know Mr. Bowman attended Central State University with the daughter of State Rep. Frederick Kimbell, the ranking member of the state House Judiciary Committee. This connection resulted in a relationship that developed over time, leading to her becoming pregnant."

"Oh, that's a fascinating connection."

"Once her father was told of the pregnancy and the impending arrival of his first grandson, well, that resulted in this young man's well-being becoming a matter of particular interest."

"How does this affect you?"

"It usually wouldn't, but they called me into Rep. Kimbell's office to find out how well I knew Warden Hudson. Mainly to use my relationship to get his help to ensure this young man's safety, along with securing his well-being until he finishes serving out his sentence. However, once I told them I interviewed this young man and didn't believe he belonged in prison in the first place, they offered to help in my re-election effort. Help that I need after the conservatives redrew my district lines. Mainly because I now have constituents I'm not used to dealing with, let alone representing—members of the black community. They also showed me Mr. Bowman's rap sheet with little in it. It had a document from a deputy US attorney noting a friend of the court brief filed on his behalf, a detail that caught my attention."

"So is that all you know?"

"Yes, that's all they told me."

"Okay, what do you know about prison privatization?"

"I know it was a dumb idea that will never save the state money, so long as those prison corporations are accountable to their shareholders. The chairman of my committee told me he is considering early retirement primarily because of his problems with the cozy relationships and overly generous campaign donations that members of his caucus were too enthusiastic to accept. Donations those corporations gave in return for supporting the prison privatization legislation."

"Ms. Townsend, things will get nasty in the capital in the next few days. Nerves will flair because of federal prosecutors' pressure on people."

"You can call me Kim."

"Kim, this is what I know. Indictments are being issued, and they will unseal them in days. The US attorney of Ohio called the supervising agent in charge of the Ohio branch of the FBI. He told us early this morning, someone is being prepared for handcuffs right now. That target is the arresting officer in the Bowman case. Kim, we've got a video of the man dead to rights planting drugs on Mr. Bowman and other black Ohioans. I also know he's facing the prospect of being walked out of his station in handcuffs."

She sat back in her chair in shock after hearing these revelations. "Ron, how serious are you right now? Why should I believe you?"

"Because my boss gave me a copy of the video of Officer Donovan planting the drugs. That's after I volunteered to be the one to walk him out of his station in handcuffs."

"My God. You are serious. The only way you would know the arresting officer's name in the Bowman case is by looking at his criminal file, which has a link to a federal one. Or you were told by someone working a connecting case who looked at the file."

"Yep."

Meanwhile, events were converging a distance away, culminating into a single moment. Michelle was under the watchful eye of her mother sitting across from her when an odd feeling came over her. She sat in what seemed like the most uncomfortable chair she could be in. What made it worse was that the pillow used as a cushion wasn't working to reduce the pressure on her back. When her mother looked at her pants, they were light-colored enough to notice they were wet. Instantly she knew, and Michelle eventually realized...

"Oh, God, my water broke!"

This caused both women to look at each other in shock until they came to their senses and started taking action.

Fortunately for them, they were close to a hospital. Her mother nervously dialed 911 to call an ambulance. The pain grew as her breathing became labored but consistent, and the wait seemed like an eternity. When the ambulance arrived, the paramedics were professional and thorough, asking questions while applying all the training they had to get her to the hospital safely but as fast as possible.

Arriving at the hospital, the nurses and doctors were waiting for her, to her mother's relief. However, the only thought that seemed to cross her mind at that moment was to call Dad. She looked at her mother, squeezing her hand as she lay on a gurney, sweating profusely as her mother looked on. Her mother knew what she wanted without her having to say a word.

"I already called your dad," she whispered.

The pain overwhelmed her, making her feel like her insides were being squeezed, twisted, and pulled. She was then rolled into a room with bright lights and medical equipment. Just as the pain grew ever more intense, the lovely lady with the epidural showed up. The calls to push, push, push a little more rang out. Time seemed to stand still, but four hours had passed when she heard the best sound of her life: the cries of her son. He was covered in body fluids, cold, and shaking, and she looked at him, smiling, with a sense of joy and relief.

An odd set of events occurred with the prison's closed-circuit video system, strange even for Redmond, a place known for strange occurrences. The video feed from the prisoner intake area recorded a bus from the 1950s pulling up. The video showed prisoners getting off the bus with pale transparent skin, along with short or no hair at all. The prisoners were dead, but walking around as though they were alive, all as the guards looked on in terror.

The closed-circuit video system also recorded Civil War-era Union soldiers running drills in the recreation area. The prison archivist reviewed hours of video to figure out what was happening.

The place got so weird, the guards raised the possibility of inviting ghost hunters in to get a clearer picture of what was going on. Warden Hudson seriously considered this, but his better judgment kicked in and he shot it down. Meanwhile, the inmates were mainly oblivious to what was going on.

Joseph A. Green, Inmate 30678, lived by his routine like all other inmates at Redmond. He was one of a kind, with swastika tattoos covering most of his body. He may have once held racist attitudes, but time has a way of changing a man, especially one doing time in prison. He was a fixture on C-block and well-known to all the guards and inmates alike, mainly because he swept and mopped the floors. His routine was so consistent, the guards could set their watches to his schedule. His most important quality was the other job he held, the one Jon was most interested in. Joseph was the inmate trusted to deliver books and mail to all the inmates in the C-wing.

On the Redmond Prison grapevine, some suspected that Joseph got his job and had so many privileges by being a snitch. Whether it was true, the Black and Latino inmates didn't know, but the Skinheads seemed to believe it. They felt he wasn't at Redmond long enough to justify the level of privileges he was getting. These suspicions put his life at risk and forced the guards to give him a job where they could monitor him to ensure his safety. Once he completed all his assigned tasks, Joseph could smoke a cigarette before returning to his cell.

Jon's interest in him first peaked because he couldn't quite figure out what could persuade a man to put a tattoo on his face. He saw him every day and held brief conversations with him. Delivering books from the prison library forced Jon to strike up conversations with him, still careful to abide by Freddie's rules. This relationship caused him to look past all the racist tattoos and see the human being behind them. Jon learned he got all those tattoos when he was young and stupid.

One day, Joseph showed up at Jon's cell with a guard, and both men smiled. Joseph had one package in his hand, while the guard had another package and an envelope. The guard was the first to speak—the same guard who told him about the job in the prison garden.

"Bowman, Inmate 70597?"

"Yes, sir."

The guard opened the envelope and began reading it.

"This letter is from your attorney, Mr. Merit. 'The guard delivering this letter has my permission to read it to you. During our last conversation, you requested reading material that involved science fiction books, specifically anything about traveling through or exploring the galaxy in a cool-looking spaceship.'" After reading that statement, he signaled for Joseph to hand him the package he was holding, then he continued reading while smiling. "'Contained in the second package and envelope is a popular men's sports magazine you may like based on my advice to you during that conversation we had. I feel you might like the swimsuit edition of that magazine.'" On the cover were two scantily dressed women in bikinis.

The guard stopped reading and looked closer at the last part of the letter. Then he laughed to the point of crying before showing it to Joseph, who was standing beside him. As he handed it back, he started laughing. Jon looked at them in confusion. They both looked at him and said simultaneously, "Padawan, stay strong in the force. Do not succumb to the love that I shall not name." Laughter erupted from the group.

Before leaving, the guard carefully reminded him that the magazine was likely contraband, but he could keep the magazine if it stayed hidden and didn't cause any problems. Both men turned to walk away, and as they got a few feet away, Jon could still hear them laughing. He had to smile and laugh himself.

After searching for nearly five minutes to find a hole in his mattress, he finally found one. Opening it just wide enough, he stuck the magazine inside, ensuring he could get it out again. However, he had to peek inside and take the time to admire the women before hiding it. Then he turned his attention to his science fiction books before falling asleep a few minutes before lights out.

Unbeknownst to Jon, the hilarious scene he had with Joseph would be his last. It would also be the last time Joseph would have a smile on his face. Unfortunately, he would die within eleven hours. The next day, tragedy struck. It started when an accidental leak occurred between the deputy district attorney of Mansfield, Ohio, and the defense counsel during the discovery process in a rather important drug case connected to the Redmond Civil War. The leak revealed to the defendant that Joseph was the snitch who ratted them out, breaking up a rather lucrative illicit drug network.

Once someone mentioned this name to a friend with connections in Redmond, the news made its way through the grapevine, eventually being whispered into the ear of the leader of the Skinheads. Fueled by anger and a burning desire for vengeance, he moved with lethal speed to punish Joseph for his betrayal. Knowing his routine, they meticulously crafted a plan, carefully setting a trap after acquiring a small but potent chemical substance that burned ferociously and left no trace. The goal was to make him suffer before he died.

They waited and watched him, allowing him to follow his daily routine, delivering the mail along with books as he usually did. Jon saw him make his rounds on the C-block just like every other day. However, on this day, when he made his way up the stairs toward A-block, upon reaching the first cell, one of the inmates hastily stopped him and asked him to come closer in a loud and angry voice. Shouting blared out at him, a single word that would terrify any inmate behind the walls to hear: "Snitch, snitch, snitch! Joseph is the low-down rat responsible for the Redmond Civil War." He hastily abandoned his position in front of the first cell on the block, walking fast and instantly revealing his guilt to his tormentors. Suddenly, an inmate doused him with a small bottle of an unknown solution he had concealed behind his back.

The solution was clear and odorless, so he wiped his face with his shirt and thought nothing of it. An odd sensation came over him, a slight but persistent burning of his eyes. It should have been a sign that it wasn't water, but he paid no attention to it. The guards saw nothing on the security cameras because just as he was being doused, the lights flickered, and an image appeared on the closed-circuit monitors: Christopher Davis, the Axeman, holding his axe, appeared only long enough to distract the guards.

Returning to C-block after finishing his rounds, Joseph walked to his usual corner to smoke his cigarette. He had his single cigarette stuck securely behind his left ear. He brought it to his mouth. He held the lighter in his hand, pushing the button to trigger it. Sparks appeared before the flame rose steadily until it was continuous. The cigarette seemed to absorb the flame as puffs of smoke filled the surrounding air. Then an image of a man phased in and out. The pale, axe-wielding man frightened him so much, his cigarette fell onto his shirt. Once his shirt caught fire, he tried frantically to put it out, only to see it get worse. As the guards surged forward, their shouts echoing through the air, the flames grew, consuming the man in a fiery inferno. He was a desperate, panicking figure when they reached him, but by then, it was already too late.

Unknowingly, he was feeding air to the fire. The inmates watched in astonishment as flames engulfed him, turning him into a human fireball. When the guards finally unlocked the doors to reach him, the smell of singed flesh hung heavy in the air. He lay there, his skin blistered and red, a testament to the fire's brutal touch. He lingered, clinging to life in pain for nearly two days, enduring skin grafts to remove burned skin. He gave up the ghost and died late on a dreary Sunday night.

Chapter 11. Lost Souls

After a short two-hour and twenty-five-minute drive from the capital in Columbus to West Cleveland, Darnell Jackson thought long and hard about what to say to Mrs. Darlene Freeman. His assignment was mainly a reconnaissance mission to discover more details about Jon's character, trying to see if this young man was worth the expenditure of political capital to save. Riding through the black community of West Cleveland, he had flashbacks of the neighborhood where he grew up. Familiar sights reminded him of his childhood, with its rows of sporadic, vacant, and dilapidated houses. The sounds of cars honking and people chatting filled the air, blending with the distant hum of city life. The stench of trash from a nearby waste dump that they always put in the black community because those in power figure other lives are worth more.

As he drove through the neighborhood, he couldn't help but feel a sense of nostalgia, as if transported back to his early years. The conditions here mirrored his upbringing, evoking emotions and memories. It was the reason he entered politics in the first place. He wanted to make a difference. When he compared the conditions to his upbringing, the similarities were glaring in the concentrated poverty. Pockets of blighted houses scattered between the manicured yards of those who could still afford to maintain them, along with the single-story houses sitting at slight elevations.

He pulled up in the driveway of one of the more fixed-up houses on the block. Mrs. Freeman sat on her porch staring at his car. He looked at the house number on the mailbox to confirm he had the right house. He turned off his car and grabbed the keys before getting out while closing the door behind him.

"Mrs. Freeman?"

"Yes."

"My name is Darnell Jackson. I called to talk to you about your son Jon."

She stood up to greet him properly, shaking his hand. "Mr. Jackson, please come in."

Stepping into her house, he immediately noticed the gallery of pictures lining the walls. He focused on the ones of her and her son on the wall. She recalled the stories behind them as she noticed what he was doing. Tears rolled down her face, and she remembered the happier moments while talking about the sad ones. Just listening to her, it was apparent how much love she felt for her son, and it wasn't hard to feel her pain over what happened to him. He listened with interest as she told him about how he helped pull her out of a deep depression after she went to visit his father in prison.

She told him how funny and intelligent Jon was by showing him old report cards she kept from middle school and high school. One statement stood out in his mind: "Mr. Jackson, I know all mothers say their sons are angels, even when they're closer to devils, but my baby, my son, is different." She was adamant that her son knew nothing about opioids. "I know my son, and I he may know about marijuana, but he knows nothing about opioids." The last detail she provided would prove to be the most important nugget of all, a detail that made the entire trip worth it. She explained she couldn't believe he was guilty of having opioids, "because he used to flush my doctor-prescribed Happy Pills down the toilet when he noticed I liked them too much."

As the conversation continued, she told him about how afraid she was raising her son in the neighborhood she lived in, almost alone. "I was fearful of working late and having to catch the bus at night, afraid of walking down the street alone, praying to God with every step I took, asking Him to protect and keep me safe. My fear only went away when I married his stepfather, one of the few black police detectives the community knew and liked. Once that happened, nobody dared bother me, and the community kept a protective watch over us."

After listening to her for nearly an hour and a half, he left Mrs. Freeman's house knowing he had to get Jon out of Redmond because he truly didn't belong there.

Back at Redmond, C-block became festive when people learned a jury cleared Kenny of all charges during a retrial that nobody talked about to avoid jinxing his chances. The trial ended in an acquittal after a jury reviewed existing evidence from the previous trials and the fresh evidence discovered. The thought that ran through Kenny's mind after the trial was to leave Redmond and never to return, especially after seeing the sky as a free man.

For Jon, this event was a bittersweet occasion. He was losing a critical elder who was helping him survive in Redmond. The thought of losing Freddie through parole filled him with dread. Remaining strong through being thoughtful and listening to solid advice helped him up to this point, but he knew he might have to go the rest of the way alone. Only time would tell if his fears would come true.

The exoneration did trigger a positive side effect. It revealed prosecutorial misconduct by District Attorney Thomas Bounds, the prosecutor trying the case at the time. Now that he was a sitting judge, all of his cases as a prosecutor and as a judge would also be reviewed for bias and misconduct. This then called into question other Ohio jurists' bias, giving the Ohio justice system a black eye that they could little afford at a time when the feds were already looking at them side-ways.

Meanwhile, sitting at the table in the usual spots, it was uncharacteristically silent. They all missed Kenny, but were happy he wasn't in Redmond, he was somewhere else, enjoying his new life as a free man. That's when an excruciating shot of pain flooded through the nerves in Jon's mouth. He spit out a broken tooth along with blood into a napkin palmed in his hand. It seemed like biting down hard on a piece of baked chicken had consequences—a level of pain he would become intimately familiar with. Anything hot or cold he ate or drank would be an unyielding source of pain for the next two weeks until the prison dentist could see him. That made for an interesting first week back.

Freddie, however, seemed to notice everything, even the smallest detail that others would dismiss as insignificant. If no one else noticed the pain in his friend's face, he did. Pain that he tried to conceal and take without a sound. "Hey, young man. Are you alright over there?"

In too much pain to lie, Jon had to tell the truth. "No, no, I'm not alright." He held his jaw, trying to ease the pain. "I think I broke a tooth biting into this chicken."

"How much pain are you feeling, on a scale of one to ten?"

"I would say it's about a nine. I think I can take it for a while."

"No, you can't. A toothache can wake a grown man from a sound sleep, bringing him to tears." Freddie smiled, showing him his dental implants. "Padawan, I know this from my lived experience." The other guys also showed their replacement dentures. "No matter how tough you think you are, no man is tough enough to take a toothache for long. You must get on the list to see Doctor Harris. The sooner you get on the list, the sooner you'll get seen and treated. You would be wise to listen to your elders, and we advise you to deal with this problem. Besides, I don't want you using this toothache as an excuse for why you lost another chess game to me."

Listening to Freddie, Jon could only smile and do as he was told.

"I should warn you that Doctor Harris is the weirdest doctor you will meet."

"What do you mean?"

"Oh, you'll find out."

The next day, following Freddie's advice, Jon made it clear to the guards that he was in severe pain and must see Doctor Harris. Suffering through the pain for another week, he watched his name slowly move up the waiting list. By the time Doctor Harris eventually saw him, the pain was throbbing and constant due to the cold temperatures of the waiting room and the prison itself. The dental assistant took care of the paperwork. Eventually, they led him to a room with a dentist's chair and other equipment and instruments. It was still cold as hell, which all doctor's offices seemed to be. He sat in the chair and waited for the doctor. Within a few minutes, he walked in, a middle-aged man with graying hair.

Looking at x-rays of his teeth, Jon could hear groans of anger. The doctor rotated in his chair to look at him. "Mr. Bowman, your lack of vitamin D has weakened your teeth, and you'll lose one. I've seen this all too often, and I blame the state for the lack of adequate nutritional food served to you all. I'm going to have to do a root canal." And that's when he asked an odd question. "Do you like stories?"

"Yes, I love them."

Numbing his jaw and waiting a few minutes for the drug to do its job, Doctor Harris started telling the story of his predecessor.

"Doctor Kalvin Giovanni worked at Redmond for nearly thirty years. Even though he was skilled at his job, there were problems caused by unexplained and excessive deaths on his watch. Doctor Giovanni over-anesthetized many of the inmates under his care."

Jon's eyes widened in fear, trapped with no escape. He tried to speak up, but could only mumble incoherently. *Doc, this is not what you should tell me right now when you're sticking me with things and pulling at my teeth.*

Doctor Harris continued his story, stopping a few times to figure out what he was mumbling, giving him details he didn't want to hear. He described how Doctor Giovanni conducted medically unnecessary procedures on inmates who had no family and inmates convicted of heinous crimes, inmates nobody would miss if they died. The dentist's office, built surprisingly well, contrasted with the prison, a cruel irony given the number of inmates murdered there.

"Doctor Giovanni made one critical mistake toward the end of his career. When his screening process failed him, he took the life of an innocent man. An autopsy would reveal the actual cause of death. So he locked himself in this office. The county coroner beat on the door, demanding to be let in along with sheriff's deputies and prison guards.

"Sitting in his dentist chair, Giovanni quietly turned on a classical selection of Bach's music before swallowing sedatives. It seems he felt overdosing on them mixed with alcohol was a better option than facing the music of his unprofessional and cruel behavior. Some inmates and prison staff swear they still see Doctor Giovanni's spirit wandering the halls of Redmond, white coat and all. While others are skeptical, I keep an open mind."

Doctor Harris told this crazy story while methodically working on his patient without missing a beat. A week later, during follow-up care, once he regained the ability to talk, Jon just had to ask the question.

"Doc, why did you tell me that crazy story about Doctor Giovanni?"

Doctor Harris responded with a smile. "I share that story with my patients for a reason. If you're tough enough to take me telling that story, stuck sitting in my chair, then you're tough enough to take anything I can do for you. Young man, Redmond Prison is an odd and crazy place. Stay strong, and above all, stay alive. Come back if you have any more problems I can handle."

Walking out of Doctor Harris' office, Jon was relieved and felt no more pain, although he was afraid it might come back. Escorted by a guard back to his cell, he gave a quick head nod to all the guys on the way, acknowledging they had given him excellent advice. A fight between two other inmates broke out, inmates he didn't know. This caused the guard escorting him, within a split second, to help his fellow guards. During the melee, somehow Jon got hit in the head. He felt a sharp pain while falling to the ground, and eventually slipped into unconsciousness.

He woke up in the prison infirmary, lying in bed, unable to move his limbs. He was blind, but could hear everything around him. In a nervous scream, he yelled out something no one could hear; he tried to talk, but no one could understand. Noticing that other inmates were talking to nurses as if everything was fine, he yelled in vain, receiving no response or even a sign they heard him. That's when a nurse came over. He didn't know it, but this nurse was unlike the others. She was older, and her skin was pale, as though she was more dead than alive, with a subdued demeanor. Her uniform was older and somewhat faded. She shushed him, then whispered, "You must respect this silent place as long as you stay here. You're in a coma; that's why you can hear me but can't see me. If you sit up, you should be able to see me."

He sat up, listening to her advice, and was inundated with images, disoriented by his vision. Then what he was seeing came into focus. Looking at his legs, he noticed something odd about them. Turning his head, he realized his spirit had partially left his body.

"Don't get nervous; this is normal. If you stand up, you will fully understand what's happening to you."

He realized he was looking at himself outside of his body.

"How is this possible?"

"It's likely because everyone's body is the container for their soul so long as they physically walk the Earth among the living. The first rule is to return to it if your body is still alive. You shouldn't risk staying away from it for too long."

"How long have you been here?"

"An inmate who wanted to have his way with me killed me in this room, or a similar room at the old Redmond. Something that I couldn't allow him to do without a fight."

"Why don't you leave?"

"I can't leave until I find someone I lost. The man I lost loved me and killed the inmate responsible for taking my life. The last thing I remember is guards putting him in solitary confinement, and he disappeared."

"Do you remember what his name was?"

"Yes, his name was Daniel. He was an inmate I was secretly having an affair with."

"What's your name?"

"My name is Carol."

"Well, I've been in solitary confinement once since I've been here. While there, I met a spirit that may be the man you're talking about. He seems to be stuck there, unable to leave. I'll tell him to see you if I can get him to go."

With enormous excitement, Carol's entire demeanor and mood changed. Her appearance seemed to be linked to her mood. Since she felt better, she appeared better. There was even a slight smile on her face.

Suddenly, a force pulled on him in ways he couldn't control. He looked at her frantically, wondering what was going on. Carol looked at him, a little sad but honest.

"Calm down. You're being pulled back into your body because you're regaining consciousness. Please, please keep your promise."

"If I am nothing else, I'm a man of my word."

With that, he was gone, cleared to leave the prison infirmary. He thought he was returning to his cell, but eventually realized he was heading in the wrong direction.

"Hey, boss, where are we going?"

"You're going to solitary, and I'll get you something to eat when I'm done taking you there."

"What did I do to get stuck in the hole? I did nothing wrong."

"I know, but word is, it's to keep you safe. It seems you have friends in the state legislature you don't know about. Sending you to the hole is the warden's temporary solution to his current problem of keeping you safe here."

"Hey, man, how long will I be stuck there?"

"Maybe a week until we can develop a better plan for you."

One hour earlier, before they released Jon from the prison infirmary, there was a hastily scheduled meeting with Warden Hudson in his office at the Redmond Administration Building.

"Julie. Julie, where are my notes on the cost estimates for the backup generators for the D-wing?" the warden asked in a loud but respectful manner.

His secretary strolled in, smiled, and appeared unfazed. "Sir, they're underneath the current year's budget proposal behind you. I placed it under the old Redmond portrait to ensure you wouldn't lose it."

After turning around, he moved the budget proposal to the side. "Oh." Then he turned back around with a smile. "Julie, what would I do without you?"

"Sir, you would have a nervous breakdown. Also, you have guests."

"Who is it?"

"It's State Rep. Kimberlee Townsend and Agent Ron Coleman."

"Send them in, send them in." Welcome, "Agent Coleman and Miss Townsend, how are you two doing?"

Almost simultaneously, they answered, "We're doing fine. Warden Hudson, how are you?"

"I'm fine. Hopefully, your visit with us today won't be as exciting as your last one."

Ron, speaking first, said, "I sure as hell hope it's not as exciting. We're here because of an inmate named Jon Bowman."

"I see a lot of inmates. Let me check our files. Julie!" he yelled. "Please pull the file on Jon Bowman." A few minutes later, she returned with a folder. "I remember that name," he said, looking at the mugshot attached to the file and reviewing his notes. "My impression of him was that he doesn't belong in here."

"Warden, that's why we're here. We now have evidence that he doesn't belong in here. The Ohio branch of the FBI has video surveillance evidence of the arresting officer in his case planting drugs in his car, evidence that should exonerate him."

"Well, I'll be damned. The friend of the court letter filed by a deputy U.S. attorney."

"Charges against the arresting officer are coming soon. We need this young man in protective custody or some protective monitoring until we resolve this issue."

Then Miss Townsend spoke. "This young man has a friend in the state legislature besides me."

"Who's the friend?"

"Democratic Ranking Member of the State House Judiciary Committee."

Taking all the information in, the warden placed his hand on his chin while looking down at the floor. A hush fell over the room. He picked up his phone and pushed a button that immediately put him through to the senior guard on duty in C-block.

"Hello, C-block. How can I help you?"

"This is Warden Hudson."

"Warden, what can I do for you, sir?"

"I need an inmate temporarily moved to solitary under protective custody and monitored every four hours. This status should last for only one week. However, the deputy warden or I can review and extend this status. Do you understand my instructions?"

"Yes, sir."

"Good, I also need you to make sure that you document this order in your shift report for the record."

"Yes, sir."

Meanwhile, Freddie was preparing for his parole hearing—mostly preparing to be disappointed, as he was every couple of years before the parole board. He looked in the mirror: the gray hairs had become more plentiful on his head, the wrinkles on his face more pronounced. Life on the inside got a little more challenging every year as he worried about dying on the inside as well as being terrified about life's unknowns on the outside.

The next day, looking over at the empty chair at their table, he said, "So, guys, what's going on with our young friend?"

"Word is he was in the prison infirmary after getting knocked out by that shot to the head. We later found out the warden moved him to solitary for his protection. We haven't been able to find out why."

Just then, a guard approached the table. "Hey, Freddie, the warden needs to speak with you about your young chess partner."

They made their way to the warden's office. Upon arriving, the warden already had two people in the room, but when their conversations ceased, the room went silent. He recited his inmate number, which he sometimes tried in vain to forget.

The warden reviewed his file, which was already open. "Freddie, my guards tell me you're a man who has gained much respect here. I've been told you've been mentoring younger inmates who were smart enough to ask for your guidance and counsel. Jon Bowman, it turns out he didn't commit the crime he's stuck in here for. I have it from a solid source that a video exists of the arresting officer in his case planting drugs in his car, proving it. I've also been told that you and your entourage are solely responsible for keeping him alive long enough to reach this point. Because of this, you're getting paroled. The parole board will get a letter from me. Please provide some information before I send it. Who in your entourage is younger and capable of leading them? Who do you trust to continue your work and keep this young man alive while he's stuck in here?"

Immediately, two names came to mind. "Sir, inmates Gary Washington and Craig White. They're young enough to take over for me, and they've been here long enough to know how I roll. So that's why they put him in solitary?"

"Yes, and now that you've provided me with some options, I can return him to the general population. I'll keep him there for at least a week to implement more safeguards."

Chapter 12. Soul Hunter

Sitting in his tiny cell in solitary confinement, Jon felt like a man thrown away by the world. He was consumed by an ever-present fear of being forgotten. Surviving his first day in solitary, waiting to eat dinner, he wondered if he would get any visitors of the ghostly persuasion. The next day, late in the evening after eating dinner, an unexpected visitor appeared. A chill swept through the room, and Jon turned and saw a spirit that startled him. The hairs on his arms stood up, reacting to the sensations he was experiencing. The spirit appeared transparent but visible, hovering around him before speaking.

"What are you doing back here?"

After a momentary pause, Jon responded, "The warden sent me here for my own good. Just like you, I'm wondering why I'm still here. Why are you here?"

"The pull of this place is too strong, keeping me here despite my desire to leave."

"The last time I was here, I wanted to ask you something. What is preventing you from moving forward?"

"The guard is stopping me, along with something else."

"Is your name David?"

The spirit came to a firm stop. "Where did you hear that name?"

"I heard it in the prison infirmary."

"It's been so long since I've been called by my name, I almost forgot it."

"Well, you should know there's someone looking for you. That's what the something else is, someone named Carol."

"Did you see her?"

"Yes, she's been looking for you for a long time. She told me how much you loved her, along with how you killed another inmate who took her life. She explained that's how you ended up in solitary."

"Please, please, I need your help to get out of here."

"This problem of yours... I've been thinking about your situation since I left the infirmary. I think the best way to help you get out of here is to trick the guard into releasing you by saying your name. Simply telling you that you're free to go. Before I'm released from solitary, you have my word that I will get the guard to do this. If I'm nothing else, I'm a man of my word. I need something from you."

"What do you need me to help you with?"

"I need to know about the ghosts in here. Mainly how to avoid them or, at a minimum, prevent them from hurting me."

"My first warning is to stay away from the Axeman, Christopher Davis. What's known about him has spread far and wide by those of us amongst the dead. He's like a shark, capable of striking with deadly force. But a shark must keep swimming to ensure its survival. If Christopher stops killing and stealing souls for his boss, he'll face a second death. Angels will arrest his soul, condemning him to an eternity of suffering in Hell.

"After his death on the bridge, his soul, like all souls, embarked on the journey to the afterlife. He went to the place in between Heaven and Hell, where his soul hung in the balance, a desolate landscape devoid of light and life. There, the judges weighed and analyzed every decision, every action, and every moment of his life. The beings in that desolate place assessed his deeds and decided on his ultimate fate. The angel gazed into his heart, piercing the darkness that had settled there, and found only the venomous brew of anger, revenge, and rage.

Condemned to Hell, Christopher Davis had no choice but to accept his fate. Once there, the Devil, with a fiery gaze, peered into the condemned soul, seeing the smoldering anger and rage festering within. He recognized him as a person he could manipulate, and with a voice as smooth as honey, whispered an offer that he knew would sway him.

"Their agreement stated that his life would return to him, but at an unspecified cost. He wondered, but didn't question the fine print. The power was contingent on him agreeing to act as the Devil's emissary, bringing souls to the Devil. He sought to consume them, gaining power to challenge God and claim his place. This deal was problematic because the Devil lied. God alone has the power to create life. The Devil can only manipulate the dead, granting the appearance of life to take life from the living. The Devil gains power by taking lives through his followers. Emissaries draw life from the souls they take, keeping some, sending the rest to the Devil.

"Christopher would later learn that he stayed alive as an emissary only by taking the souls of the living, some of the lifeforce going to him, most of it going to his boss. If you make a deal with the Devil, it's always good for the Devil, and bad for the person who sells their soul. Oh, and the fine print can be a bitch. That's how Christopher Davis became the Axeman, condemned to haunt Redmond as long as the prison and any replacements with the same name stand. Nearly all the other spirits trapped in this place are a threat, but most are less of a threat compared to him."

So, at the end of his week in solitary, being a man of his word, Jon asked the guard who released him from his cell for an odd favor. "Sir, can you say, 'David, you are free to go'?"

The guard hastily looked at Jon, confused, then looked in his cell, only to see no one. Despite this, he humored him, thinking he might have gone a little crazy being isolated, even if it was only for a short stint of time, and complied with the request.

After meeting with Warden Hudson, Freddie felt a twinge of doubt, wondering if the warden's grand promises would match the reality of the actions that followed. Now standing before the parole board, he noticed the stern expressions on the faces of the men and women evaluating him. He scrutinized the tone of their voices and the way they phrased their questions, hoping to determine their interest and assess his chances of success.

"Do you feel any remorse for the crime you committed?" was the first piercing question they asked.

Offering the most fitting answer that sprung to mind, what he said reflected his genuine convictions. "I admit I did what this state convicted me of, and the consequences have been severe, taking away a large part of my life. I'm genuinely sorry."

A board member asked, "What's the chance you'll re-offend if we release you?"

He tried to appease them with every ounce of his intelligence, and his answer took him by surprise. "I arrived in Redmond as a young man. My reflection shows an aging man with more gray than black hair. All I see in the mirror is a man who is afraid of dying in here."

The room fell silent, the only sound the faint hum of the air conditioner, before the chairperson of the board spoke.

"Mr. Castile, the warden has written a letter on your behalf due to the time you've served, your age, and what you've told us today. We feel comfortable releasing you. We're granting your parole. Congratulations!"

He smiled, thanking them, and tears rolled down his face. He was mindful to be careful not to do anything intentionally or unintentionally to screw up this moment. The guys on the line seemed to know, their gazes fixed on him as he walked back to the C-block, the air buzzing with unspoken anticipation. Like the group of guys they were, whatever their flaws, they stood up, giving him a standing ovation, a gesture that even the guards respected by not interfering with right away.

The next day at breakfast, handshakes and well-wishes came from everyone. Gary Washington and Craig White knew they were now responsible for leading the once-small group of inmates. The group grew because of Freddie's reputation for mentoring some of the younger inmates. Gary said, "There's a matter of housekeeping to do. Freddie, there's one thing we've got to discuss that I can't forget to mention. We're all happy for you, but please don't let us hear that after surviving 25 years on the inside, you finally get paroled and you off yourself months later because you couldn't take life outside as a free man. If word gets back to us that you've committed suicide, when we get out, we will find out where you're buried, go there, and curse you out for about five to ten minutes after relieving ourselves on your grave."

"Wait, how many of you guys feel the same way?"

Of the nine guys standing there, eight of them raised their hands. Shaking his head with a smile, Freddie then looked at his young friend and chess partner. "Well, at least I can depend on my friend Jon to have more faith in me."

Jon, with a massive grin on his face, said "Wait, I agree with the guys on this matter. I hesitated and didn't raise my hand because I have more respect for God and cemeteries than they do."

Freddie and the guys looked at him with huge smiles and bust out laughing.

Wiping a tear from his face, Freddie said, "Yeah, I'm going to miss all of you guys too."

After Freddie left, the place just wasn't the same. Jon lost his friend and chess partner. Even though he still had his job in the prison garden, his routine wasn't the same because the morning breakfast ritual of talking with the guys seemed different, despite the best efforts of Gary and Craig.

A few days after Freddie left, Jon lay in bed looking up at the ceiling in deep thought. His thoughts drifted to how he would survive his remaining time in Redmond. When he fell asleep, two familiar spirits visited him. Carol and David appeared together. They were the happiest he had ever seen them.

Carol spoke in a whisper, "Thank you, thank you, thank you. I have him back. We can finally leave this horrible place forever."

A stairway appeared, leading to an open door. Rolling hills and a sea of flowers were visible through the door. An angel stood near the stairway, inviting them in. "You don't need to stay here anymore. Peace and rest await you for a life well lived." Then, the angel's gaze turned to Jon. "Mr. Bowman, we know who you are, and I've been told to relay a message to you. This happened because of you. Everyone has a blueprint for their life, and you are no exception. You won't understand this now, but God knows and sees all. He gives all men and women the free will to follow their life's blueprint. You could ignore it, although it never works well for those who do. Through his divine wisdom, he grants all human beings free will to choose right from wrong. So, I'm here to tell you to stay on the right path and avoid the wrong one. Continue to do what you know is right, even when it may not benefit you immediately. If you do these things, you will survive, and your life will never be the same. Blessings from Heaven will pour out to you in amounts that you'll have to figure out how to manage wisely."

The angel's appearance changed to that of a Civil War Union officer, a general. Then a horn sounded, calling Colonel Daniel French and Colonel Marcus Spiegel, as well as part of their Union regiment, to muster for roll call. The two colonels' spirits stepped out of the portraits on the wall leading to the warden's office, reappearing in C-block. This was along with six officers and 275 enlisted men who died of disease in the 120th Infantry Regiment. The quartermaster, also a ghost, issued caps and mini balls for their muskets, plus provisions for additional caps and mini balls. Then, the angel looked at Jon and pointed to a spot on the ground. Jon stepped forward, and the angel placed an Army lieutenant general's star on his shoulder. Then he barked orders, cutting through the tense silence like a whip.

"As of now, the general is in charge of you. You must shield him from the dangerous spirits lurking in the shadows within this prison, keeping him safe from their malicious intentions. This is your primary responsibility for as long as he remains here. There should be two men standing watch outside his cell at all times. Four guards will always escort him wherever he goes. Men, your secondary mission will be to hunt down the Axeman, Christopher Davis. When you find him, shoot him immediately. You can't just shoot him once to send him to Hell, because he's already dead. Keep shooting him until he has only one soul remaining. Only then will you be able to send him back to Hell where he belongs. The rounds you have will free the souls he's imprisoned. These souls power him, feeding the Devil as well.

"If stabbed by Christopher, the angels watching over this place have the power and authority to intervene, preventing your souls from being absorbed and taken by him. However, you must ask for God's protection and grace. If you ask, you shall receive, but you will be out of the fight. Those of you who fall in this fight will be relieved of the burden of staying in Redmond. The reward for your courage and sacrifice is a place in Heaven. However, we will summon you again if needed."

While these events unfolded at Redmond, a distance away, Michelle stood in the doorway of her son's nursery, watching him sleep, still in shock that she was now someone's mother. Sometimes, he would surprise her, sensing she was there and opening his eyes to stare at her. But she still just couldn't stop watching him sleep.

A surprise visitor showed up.

"Dad, what are you doing here?"

They both whispered, trying not to wake him up.

"I had to look at him for it to sink in that I have a grandson." He kissed her on the cheek as she stood there, leaning up against the door frame. "Wait, are you watching him sleep?"

Her face lit up as a huge smile came over her. "How did you know?"

Looking directly at her with a huge grin on his face, he said, "Where do you think you got it from? I used to do the same thing when you were a baby, and this is God's way of bringing everything back full circle."

"What's going on with that other issue?"

"Your young man got railroaded, from what my staff has gathered so far. I'm working with another state House member who knows the warden of Redmond. I must leave now to return to the capital for a meeting on that issue."

He kissed her on the cheek before quietly leaving. He noticed his wife sleeping on the living room couch, but decided not to disturb her. His daughter continued to watch her son sleep. A few hours later, arriving at the capital, he walked past everyone in a blur, waving periodically at those faces he recognized. Walking into his office, Darnell greeted him with an exuberance that shocked him because it was totally out of character.

He realized Agent Ron Coleman and State Rep. Kimberlee Townsend were already waiting for him, and he sat at the head of the table.

"How's everyone doing today?" All around the table, everyone responded. "This state has an enormous problem. Agent Coleman will lead the discussion."

"Sir, this is the first time I've met you. Your reputation for service and help in law enforcement matters is well-known and appreciated in this state. I've already briefed your chief of staff, Mister Jackson. You likely already know about pending indictments linked to investigations of private prisons in this state. I can't reveal much about that because I'm out of the loop. What I can tell you is that young man you are interested in is innocent of the charges the state convicted him of. Evidence exists of the officer planting drugs in his car, as well as on other young men fitting the same description and profile. I've seen the video surveillance of this officer, and I've volunteered to be the one to take him into custody on the condition that I could obtain a copy of the surveillance video. My boss gave me a copy, but told me to stick it in a locked drawer. I cannot reveal it until the officer's trial or plea deal."

"How long will it take to exonerate this young man and get him out?"

"Unfortunately for him, the wheels of justice turn slowly. Too slow for my taste. We'll just have to deal with this the best we can. Why is Lady Justice so blind when the truth of a mistake is clear? Why is it so slow to fix an error when it's clear it's made one?"

That's when Rep. Kimbell showed his age and wisdom by answering the question. "Attorneys make careers from prominent legal cases and destroy them by lapses of judgment and personal ethics. Darnell, I think we have enough information to contact the attorney of record regarding this case. Share what we know with Attorney John Merit, and make sure he's ready to notify the court that additional evidence exists when the time comes."

Jon sat in the Redmond prison library, reading through reports of unexplained deaths in various areas of the old Reformatory and similar reports in the new one. He was trying to figure out the best place to position his small ghost army, when his old friend came to mind, and all those games of chess they played. Freddie would always say, "Young man, think. Think a few moves ahead. That's how you'll win, that's how you'll survive." It seemed like that wasn't only about the game of chess, but also about the game of life.

He started noticing consistent patterns of where inmates died. Reports of strange deaths in the inmate bathrooms. Many in the Redmond kitchen. But the report of an inmate attempting to escape who drowned in a small lake near the old Redmond stood out. The death was bizarre, given that he knew how to swim before coming to Redmond. What made this inmate's death suspicious was the fact that one of the witnessing guards swore he saw a man with an axe walk into the lake.

Shortly after this inmate entered the lake, trying to escape, the guard recognized Christopher Davis from the vivid descriptions of him by other guards. He detailed the inmate's fight to stay above water. Unable to provide any help due to being overweight and not a swimmer, his options were to shoot him or see if he would drown for his stupidity. He knew if, by some miracle, he survived, he would likely be on the run for a couple days. This guard also reported seeing the same axe-wielding man who had entered the water standing behind the inmate, forcing him underwater, holding the wooden handle of his ax against his neck, watching as he man struggled to breathe.

After reading this, the lights in the entire library flickered and then totally went out. They flickered back on, revealing Christopher's axe raised and a chilling look in his eyes, sending shivers down Jon's spine. Face to face with a ghostly killing machine, he froze before regaining his senses and courage. His gaze swept over the Union soldiers guarding him, and realizing he had a choice, he swiftly gave the order. "Fire, fire, fire, got damn it!"

In quick succession, two-man volleys rang out. *Pow pow.* Then pow from the second volley, stunning Christopher, who was used to attacking his prey, not his prey attacking him. The rear soldiers waited before firing to ensure the guards in front had enough time to reload. Watching this play out, Jon scrutinized every minute and detail, watching nervously as his heart beat at a feverish pace. Fear welled up inside of him as he struggled to show no emotion, knowing he had to remain strong. He watched as spirits left Christopher's body, a smoky fog filling the air. Christopher, in shock, retreated, even though he was still strong enough to keep up the fight.

Two hours had passed, and Jon was back in his cell, the silence suffocating. The room was still and silent, the only sound the soft rustling of sheets as he lay in bed, lost in thought, trying to think of a strategy along with creative ways to execute it. All to hunt down Christopher. He analyzed the details of the skirmish that he had just been through. He now knew the men and weapons under his command were effective. But he didn't have a strategy, and that's when the wheels in his mind started turning.

He had to figure out how to create a communications network. Then it hit him: he could develop a system through couriers similar to those used during the Civil War. He had enough men for it to work. Then his eureka moment came when he realized these men weren't living people, they were ghosts who could walk through walls. His mind wandered to American History class in high school, where he was one of the few students who paid attention.

The demand for action was apparent from the information provided. He moved subtly, carefully avoiding any actions that would make him seem crazy or unstable. Realizing that many attacks occurred in the bathroom, he ordered men to stand guard. Rumors about the Latino inmate who started the Redmond Civil War led to orders for men to be sent to the yard, which reminded him of the crazy brawl that ensued and the side business that he'd taken care of during it. Despite scant reports of attacks, he returned to his plan and assigned men to the prison laundry. He also assigned men to the crystal palace, the prison's nerve center, where all the security monitors were. But the most critical area of the prison was where he placed many troops because of the concentration of inmates at any time: the Redmond cafeteria. So many people in one place could easily make for a mass casualty event, which had to be prevented.

Chapter 13. The Hunter Becomes Prey

Jon lay in bed looking up at the ceiling, as he had done many times before. Looking at the gray of the four walls, he closed his eyes, and for a moment, he was back at Central State University. He could feel the weight of his backpack and the anxiety of late assignments as he headed to class. He reminisced on the times he sat on the green grass of the quad with Michelle, admiring the glow of the moon and stars while looking into her eyes.

A ghost appeared halfway in his cell and the adjoining one, and he instantly knew this ghost had something to report. He sat up in bed, his mind racing with anticipation. The ghost appeared to be a relatively young Union soldier wearing his Union blues, standing at attention until ordered to do otherwise.

"Soldier, at ease. What do you have to report?"

"Sir, we spotted Christopher in D-block and gave chase. We fired on him when we caught up with him, freeing six spirits. We retreated to avoid getting attacked. Not because we were afraid, but because we were fearful of being taken out of the fight."

After thinking about the report he was getting, Jon felt that a hit-and-run strategy may be wise against the stronger adversary, if only to soften him up before a frontal assault. He looked down at the floor in the dark, pacing. Then, in a whisper, he issued his order. "Young man, tell the men they did an excellent job in this skirmish. Tell them to keep it up. My order, as of now, is to pursue a hit-and-run strategy. Search for Christopher Davis, and when you find him, engage aggressively, then retreat to a safe position. Is that understood?"

"Yes, sir." Then he saluted and left. A fast-paced game of whack-a-mole ensued.

Following the narrow, darkened corridor leading to the kitchen, a guard was doing his routine spot check of the area. He flipped the switch to turn on the lights. Looking around, he saw nothing out of order. Then a cold sensation came over him, and an intense unease consumed him.

"Hello, is anyone in here?"

You hear these words in a horror flick. You know someone's about to be killed in some cruel and unspeakable way. There was no response. He wandered through the kitchen to the manager's office by the walk-in freezers.

Just a few feet away, a slight, ever-so-insignificant flicker of the kitchen light occurred. In an instant, Christopher appeared. He caused all the stainless-steel knives to fly off the magnetic wall mount through sheer force of will, hovering in midair. Just as the guard walked back into the main kitchen area, he heard the clatter of pots and pans. His eyes widened in terror as he saw the gleam of steel flashing through the air, each knife aimed at him with deadly intent. Moving on reflex, he moved his arms in front of his face to block what was coming. A searing pain ripped through his arm as a knife sliced through his flesh, the blade's tip protruding from his wrist. Stuck firmly through muscle, it nicked one of his arteries, causing blood to gush down his arm to the floor below. A searing pain ripped through his chest as another knife plunged in, mere inches from his heart. Another darted incredibly fast, slamming into his leg with a sharp impact. Then one plunged into his stomach, a sharp, searing pain that made him gasp.

Losing enormous amounts of blood, he knew he was in trouble. He grabbed his radio, hardly able to speak. "This is Corrections Officer Wade Donaldson. Code ten-twenty, in the cafeteria subsection kitchen. I need help! I repeat, code ten-twenty in the cafeteria subsection kitchen area. I need help right now, got damnit!" He passed out from the loss of blood.

The remaining knives suddenly dropped, and Union ghost soldiers showed up just in time to distract the Axeman. Firing in quick succession, they freed several spirits before retreating.

Christopher, never one for many words, stood there confused, trying to understand how his fortunes could turn so fast. One day he was torturing the inmates of Redmond, the next he was being attacked by Civil War ghosts. It was a strange turn of fortune indeed. That's when he disappeared, angry and seething with rage, wondering how to explain his losses to his boss. He knew that, in time, a reckoning would come.

Meanwhile, the guard, though seriously injured, would live and fully recover. However, he had trouble explaining his strange ordeal to his superiors and other guards. Officer Donaldson learned about the security cameras later, when the system backed up his crazy story. Everyone watched the video after the hospital admitted Wade. Attitudes changed significantly, and Warden Hudson expressed them perfectly when he visited him in the hospital.

Walking into his hospital room and greeting his wife and kids, the warden's voice resonated with sincerity. As he spoke, the words hung like a promise, and Wade felt a profound sense of wonder wash over him.

"Wade, I've seen something unusual. I've just seen a video of knives floating in the air with no human being anywhere holding them. I then witnessed those knives fly like mini guided missiles. Those knives repeatedly stabbed you with lethal force."

"Wait, sir, there was a video of that?"

Looking directly at him with a huge smile, the warden replied, "Wade, I just watched the video of what we're affectionately calling the Miracle at Redmond. Not only does video exist, but you are the most fantastic part of it. After what you've been through, you can take early retirement with full benefits if you so choose. The option is available, and your decision can wait. As far as I'm concerned, Redmond Prison is the most haunted prison I've worked at. However, if this statement leaves this room and finds its way to a news reporter, I'll deny it. Based on my observations, I can only come to two conclusions. It takes either a close bond with God or an unyielding will to survive the challenges you've faced. All we know is you're too stubborn to die, because you shouldn't be here."

Hearing that, everyone in the room couldn't help but laugh, almost to the point of tears, including Wade, even though he was still in a lot of pain.

"We're all glad you survived this fantastic incident."

He then presented Wade's wife with get-well cards from the guards and placed a potted assortment of flowers on the counter nearby. He then had terse conversations with everyone before leaving, knowing Wade's family didn't need him staying too long.

The inmates, oblivious to the drama unfolding at a distant hospital, remained relatively insulated from the personal lives of the guards. They were only familiar with the daily routines. Even though parallel stories were developing, Jon was laser-focused on the reports he was getting from multiple sources. He still tried to keep up appearances to his fellow inmates, including his friends, that everything was normal. His problem was not enough sleep, and he knew it would eventually catch up with him.

A report came in from another soldier about five inmates who mysteriously overdosed thirty minutes after taking some unknown substance that was smuggled into the prison. The soldier reported that the Axeman tried to take advantage, but they stopped him.

"It seems he would have had to be standing there next to them to take their souls. He may have been a little desperate. We're trying to keep him on the run, leaving him no time to settle down. Three men fired three shots, and only one found its mark. Right before our eyes, the spirit separated from the body, appearing as a swirling mist that pulsed with soft light, then gathered itself before disappearing into nothingness."

"Keep up the chase; make sure he never gets a moment of rest."

With that said, the soldier turned and walked through the bars of his cell, causing Jon to wish he could do the same thing. Then he remembered what it would mean and what it would cost him—his life—so he focused on other things.

It was forty-five minutes before the lights turned on, and the room was silent and dimly lit. Jon's eyes opened to see the creaking springs of the bunk above him. He tossed and turned, realizing he couldn't fall back asleep. He sat up, allowing his feet to hit the cold concrete floor of his cell. Eventually standing up and stretching to get the blood flowing, he stumbled to the sink and looked in the mirror. He tried, but not very well, to shave while standing at an angle using the light from the C-block hallway. In prison, a man has plenty of time and few worthwhile activities to fill it with. That's why he found it odd when the time came for the lights to come on and they didn't. In the darkness, there was only enough light to see the faces of the other inmates. The half-moon, still visible through the prison bars across the way, cast an eerie glare into the room.

A tall, stern-looking guard passed his cell, and Jon asked, "What's the commotion?"

The guard halted his brisk walk, the sounds of his shoes crunching on the pavement replaced by the stillness of his sudden stop. "A transformer blew somewhere, and it's messing up our schedule," he responded in an angry tone. He dismissed it as a terrible omen for the rest of the day, and continued on his way, a knot of unease forming in his stomach.

The guard's words held some truth, he realized, anticipating they might have to eat breakfast in their cells, or worse, it might be late. So he sat back on his bed, closing his eyes to meditate and think.

The prison yard was a scene of chaos as the Axeman, his eyes wild with rage, fought back against a contingent of Union soldiers, their rifles pointed at him. Jon had forgotten he assigned a contingent there. The fight started when the Axeman was spotted and immediately fired on, taking a round to the shoulder. He refused to withdraw, and instead charged his first two attackers, swinging his ax wildly like a madman and stabbing one of them. He forced the soldier to ask for grace and allowed the other soldier to escape. This request for grace caused angels to appear with a fantastic aura of light around them. They angels granted the request, allowing the soldier to escape the fight.

Two more soldiers appeared as reinforcements, maintaining the effort. Extremely stubborn and refusing to give an inch, the Axeman refused to retreat. He disappeared, then reappeared, trying in vain to make it harder for his attackers to get a lock on him. Mimicking a wolf's determination to hunt its prey and an eagle's focus, they fired with steady aim and a seemingly sixth sense of where their target would be. Within a split second after reappearing, he took a round to the chest and another to the thigh. Filled with frustration, along with enormous rage, a powerful explosion rocked the area, causing a major power outage in the C-block. The intense feelings of ghosts or spirits could sometimes cause tangible changes in the physical world of the living, like moving objects or creating strange sounds...or detonating an electrical transformer.

\#

In the bowels of Redmond Prison, far from the public's prying eyes, a fierce guerrilla war was being waged. The Axeman, appearing and then disappearing, tried in vain to secure new victims for his sadistic boss. Gradually, Jon's strategy was working. The Axeman knew he was losing souls at a fast rate. He was angry, but over time, he became increasingly afraid, terrified of his boss's reaction to his failure. If only he could find inmates, flawed visitors, or both, where no soldiers were. Roaming the halls of Redmond, trying to avoid being spotted by the sentries that were aggressively hunting him, the Axeman found himself in a position he wasn't used to. He slowly, carefully walked through walls and peered around corners to avoid detection. Even without directly confronting them, he could feel a palpable darkness emanating from certain inmates, an evil aura that hung in the air.

Simultaneously, he intimidated the hell out of those poor souls who he felt were weak in spirit, sensing their fear and feeding on them hastily before moving on. Deformed by years in a watery tomb, his face was so disfigured that it was impossible to tell who he was. His demeanor reflected his inner turmoil, a constant wretchedness visible to all. The creatures of the lake were feasting on his flesh, their sharp teeth tearing through him. The sight of his twisted and disfigured remains sent a shiver down anyone's spine. His breath came in ragged gasps, and he felt the strength draining from his limbs. He needed to find shelter to regain his strength. So, he went to the one area of the prison where most spirits could go, but few roamed.

The building next to the prison administration was buzzing with visitors, a mix of hope and despair hanging in the air. This made this building the perfect place to hide and regroup, while also allowing him to get new souls to steal and victims to torment.

Meanwhile, unbeknown to the Axeman, in a courtroom miles from Redmond, Steven Crawford stood next to his lawyer as the jury foreman read their verdict. "Guilty, guilty, guilty." The words seemed to roll out of the jury foreman's mouth. His voice and the sound of those words reverberated throughout the courtroom, weighing on Steven's soul. The click of the handcuffs, the cold metal digging into his wrists, announced the end of his freedom as the bailiff led him away. The jury's verdict would stay stuck in his mind until they transferred him to Redmond. He was determined to show no emotion throughout this process as the bailiff led him away. Refusing to give them the satisfaction of seeing his pain, he remained silent. His thoughts drifted inward, focusing on memories and introspection. His mind raced, fixated on the rapid descent of his life into a chaotic mess, like a dog had just deposited a steaming pile of waste.

When Steven Crawford, Inmate 30609, got to Redmond, his demeanor revealed that he was a despairing man. His fall from relative obscurity happened how most men fall from grace. It was due to the love of a woman. She was incredibly wealthy and stunningly beautiful. Her name was Kathryn Johnson, and to be honest, she only became rich a few years after entering her marriage due to shrewdly saving money from the limited access she had to her husband's vast wealth—mainly for fear of being traded in for a younger model.

She discovered he was an abusive and womanizing man. After years of telling herself, *I can change him*, only to fail miserably time after time, she finally realized the futility of her effort after hearing a song on the radio. The frantic clicking of her mind broke the moment's silence as it raced toward a place of darkness. Creative thoughts enabled her to develop an elaborate plan to relieve herself of her husband's company permanently.

Her plan called for persuading a useful idiot—in this case, Steven Crawford, a handsome but unsophisticated handyman—into having an affair with her, then selectively letting morsels of information slip that she wished she could get rid of her husband. She dropped the detail that he had a rather large bank account and a more significant insurance policy, one that she was the sole beneficiary of. She deliberately left the details of his potential share of the profits unclear, her words a carefully crafted veil. "I'll pay handsomely to anyone who can solve my problem," she said, her voice echoing doggedly. They calculated every step, ensuring no tangible proof of their relationship survived.

They needed to keep their love a secret, as the insurance company would likely deny their claim if they knew she had any involvement in her late husband's death. She slowly and deliberately manipulated Steven into killing him. Mr. Crawford's criminal record, riddled with offenses like theft and gang-related violence, made it reasonably easy to figure out why he would do such a thing. Though it's a controversial tactic, the use of one violent person to neutralize another violent person has been a recurring theme throughout history. It was to no one's surprise that this happened with these two. However, the key was to develop a motive to implicate Steven and exonerate her, leaving her free to enjoy her dearly departed husband's money without having to keep Steven around. That's when she discovered a guilty vice one day in his apartment, an old picture of him at a card table playing what appeared to be poker.

"Do you play poker?"

"Yes, or, to be honest, I used to until I had problems with the game."

"What problems do you mean?"

"Well, I played in high-stakes games and was quite good at it. Until one night, I played with the wrong people and had an excellent night that they didn't appreciate. It alarmed me when I realized they were involved in organized crime and angry at me for taking their money. After that, I had trouble getting into games free of mob-connected criminals. On top of the buy-in fee problems, I simply couldn't get into a game worth playing."

Realizing that this was her opportunity to put her lover and her husband in a room together, the calculations and simulations started randomly running in her mind. "My husband plays poker. I'll give you the buy-in fee, but you can never mention you know me. Just tell them you found out about the game from one of the golfers at the club."

#

#

After many poker games over a few months, a relationship developed with Kathryn's husband. Steve was cautious not to slip and reveal to Mr. Johnson his secret relationship with his wife. All the players won and then lost money. Laughter filled the room as the alcohol flowed freely, and everyone enjoyed their time together. The day began innocently, but would take a tragic turn, ending with an unusual night.

It had been a few months since Steven had joined the staff at the golf club. He traded in his club life for a toolbox and a few hours of work each week, taking on whatever odd jobs he could find as a handyman. He mainly interacted with the club's female members while their husbands were at work.

One day, Steven was called to the Johnson house to repair a window that a stray golf ball had broken. As time passed, the purpose of his being there faded into obscurity. Mrs. Johnson's acceptance of help would have displeased her husband. That's how their illicit affair began, a secret pact sealed with a whispered promise. The way they met was unexpected, a twist of fate leading to a deep and lasting connection.

Back to the unusual day where the unexpected occurred. Kathryn was getting impatient. She wanted the job done. The sooner, the better. So, taking the initiative, she got a small vial of some unknown poison that was clear, odorless, and highly toxic. It was likely that her husband was at work, possibly involved in inappropriate behavior with his secretaries—secretaries who seemed to be better at their *other* job than their actual job.

Mrs. Johnson was home, getting her satisfaction. Afterward, she lay in the guest room bed with Steven and reached over to grab the small vial wrapped in a paper towel. Handing it to him, she explained, "Pour a small dose of this into his drink, and after a few minutes, it will look like he had a heart attack."

"What is this?"

"You don't need to know. What's important is that you get close enough to use it."

A few hours had passed sitting at the poker game with Kathryn's husband and another man that night. The other man seemed nervous, looking more at his phone than the cards in front of him. When the phone rang with a funny-sounding ringtone, he answered it, a few droplets of sweat rolling down the side of his face. He hung up and slowly turned, his eyes scanning both. "Sorry, but I need to go. You'll have to make the most of your time and have fun without me. My wife is expecting our first child. That's why I've been a little nervous and distracted."

After he left, the room got silent.

"So, now what do we do?"

Steve wasn't ready to go home yet, so he responded, "Let's keep playing."

"Okay, then do me a favor and grab two cold ones from the fridge."

Walking in the kitchen, standing near the stove next to the refrigerator, Steve opened the door and enjoyed the cold air flowing out for a few moments. His eyes scanned the shelves to find the bottles of beer. Using a bottle opener to loosen the cap on one, he took the small vial out of his pocket as he wavered on whether to use it. Knowing he had little time, he had to decide. When he finally did, the realization of his commitment dawned on him suddenly. He poured too much of the vial's contents into the open beer bottle. He tried to be careful about putting the cap back on tight enough not to raise suspicion from Mr. Johnson. He popped the cap off his bottle, a satisfying click echoing in the stillness, and took a small swig, just enough to stay sharp and avoid mistakes.

He returned to the room with the two bottles and handed one to his host. He sat down and looked at his cards. Mr. Johnson took his sweet time taking off the cap of his beer. After he did, he took a long gulp before taking his seat and placing the bottle back on the table.

Then he said something shocking and terrifying. "So, how long have you been sleeping with my wife?"

Thinking fast, Steve did the only thing he could do and played dumb. "What do you mean?" he said in a calm and collected manner.

"Playing dumb with me won't work because I've got cameras in most of the rooms of this house. They're all linked to my home office's central computer and storage device. I figured the video was worth having in case I wanted to trade her for a younger model. The sight of a cheating spouse on video, coupled with a watertight prenuptial agreement, is a lawyer's dream scenario."

Fortunately for Steven, and unfortunately for Mr. Johnson, the poison was fast acting. Before Steve could explain or even make up a lame excuse, Mr. Johnson was clutching his chest in pain. Within minutes, his heartbeat slowed from average to nothing. Sitting in his chair, he slumped over, facing forward, his head resting on the table before him. His bottle of beer fell over, allowing the remaining contents to spill out, only to be absorbed by the tablecloth covering it.

Never known as the brightest kid in school, Steve did have a few brain cells working. Panic surged through him as he raced through the maze of rooms in Mr. Johnson's sprawling house, desperately searching for his home office. The piece of evidence, a key to unraveling the mystery of Mr. Johnson's death, was his only hope.

He finally found the room. A polished desk gleamed under the overhead light, with a laptop resting silently on its surface. He figured this must be the place. He peered under the desk, the dim light from the overhead fixture illuminating a small, silver USB drive. Carrying the laptop and the USB storage drive, he left the room. He hoped that all evidence of his affair with Mrs. Johnson that Mr. Johnson might have secretly had was on the USB drive so he could destroy it. He then bolted, desperate to escape the scene and put some distance between himself and a dead man, hopefully avoiding becoming the prime suspect in his death.

\#

Karma had a way of coming back to bite him. In his haste to leave the house before sunrise, as an amateur in the job of murder, he made mistakes that led to his arrest and eventual conviction. He rushed out of the house so fast he didn't grab the two beer bottles with his prints, especially the one with the poison residue. He also was unable to wipe down anything he may have touched, including Mr. Johnson's home office safe that he accidentally found open with fifty thousand dollars. Money that conveniently made its way to Steven's apartment, which detectives found. In addition, a witness testified that the victim was still alive with Steven when he left, leaving the police with an open and shut case of murder. The punishment for the crime was a fifteen-year sentence in prison, plus additional time on other charges.

The allegation that he was having an affair with Mrs. Johnson became impossible to prove when witnesses revealed she was in a club at the time of the murder. This was corroborated by video evidence and receipts, conveniently providing her with an air-tight alibi. Plus, if he had raised the point, it would have triggered a murder-for-hire component that would have put the death penalty on the table. So his lawyers had to advise against even bringing it up. Since no evidence existed, he had done an excellent job of getting rid of it. Mrs. Johnson never returned to the house that night because it was boys' night. She didn't return until the following day, resulting in their housekeeper finding her husband's body.

Satisfied that Mrs. Johnson was not involved with her husband's death, homicide detectives closed the case, making no further arrests. Estate lawyers transferred all of Mr. Johnson's assets and money to his only heir: his grieving wife, Katheryn. She had successfully manipulated someone else into killing her husband. She made only one mistake. After learning of Steven's suicide attempt one month after his conviction, she agreed to one conjugal visit at the Redmond Prison. She was assured by her lawyers that even though the optics looked bad, the police had no evidence to charge her with anything.

Using the influence that her newfound wealth afforded her, she arranged for a rarely granted conjugal visit with Steven, even though he was a new arrival. Riding in the car to the prison, there was an odd sense of warning. A voice, a raspy whisper, sent chills down her spine as it uttered, "Don't go." In Redmond, towering buildings cast long shadows, obscuring the sun and creating a sense of unease that made even the trees seem ominous and menacing. Despite this fear, she pressed on.

Chapter 14. You Don't Belong

Kathryn walked through the gates, being directed through various locks and ordered to turn over all items that could pose a risk. The room they led her to seemed small, but it was nice enough and served the purpose. Steven arrived minutes after her. He looked fine, but his mood was somber. His rather short incarceration had left him brutalized by prison life. The guard explained the rules of the visit and how much time they had, then left the room in a hurry. She knew she was on the clock and her tone changed fast.

"What's your problem?" Her face contorted with anger, the lines around her eyes and mouth deepening with every breath. "You need to toughen up, keep your mouth shut, and, above all, remain strong." She said this as she peeked through the curtain to ensure the guard was gone. Then she turned around to look directly at Steven standing before her. With no warning of her intentions, she slapped the hell out of him with a level of force and power that stung, leaving a red mark on his face.

"Hey, what was that for?" he asked, holding his jaw.

Looking sternly at him, she replied, "Don't you ever try to take your own life." Then she whispered in his ear, "Since you took care of my problem, I now must take care of you. Fifteen years may seem like a long time, but you will be out before you know it. Let me explain to you what's going to happen when you make it out. You will get picked up in a limousine and taken to a private airport. We will transport you to Switzerland and take you to a bank where fifteen million dollars is waiting in your account. Payment for each year you spend in this place. All you have to do is stay alive."

Unfortunately for them, that room would be the last place either would see while among the living.

After taking the hair pin out of her hair that kept it wrapped in a bun, she allowed her flowing brunette hair to fall to her shoulders. She unbuttoned her blouse, revealing her shapely figure. Steven watched with anticipation as she then took off her bra. He caressed and kissed her as they fell on the bed. The temperature in the room seemed to increase, but they paid no attention while making out on the bed. The standing lamp in the corner toppled over as they locked in a passionate embrace. The lampshade fell off, causing the bulb to break. Neither of them seemed to notice what was going on behind them while Kathryn sat on top of Steven, moaning with satisfaction.

Like a silent ghost, the lamp glided upward until it rested a hair's breadth shy of six feet. Then, with lightning speed, thrown like a spear through the air, it pierced Kathryn's back and then impaled Steven while she rode him like a horse, leaving them stuck in their compromised position. Gasping for air and unable to scream, shock and panic set in. As blood gradually leaked from their bodies, soaking the sheets and bed underneath them, the Axeman materialized from the shadows, his axe gleaming in the dim light. As they sat stuck together, clinging to life as fear gripped their hearts, the Axeman looked them both in the eye and decapitated them with one swing. Their heads fell to the ground and rolled across the floor. Their heads, eerily still, sat side by side near the chair, their eyes wide open, frozen in a gaze that seemed to pierce through anyone entering the room.

Kathryn and Steven felt a sense of weightlessness as their spirits departed from their bodies. The first ghost they would see was Mr.

Johnson's spirit. Standing in front of them with a huge smile. He didn't say a word at first. All he did was clap. Then he said, "I've got to say, I'm honestly shocked. Not in a million years did I see this betrayal coming. I know I should have, considering the number of times I cheated on you with my various secretaries. But it never crossed my mind that you were capable of manipulating another man into murdering me. I've been following him since he poisoned me. The moment I looked at you, I realized with the force of a lightning bolt that you orchestrated my demise. They say justice is blind, but payback...oh, payback can be a real bitch."

That's when the Axeman absorbed their spirits, gaining new strength. His attempt to absorb Mr. Johnson's spirit failed. Then, a door appeared engulfed in fire with a handle made of a snake that seemed alive. When it opened, a shadowy figure stood in the doorway but didn't walk through it.

The Axeman was temporarily stuck in place, and then a voice from the bowels of Hell spoke. "I claim your soul. As my servant, you live, but only to serve me. Disobey, and you burn forever." Without a word, the Axeman stopped, lowered his arm, and allowed his ax's metal end to rest on the floor. He stood over Mr. Johnson, a cold, calculating look in his eyes as Mr. Johnson's pleas for mercy rang out. When the shadowy figure made his presence felt and his power known, demons flew out from behind him and surrounded Mr. Johnson's spirit.

"Mr. Johnson, you should be on your knees, begging me to spare your soul. Let me caution you that your soul belongs in Hell with me, and there is no way around it. My demons sensed your anger and asked what was your heart's desire. You responded by saying you wanted to watch those responsible for your death die, having the satisfaction of knowing they would never see it coming. So those demons, on my orders, told Christopher to kill your wife and her lover. Your wife didn't have a mean or murderous spirit in her body until she met you. You drove her to this. You caused her to sin by being an accomplice to your murder. If she was married to anyone else but you, she would have lived a relatively dull life. Choosing you to be her husband was her first mistake. The abusive, unfaithful a-hole that you've always been as a man, that destroyed her life. Agreeing to this conjugal visit was her second, and fatal, mistake. Mr. Johnson, justice truly is blind, but to use your words, payback...oh, but payback, she can be a real bitch."

As the shadowy figure turned to walk away, Mr. Johnson's screams echoed. "Who are you? Who in the hell are you?" Four demons then grabbed him by the arms and legs, dragging him through the open door to what looked like a smoldering volcano leading to Hell.

"You know who I am. They say the biggest trick the Devil ever played was to convince the world he doesn't exist."

The screams of a corrections officer shattered the silence of the Tuesday morning. The clock ticked past nine forty-five in the morning as Calvin Winslow stumbled upon a sight that would forever haunt his dreams. He had worked for 20 years at Redmond. Assigning the guards close to retirement a relatively safe job was standard, knowing that no job was secure in prison. The goal was to make their retirement date and make it to a lush tropical beach, sipping a Long Island Iced Tea with a funny-looking umbrellas sticking out of it.

Affectionately nicknamed the "Dewdrop Inn" by the guards, the marital unit was a place of love and laughter. The Dewdrop Inn was mostly a place that the guards used as leverage to compel inmates to be on their best behavior. That's if they wanted to see their spouses or female companions.

On this day, after checking in with the watch officer, Calvin asked his usual question when he took over for another guard. "Who do we have checked in?"

"We've got one couple checked in, and they're scheduled to check out right now. Do you want me to secure the prisoner and process them out?"

"Nope, that's okay, I'll handle it."

Usually, it was a two-man job, but if done right, one man could do it so long as the extra guard is a scream away for backup. Grabbing the keys that unlocked multiple rooms along with most handcuffs, Calvin walked the few feet to room twenty-five.

The room was oddly silent. His experience was that most couples squeezed in the last few minutes of their time. Guards had caught many couples in the act, mid-stroke. After knocking on the door, oddly, there was no response. Usually, he would hear voices of the "oh God, oh God, do it again" kind. He was cautious and opened the small door to the square window, allowing guards to observe prisoners safely and securely. What he caught a glimpse of shook him to his core. Fumbling with his keys, his hands shook so much that he missed the keyhole before finally connecting.

Turning the key, he heard the gears move as the lock released and opened. The first thing he saw were two heads sitting on the floor in a small pool of blood, unblinking eyes filled with an unsettling gaze staring directly at him. From the doorway, he could see two decapitated bodies on the blood-soaked bed, pinned in place as if to ensure they wouldn't escape. Knowing better than to step inside the room out of fear of getting chewed out by homicide detectives if he contaminated the scene before forensics had time to process it, he wisely stayed in the hallway,

screaming at the other guard.

"Lenny, Lenny, get over here! Get over here now!"

Feeling under the weather, Lenny looked at the scene and left. He lost his lunch soon after, throwing up down the hall in a potted plant near a window. After he finished, he took a deep breath and composed himself, wiping his mouth with a crumpled napkin he pulled from his pocket.

"Man, you've got to call this one in."

He reached for the radio on his right shoulder and squeezed the button to talk to dispatch in the control room. "This is Officer Wilson. I have a ten thirty-four."

"What's your ten-twenty, Officer Wilson?"

"My ten-twenty is the Dewdrop Inn."

"Officer Wilson, what's the problem?"

"Well, I've got a one-eight-seven in a room that's become a roach motel. A couple checked in, but they won't be checking out."

After time passed, the first group of officers showed up. The sight before them left them speechless, their jaws hanging open in disbelief.

The senior guard popped in and glanced around. "Holy shit, what the fuck did I just see?" He looked straight at Lenny and Wilson. "Can I see the visitor sign-in sheet?" When they gave him the list, he spent a few minutes looking at the names of the 25 rooms. Recognizing the visitor's name and the inmate's name, after a moment's pause, the connection hit him with the force of a brick, leaving him stunned and reeling.

One of the detectives looked familiar when they arrived.

"Mike, you've caught this case?"

"Yep, I was getting ready to leave for the day when the call came in. Since it's been a slow day, I took it."

Handing him the inmate and visitor log, the senior guard said, "Look at the two names for room 25. Do you recognize them?"

He looked closely at the log for a few moments. Then, going to the room, he was stunned by what he saw. "What the fuck am I supposed to do with that? And how in the hell am I supposed to unsee it? You've got to be kidding me. Isn't that the guy who just got convicted for killing that millionaire after a poker game and the spouse of the murdered guy?"

"Yeah, I'm calling the warden. I suggest you do the same. If we don't act fast, this could blow up in our faces, becoming a media circus. We may need to consider a cover-up, because there may not be a suspect of the living kind to pin this on. Let's not forget we're discussing Redmond here. This place has a reputation for strange and unexplained happenings."

After the forensic team arrived and started recording everything, the detectives walked around with notepads, detailing what they had discovered and their opinions about what they had seen.

"Hey, Mike, look at this door lock. I see no sign of forced entry. Which means the killer was already inside. If we can clear the guards of involvement, this case has problems."

A forensic tech stood in front of the bed, amazed at the scene he was looking at. He was more surprised at what he didn't find on the standing lamp that was the murder weapon. Motioning for the two detectives to come over, he said, "Sir, we've got a problem."

"What's the problem?"

"Well, sir, after dusting the standing lamp for prints, I can't find any images on it."

"How is that possible?"

"Depending on when this room was last cleaned and how thorough the cleaning crew was. If we dust everything else, we're going to get false positives."

Quietly listening to conversations while trying not to get in the detectives' way, one stood out to the senior guard when their discussion turned to what weapon could have caused the beheading of the victims. He chimed in, "An axe could do something like that."

Mike looked at the bodies still pinned to the bed and the cleanness of the cuts on them. "It's not serrated, but clean." He looked back at the senior guard and nodded in agreement. The other detective then asked how many deaths had occurred here involving an axe. Almost simultaneously, Mike and the senior guard answered, "Christopher Davis, the Axeman."

They both looked at each other, and Mike spoke first. "This woman died of a broken heart."

The senior guard nodded, his face etched with years of experience. "Sounds like we're on the same page. He couldn't hack it in prison, so someone stabbed him. A prisoner, we couldn't identify who he was."

"That sounds like a plan. Then the only question is, will the medical examiner's office sign off on these causes of death?"

"He's done it before. So long as he gets assurances from our bosses that this is in the public's interest. Seeing as how we've got unusual causes of death, no living suspects, and a potential media circus that no one wants to deal with, we'll have to handle this under our CYA procedures."

The junior detective asked, "What's the CYA procedure?"

"Oh, that's the cover-your-ass procedure. We law enforcement officers can't lie in an official police report. So we have to file two reports—one that's the truth as we know it to be and one that gets told to the public—while being careful to ensure the truthful report gets improperly filed and never sees the light of day for at least twenty to thirty years."

Arriving at the newly built green building in the Mansfield, Ohio, court district, Darnell was blown away by the building's cool look when he walked in. He had little time, so he scanned the directory until he found *John Merit, Attorney at Law, Suite 210.* A few minutes later, he stood in front of the door. He wasn't sure if he was in the right place until the receptionist greeted him with a smile.

"I'm Darnell Jackson, from Rep. Kimbell's office. I need to talk to Mr. Merit for a bit."

She waved him in. "He's got a few minutes to see you. He's in a hurry, and he has court soon."

A warm smile lit up his face as he gazed at her. "You're a lifesaver!"

Walking into his office was like walking into a small library. It was a sprawling space packed with books from floor to ceiling, towering bookshelves lining almost every wall, not o mention the books piled up on his desk. Mr. Merit stood up to greet him. He shook his hand, and then they both sat down.

"So, Mr. Jackson, what can I do for you?"

"What can you tell me about your client, Jon Bowman?"

"I can tell you he's a young man who shouldn't be in Redmond Prison. He got railroaded."

"How can you remember his case without looking at your case file?"

"Easy, because the district attorney and judge showed bias against my client. The police didn't even find the young man's fingerprints on the bottle of pills. This along with the judge limiting my ability to cross-examine the arresting officer in the way I needed to impeach his testimony. I also remember this case because of the weird way I got paid."

"How did he pay you?"

"He didn't. His county lockup cellmate generously paid my fee instead of him on the condition that I took both cases."

"Are you freaking kidding me?"

"Nope."

"Why would he do that?"

"Because he needed a connection on the outside that he didn't have. It seems he also sensed the young man didn't belong behind bars."

In shock, all Darnell could do was shake his head, stunned. He felt compelled to ask another question. "How did he get your card in the first place?"

"A woman I know who's a sergeant at the county jail has many of my cards. She gives them out to young brothers who she feels shouldn't be there."

"Seriously?"

"Yeah, it's an easy way to generate word-of-mouth business. Mr. Jackson, why are you asking me these questions anyway? Why is Rep. Kimbell's office interested in this case?"

Sitting up in his chair, Darnell looked directly at Mr. Merit. "Mr. Merit, you must get legal help on the Bowman case and possibly others. I say that because you'll have to wage a legal war to get that young man out."

"Darnell... Can I call you Darnell?"

"Sure."

"The only way to get him out is with fresh evidence. I have no clue where that will come from or where to look." He stood up to get ready to leave.

"Mr. Merit, that's why I came to see you. The officer in your client's case is going to be indicted for planting drugs on many black men during routine traffic stops."

Mr. Merit just stared at him. "You're joking. Please tell me you're not kidding me."

"Nope. And that's not all. There's a video of your client's traffic stop. There's a video of Officer Donovan putting drugs in your client's car. Even though I haven't seen the video, I have it on excellent authority that they've got the goods."

"To get this evidence, who should I target with a court order?"

"Mr. Merit, I suggest you subpoena the Ohio field office of the FBI."

That's when Mr. Merit stood up and started doing what amounted to his happy dance. Realizing that he was due in court soon, he composed himself and sat back down at his desk. "Mr. Jackson, where can I find you if I need to contact you?"

"Call the state house. Ask for State Representative Kimbell's secretary or me by name. They'll know where to find me. Mr. Merit, you should also know that this implicates people at the highest levels of government. Judges, law enforcement officials, and politicians involved in the state legislature. This corruption is like an octopus. At the center are for-profit prison corporations whose tentacles reach far and wide. Indictments are coming, and many influential people are on edge."

#

On a serene block of a relatively normal-looking street, in a community where the houses were indistinguishable, all painted the same shades of beige and gray, with identically manicured lawns, Officer Donovan woke up depressed about being placed on desk duty after his grand jury testimony. Standing in the bathroom, looking in the mirror, he was worried. He beat charges before, but these were the feds he was dealing with. It was still dark outside at around five o'clock in the morning. Early, before the sun rose and most people were up. He was totally unaware that this would be the worst day of his life.

He wouldn't learn about the grand jury's true bill until five hours after his drive to the station. A United States attorney had decided that the document would stay sealed until ten o'clock. The United States attorney warned the chief of police about the impending indictment. Everyone at the station knew something serious had gone wrong when the city manager appeared and entered the chief's office. A thick silence fell as he arrived, broken only by nervous shuffling and hushed whispers. Everyone knew danger was near. Alerted by a tip, reporters waited outside with cameras flashing and notebooks ready.

Donovan hadn't even touched his chair when his eyes caught sight of the city manager and an HR representative deep in conversation with the chief. This was always an omen, never a reassuring sign for any officer under a cloud. When he was called into the office, the chief was the only one to speak at first. "Anthony, how are you holding up?"

"I'm doing the best I can under the circumstances."

"Well, I've got some terrible news for you. I'm going to need your gun and your badge."

"Sir, I'm going to beat this. I've done it before."

"Anthony, this time, it's different. This time, it's the feds. They have evidence that our lawyers can't get thrown out. They've been looking into your record of arrests over the years. Your record, combined with dispatch logs, uncovered racism and bias that this department can no longer afford to tolerate. At ten thirty, you will no longer be an officer with this department."

That's when the city manager spoke. "We have no choice but to cut you loose to rebuild this department. This is damage control. We're at risk of a consent decree from the Justice Department in Washington coming down on top of the potential lawsuits. Your pension is safe, but a conviction on these charges could lead to jail time. I'm not sorry for what you're going through because I've been here long enough to know you and your record. This has been a long time coming and way overdue. You brought this on yourself and this department. Now we have to accept the blame and the consequences for not cleaning up this toxic racist atmosphere sooner."

Agent Coleman knew his day would be unusual when his white Labrador retriever, Dino, woke him up by licking him. This behavior was out of the norm for his dog. Getting up and slowly getting dressed as the sun rose, he eventually piled into his car with all his gear, or more so his dog's gear, for doggy daycare. After dropping off his dog, he grabbed a breakfast sandwich and a cup of coffee at a nearby shop. His feeling of grogginess was almost gone. When he called his boss, that led to a short and depressing conversation.

"Is the show on?"

"Yes, the U.S. attorney has unsealed the indictment that was returned against Anthony Donovan, and you're directed to take him into custody."

Having almost perfect timing, Coleman arrived at Officer Donovan's station at 9:55. He made his way past the few news reporters in front of the station, pushing them away while saying, "No comment, no comment." He was trying hard to avoid unnecessary fanfare. It was terrible business to take a fellow officer into custody under these circumstances, and he knew it. It weighed on him, and in the back of his mind, he was constantly thinking about the reactions of the other officers. Officers who knew and worked with Donovan over the years.

Officers who would have to witness his hard fall from grace. It would be a morale killer, but he knew this awful task had to be done.

When he walked in, he flashed his badge and asked to speak to the chief. An officer led him to his office. Cops stopped what they were doing as he walked past. A strange stillness hung in the air as if time held its breath, sensing something extraordinary was about to happen, as if someone or something was about to die, even though they were still alive. Making his way to the office, he talked to the chief and the city manager. He was told they had already taken Officer Donovan's badge and gun. He then asked them to point him out, even though he had a photo of him already committed to memory. Suddenly, the room seemed to go mute, and you could almost hear a pin drop.

Exiting the office, he walked a few steps to the man sitting at the nearby desk.

"Officer Anthony Donovan?"

"Yes."

"Please stand up." Coleman leaned over to whisper in his ear, "Please don't make this any worse than it already is for yourself." Then he stood straight. Officer Anthony Donovan, the crisp morning air biting at his cheeks, heard the words, "You are under arrest," the metallic clang of handcuffs echoing the gravity of the situation. "You may stay silent if you choose to. You have the right to an attorney." He read him his Miranda rights, which he, as an officer, was all too familiar with. The cold steel of the handcuffs bit into his wrists as he walked out in shame, head bowed. The younger officers lowered their heads in sadness while some older, more experienced officers tapped them on the shoulder, demanding that they watch and learn. Encouraging them never to allow this to happen to them, to do the job the right way. To serve and protect the public, not lie and mistreat them. Despite the absence of a trial or conviction, the older officers—their faces etched with years of seeing the truth behind the lies—knew he was guilty. The silence in the room spoke volumes. However, the blue wall being the blue wall, they knew it protected corrupt cops more often than not, a fact they'd witnessed repeatedly.

Chapter 15. Tortured Souls

During the preparations for former officer Anthony Donovan's trial, plea bargain negotiations were also underway in case he pleaded guilty. During the pretrial hearing, the prosecutor showed videos of several traffic stops. The courtroom gasped when the undeniable proof came out. Anthony, eyes wide with horror, gave his attorney a quick tap on the shoulder, whispering to him, "This is not good." The sheer volume of incriminating material is overwhelming. How screwed am I, do you think?"

His lawyer looked at him. "From a legal standpoint, you're screwed. The damning footage in that video, showing your every incriminating move, will guarantee a guilty verdict on all counts if shown to a jury. You already know how bad it looks with you being a former officer.

You should start focusing on self-preservation; the path ahead is difficult. If they offer a plea deal, take it. That will include pleading guilty and likely rolling over on anyone you may have information on. Anything involving illegal activity that you may know of? You better spill it. I've already been told the U.S. attorney would be interested in working something out if you've got information on these private prison corporations. You must play ball, tell them anything they want to know about anything you have knowledge of. I have to warn you though: if they catch you in a lie, they can walk away from the deal they offer you."

" During a proffer session, tell them I'm prepared to talk about a deputy district attorney who withheld discovery evidence that could have exonerated some defendants. I can also tell them how I delivered bribes from prison execs to judges."

"What? Hold on a minute, who were these judges?"

"I can't name anyone now unless they're willing to almost let me walk. My compliance is contingent on the preservation of my pension along with little to no jail time."

Looking at him long and hard, trying to understand how serious he was, his lawyer then stood up. "Your Honor, I would like to request a recess to discuss a possible plea in return for substantial information that could impact current open investigations at the U.S. attorney's office."

The judge looked at the deputy U.S. attorney. "Do you agree with this recess?"

Smiling like the Grinch who stole Christmas, he answered promptly, "Yes, Your Honor." He knew that showing the video was a scheme to scare Anthony into flipping on anyone who may have been his accomplice.

Then, with the bang of the judge's gavel, "We're in recess until ten o'clock tomorrow."

The two lawyers met between the desks in the middle of the room. Standing there, the deputy U.S. attorney asked eagerly, "So, what kind of information do you have for me?"

As word got out that Anthony was spilling his guts to the U.S. attorney's office, many lawyers, along with state judges, contemplated their futures. Nerves frayed as the list of early retirements mounted. Back at the capitol, in a conference room in Rep. Kimbell's office, Agent Ron Coleman put together a private showing of many traffic stop videos used in Anthony Donovan's hearing. The video was nearly two hours long and very enlightening, especially regarding how police officers serve and protect specific segments of the public only to bully and mistreat others, primarily black American communities.

Rep. Kimbell, Rep. Townsend, and her chief of staff quietly watched in horror along with Darnell and various members of the two legislators' staff. The recurring injustice of drugs being planted on innocent young black men was sickening. Agent Coleman interrupted occasionally, pointing out that this was surveillance work over two years. He knew this point had to be emphasized because this officer's conduct could have been going on for a decade, assisted by other officers. The actions of one man, with the help of others, ruined lives. Men working for a system that worked for one group of people while simultaneously destroying others.

Before the video ended, Rep. Kimbell's secretary entered the room, handing him a note. After reading it, he waited until the video ended. Darnell was the first to speak after someone turned on the lights. "We have to make prison reform an issue in people's minds. Especially since most conservatives would rather lock brothers up and throw away the key."

Rep. Townsend said, "Since we don't have majority control of the legislature, there's not much we can do right now."

Rep. Kimbell interrupted them, standing with a broad, beaming smile illuminating his face. He spoke with his comforting baritone voice: "Ladies and gentlemen, I've just learned that we *used* to be in the minority. It seems five conservative members of the state house couldn't take the heat from this political firestorm, and they just resigned. All of them had close ties with prison corporations. Losing the conservative majority in the state house has directly resulted from the recent events."

The cheers from the room reached the hallway. Rep. Kimbell reminded them not to celebrate the misfortunes of others too joyfully. "One day it could be your misfortune others are celebrating."

Ron, being the agent he was, couldn't celebrate. He, of course, had political leanings. However, he was supposed to be politically independent and show no bias toward either party.

The unsealed indictments caused mass chaos in legal circles as well as the halls of power across the state. Revelations of corruption continued to spread like cancer everywhere. It turned out that Anthony's story about judges getting bribes was true, and a whistleblower confirmed it. An insider just walked into the U.S. attorney's office one day and provided an address to an office building with no business sign. The building was filled with boxes of incriminating documents along with paper shredding machines.

Of course, the mention of paper shredding machines piqued the interest of the FBI agents, who carefully listened to every word the whistleblower said. They glanced at each other after taking notes. Hearing this morsel of information disturbed them. Shocked by what they had just heard, they picked their jaws up from the floor. Within minutes, they got up and ran out of the office in a mad dash, stuffing their notepads with the address securely in their pockets, to prevent obstruction of justice through the destruction of evidence.

Once they reached their cars, the race was on. A procession of black sedans flew out of the garage. Police sirens blared while blue and red lights flashed in an automated sequence. After reaching their destination in a little less than half an hour, they found the room as described. Small, full of boxes, and smelling faintly of old paper.

Meanwhile, at the headquarters of Genesis Corrections Group, the president and chief executive officer was told an hour later by the company's general counsel that a whistleblower was talking and had given the FBI details of the sensitive information's location. After hearing this, he immediately resigned as president and CEO.

When the chief financial officer was told this, he reacted differently. He calmly opened the sliding door leading to the balcony of his rather luxurious office. Then, before anyone could stop him, he jumped to his death, falling thirty stories, leaving behind shattered bones, a blood-stained sidewalk, and a disfigured blob that was once a human being. A woman's screams echoed from the distance. There's a saying: "It's not the fall that kills you. It's the sudden stop."

He left behind a wife and two children. He knew his life was over once the FBI and forensic accountants got involved. No matter how skillfully he'd hidden the transactions, the gnawing feeling that his carefully constructed lies would unravel was inescapable. The paper trail to him would eventually surface. The weight of his deception pressed heavily on him.

Back in Redmond, life went on. Jon continued to wage a supernatural war with an adversary that killed like humans breathe. The Axeman didn't eat. He didn't sleep. He only killed to live and seemed to show no emotion while doing so. As the unexplained deaths continued, the population dropped enough to cause the inmates to take notice, along with some of the prison staff.

Life at the prison took an unusual turn when the oddest death in recent Redmond history occurred. The death involved Corrections Officer Jeffery Norton, a bear of a man. He intimidated anyone he came in contact with and was extremely hard to work with, a guard who was impossible to befriend and better avoided as an inmate. He was not only inflexible, but his thinking was rigid, like a stubborn oak. In his view, rules were sacred and inflexible; to bend them was unthinkable. He couldn't help being more honest than necessary to prison oversight investigators during an inspection that nearly got Warden Hudson and the staff in trouble.

Jeff's transfer to the night shift meant swapping the daytime hustle and bustle for the quieter, more solitary hours of darkness. This was a move he was extremely bitter about. He saw it for what he and everyone else knew it was: a punishment, considering his seniority. As his anger consumed him, he took it out on some inmates. Late one night, an inmate failed to show him the respect he felt he was due. Seething with anger, the inmate spat on him, a mixture of disgust and defiance in the act.

Jeff, with his bare hands, beat the inmate to within an inch of his life. The internal damage was so severe that even though he made it to the infirmary, the broken ribs, collapsed lung, cracked skull, and brain damage would've relegated him to eating through a straw and breathing through a tube for the rest of his life had he remained on the ventilator. As for Jeff, he seemed to show absolutely no remorse, which was why, when he died, hardly anyone cared.

A few hours after the violent altercation, he walked down a narrow hallway alone. The lights suddenly went dim and flickered for a moment before shutting off entirely. With the moon as the only light, there were areas of the hallway that were pitch-black. When the Axeman appeared, he approached Jeff slowly, taking his time as he faded in and out of view, showing absolutely no emotion or sense of urgency. Jeff knew he was in trouble, but he could do nothing about it. His growing fear made his feet feel frozen. He was paralyzed with fear, unable to move a muscle. The closer the Axeman got, the more his heart pounded in his chest, a frantic drum against his ribs. A frigid chill filled the space, the air growing thin and icy, a profound silence that felt like the world held its breath.

Directly in front of him, the Axeman's intense stare, as cold and sharp as the blade he carried, made him feel his soul was bare. The Axeman brought his hand to Jeff's left ear, then his other hand for the right. With each squeeze, Jeff could feel the pressure building in his head, a crushing weight threatening to cave in his skull. His silent scream was unheard in the deafening roar in his ears. A crimson stream of blood flowed from his nose, spurting out like a miniature faucet, warm and thick.

Upon crushing Jeff's head like a grape, a peculiar realization dawned on him. Jeff's heart continued to beat, seemingly unaware that its owner was dead. With the spirit gone, the Axeman violently tore into his body, yanking out his still-pulsating heart in a spray of blood and crushing it before him. Jeff was powerless to stop him, suffering the added insult to injury of having his soul absorbed and imprisoned afterward. The Axeman turned to walk and slowly faded away, disappearing entirely as the light from the moon shifted. They found Jeff's body early the following day. During the coroner's autopsy, he found the initials *C* and *D* on both of his wrists. Everyone knew what that meant: the Axeman, Christopher Davis.

The guards tried to get back to their daily routine despite the unfortunate fate of one of their own. They expertly managed the inmates' diverse personalities and moral failings. But it was a much different story at night. New to their posts, the younger guards patrolled the grounds at night, their footsteps echoing in the stillness. Despite their limited experience, they were surprisingly capable. The event had little impact, given that sleeping inmates' heavy breathing and snores filled the night. A different warden had made an agreement years ago that the older guards would work during the day. Redmond's night-time ghosts terrified them, a detail the younger guards eventually came to learn after several guards suffered more heart attacks and strokes than normal.

Even though the younger guards hated the seniority system, since there was nothing they could do about it, they tried not to complain. As a result, Bishop MacPherson always volunteered to talk to the young guards, providing what guidance he could. His advice was always straightforward and the same.

"Redmond Prison is seriously creepy. I urge everyone in listening distance, every soul who can hear my words—this is a warning, a piece of advice you would be wise to follow. To stay alive here, you must believe this. The weight of your duty presses down like the cold, unforgiving stone of the prison's walls, a constant, chilling reminder of your responsibility. Here, the rules for the living and the dead are ancient and unyielding, etched in stone and enforced by unseen guardians. Do your job with professionalism and respect for each other and the inmates you guard, even if the inmates show little respect for you. If you value your lives, despite how badly they treat you, you will respect them because this place feeds on powerful emotions, especially anger, hate, and fear. These are the emotions that attract ghosts like moths to a flame.

"Gentlemen, above all, remember this: So long as you're here at night, you will be safe in one place and one place only. The prison chapel. My domain is the one place ghosts may not go. It's the one place that's respected by the lost souls who haunt Redmond. They treat it with reverence, tiptoeing and speaking in hushed tones as if afraid of disturbing something sacred. Here, you'll find sanctuary—a haven where the walls breathe peace, and a protective embrace surrounds you."

Devout followers of the faith heeded Bishop MacPherson's advice. Therefore, they made a point of spending quality time with him whenever their schedules allowed. Mostly for prayer, safety, and protection during their shift. The rest staggered out oblivious to the untold dangers they were at risk of dealing with.

Sundays at Redmond were never the best days to be locked up. Some of the guys felt compelled to go to church. It provided an excuse for Jon and his entourage to get out of their cells, so no one complained about going. Besides, many guys raised in the church experienced vivid flashbacks to their younger days, the hymns and the smell of old wood instantly transporting them back to when their mothers made them spend some time with God, despite the contradictions raised by ending up in prison. Bishop MacPherson wasn't a fire and brimstone preacher. He was a seminary-trained messenger of the word who chose his words carefully while always trying to maintain a consistent tone to keep the inmates calm.

This sermon aimed to not only provide spiritual guidance, but also to uplift the men's spirits, filling them with hope and purpose, encouraging them to be better and do better. They sat in their usual spot, with Gary on one side and Craig on the other. The rest of the guys sat on the worn wooden pews behind them, the silence broken only by the occasional cough. Gary and Craig, their eyes narrowed with concern, peppered Jon with questions about his fatigue, their curiosity baffling him. The remnants of yesterday's lively bleacher banter echoed faintly in the yard.

"Why are you guys asking me these questions?"

"Because you fell asleep during our chess game."

"No, I didn't," he replied, his voice tight with a nervous tremor.

"Yes, you did. And by the way, you snore."

"I suppose denying it would be a waste of time?"

Almost simultaneously, they both responded, "Yup, that's why you shouldn't even try."

"Well, how long was I out?"

"Long enough to talk a little in your sleep. You were mumbling something about Christopher Davis, the Axeman, along with issuing orders to a soldier."

They were all whispering, trying not to get caught talking through Bishop MacPherson's sermon that he was midway through.

"Your recent silence and distracted behavior have been concerning. It's as if you're miles away. We know you miss Freddie. We all do. But there's something else going on with you."

Right then, an alarm sounded, startling everyone and causing Bishop MacPherson to stop just when he seemed to get into his groove. Since this was a relatively small group of guys, everyone turned to look at the guards standing near the door at the back of the room, instantly knowing what was going through their minds. One of them used his shoulder-mounted radio, Pushing the side button to get a situation report from the dispatch officer in the control room. Straining their ears, the men heard only a distorted, unintelligible mess, a sound that raised their anxieties. When he raised his voice, they could hear a simple question. "How long will we have to wait? Wait, what the hell do you mean tomorrow morning? Well, can you at least get food for us?"

That's when Bishop MacPherson interrupted, pointing to a locked storage room to which he had the key. He whispered, "It's got emergency rations!" The dispatcher urged them to be patient. The guard looked depressed but then signed off, and everyone waited with anticipation to hear what he was going to say.

"Gentlemen, we are under lockdown. It seems a few guys held here for U.S. Immigration and Customs Enforcement grew tired of waiting. It seems they've been stuck here months past their release and deportation date. Unfortunately, their country doesn't seem to want them back. Because of this, they've lost their minds. They took two guards and a deputy warden hostage. So we're going to be stuck here for a while."

Craig looked at Jon with a huge smile. "Well, young man, we now have plenty of time and nowhere to go. Now you can explain to us what's going on with you."

He sighed, having no interest in telling a crazy story that he didn't think anyone would believe. However, realizing he was fighting a losing war, he talked. Craig and Gary listened along with the rest of the guys as Jon told them about his time in solitary confinement.

"When you're sitting there staring at the four walls of a cell that seems like a closet, you're left alone with your thoughts. That's when something odd happened. A chilly breeze seemed to come over the cell. A ghostly figure appeared before me, sending a shiver down my spine. Only I could see it, but it was real. I wasn't sure if I'd been dreaming. A conversation started, mostly about why I was there and how this ghost got stuck there. Once released from solitary, I ended up back in the general population. Well, remember, not long after that, I took a shot to the head and ended up in the infirmary. While there, I met another ghost after having an out-of-body experience."

As the story got more interesting, the guys listened more intently.

"The ghost in the infirmary was looking for someone she lost. It turned out that someone was the ghost in solitary. I tricked the guard into releasing the one in solitary to reunite the ghosts. You know that saying, 'No good deed goes unpunished'? Well, that good deed caught the attention of an angel who had a job for me: to weaken the angel of death we know as the Axeman. An emissary of the Devil who has been torturing everyone at Redmond for decades. This was never a job I wanted, but it's a job I'm determined to do."

Gary, the most laid-back and profound thinker of the bunch, spoke first. "That, young man, with eyes that hold a thousand untold tales, is quite a story. You don't seem like a person who would tell a lie without a reason. And if you were to lie, I don't think you'd be very convincing, based on what I know about you. I'm willing to give you the benefit of the doubt until I see evidence that tells me otherwise." Unbeknownst to Gary, his words would prove prophetic.

They all fell asleep for the night listening to jazz on the radio in the chapel of Redmond Prison, a small group of inmates sprawled on the cold, hard floor, their breath raspy and shallow, like a pack of wolves deep in slumber. One by one, their spirits left their bodies. Their eyes widened in shock and confusion, a stunned silence hanging before Jon calmly explained what had happened to them. Wildflowers stretched to the horizon, a beautiful sight. One of the guys pointed out the two angels standing guard near the French doors. At the back of the chapel, these angels stood like statues with military discipline. Gary was amazed, like everyone else, but through observation, he made a profound point which caused everyone else to think hard. "The presence of the angels guarding the chapel might be why ghosts steer clear of this place. I heard the guards whispering that only the Redmond chapel offered sanctuary from the restless ghosts."

That's when a familiar angel appeared, the same one that placed captain bars on his shoulders and gave him the job in the first place. Jon immediately recognized him, and the angel likewise. Once the guys grew silent, the angel looked at each of them like a drill sergeant inspecting his men, sizing them up. He looked at Jon for a few minutes, smiling, saying nothing, then addressed all of them.

"Gentlemen, your young friend was telling you the truth when he told you I gave him a job to do. He has been waging hit-and-run attacks for the past few months, attacking the angel of death. By launching these attacks, he's weakened him enough for you all to wage a more aggressive war against him. All in the hope of defeating him for a while."

As they all listened, the air crackled with anticipation, a collective breath held. Craig looked confused. "Wait, I heard the phrase 'you all' and 'defeat him for a while'?"

The angel said, "No man can fight a war alone. And Christopher is already dead. He can only die once; there's no way to kill him twice. The only place where he truly belongs is back in Hell, and that's where you can send him."

Chapter 16. Hell on Earth

"A general without an army is a well-dressed man with good military training. A general with the command of an army and the will to use it, now that's a lethal fighting force that could then defeat any threat. Well, I'm the general, and Jon is the captain. We all need you to volunteer as second lieutenants to relay orders to the men."

"What men are you talking about?"

"The soldiers you will command are the Civil War-era ghosts currently haunting Redmond. This is the army we will use to send the Axeman to Hell where he belongs."

The angel's voice, like calming chimes, reassured them as he went on, detailing the help they would receive in leaving their bodies. "This task requires an angel to help you. Otherwise, everyone would do it. That's the rule. Plus, you only have a short window before you're pulled back. Another thing to remember is if your body dies while you're out of it...well, the best way I can put this is you're screwed, and you can call it a life. We will give you some time to make peace with your fate. Afterward, we will take you to the place in between to be judged. The place to determine whether your soul will rest in Heaven or suffer in Hell."

Craig raised his hand, trying to get the angel's attention. "Hey, if you're the general of this operation, then who's in charge of it above you?"

"You all know who that is if you've read your Bible. Gentlemen, if you need to earn points for all the behavior you're not proud of over the years, here's your chance to make up for it."

That's when one of the guys spoke up, giving him the answer he was looking for. "If your boss will forgive half of the mistakes I've made, yeah, I'm in. To me, it's worth the risk."

One by one, they all committed to the war they knew had to be waged.

The last key detail mentioned by the angel before he disappeared had to do with strategy. "Gentlemen, I have limited time, but I can't go without telling you this. The men who assembled to kill Christopher the first time hanged him. Falsely accusing him of a crime against a woman he secretly loved based solely on the unreliable word of two liars. Then, in a flash of furious rage, he performed a blasphemous act so horrific that the divine authority relinquished his soul to howling demons. The men who assembled to hang him threw his lifeless body off a nearby bridge into the water below. Because his final resting place is a river, he comes from it to haunt Redmond Prison, and he must return to it."

"How will we know when he's close to surrendering. When his eyes lose their fire and his movements become sluggish?"

"You'll know when he's forced to fight a war on two fronts by trying to hold you at bay while maintaining control of the few spirits trapped in his body. In this weakened state, the Axeman will be driven back to his death and burial place. Here, he will have no choice but to stand and fight. The one above all will send you all there: a dark, foreboding place. It will just be you, using weapons of your choice, no ghost soldiers to fight for you.

"The passage of time will slow down. You will know you're winning when he throws or drops his axe and compels it to come to him, but it doesn't respond, and when his appearance returns to what he looked like on the day he died. Two angels, Samuel Davis and Paul Davis, will suddenly appear, their voices booming with divine judgment. Since this will be Christopher's last stand, he will be more aggressive. If he loses, a door will appear to Hell. The two angels who will appear will be his two sons, granted the power and protection by the one above all to arrest him, placing him in chains. Then they will drag him back to Hell."

"Wait, how did he escape the first time?"

"He benefited from the guidance and support of demons on the Devil's orders. As a result, he might escape again. We can keep him locked up there for only ten to twenty years. Our ability to detain him will have weakened by then. God grants an angel power but intentionally limits it. It's unlike the punishment for the fallen angels sent to Hell. The one above all, his punishment is permanent. He bound the fallen angels with chains of solidified glowing obsidian light, unbreakable bonds that defy the erosion of time. The angels will arrest the Axeman, but their power can only keep him imprisoned for a limited time. This allows Christopher to come back if sent as the Devil's emissary."

As they returned to their bodies, the lockdown ended, and they filtered back to their cells and the routine they had become accustomed to.

They all convened at their customary table the following day, a palpable sense of shared adventure hanging in the air as they recounted their experience, convincing themselves it was real. Jon suggested trapping Christopher in the Redmond bathrooms. He told them about the unfortunate inmate who was dumb enough to say Christopher's name three times in front of a mirror, describing in gruesome detail how he ended up being cut nearly in half by the Axeman from the top of his head down to his waist. The Axeman ran the poor slob through like a hot knife through butter. He meticulously described the man's exposed heart and brain as if laid out on an autopsy table, his rib cage opened and his vital organs laid open for all to see. Jon then explained how his plan would work. It called for saying Christopher's name three times in front of a mirror, luring him into a trap where his spirit soldiers would be waiting. The energy in Redmond was palpable as strategy and planning sessions unfolded during breakfast, a lively buzz accompanying the clinking of cups and trays.

Time passed, and Michelle was at home sitting on the floor, watching her son crawl. She quietly watched as he moved forward on the light blue carpet in her apartment. She stared at him as he started, stopped, and crawled toward her again before eventually standing to walk, even though he seemed shaky and then fell. After giving him a big hug, she thought he was growing too fast. She smiled at him, and he immediately responded by waving his arms and grinning after achieving the minor milestone of walking a few steps before falling into the wide-open arms of his overjoyed mother.

Meanwhile, at the law office of John Merit, he was diligently drafting motions for various cases he was working on. He got to the petition for a writ of habeas corpus and recalled the key elements of the Bowman case. He painstakingly detailed how he believed the justice system had failed, citing specific instances of flawed evidence and biased proceedings, his voice tight with frustration. Knowing Jon had toiled for nearly two years at Redmond's sprawling campus, marked by triumphs and setbacks, he figured he'd still be stuck there for another year while they sorted things out. He filed the documents to get things going. The paperwork was done and dropped off at the courthouse. He knew he then had to go to Redmond to see his client and tell him all about the amazing things he discovered.

The allegations against the arresting officer alone undermined the state's case against Jon. The corruption and bias of the judge and prosecutor in his case, systemic racism together with bias, caused his client's unfair treatment. There was documentation of a pattern of how other people were unfairly treated as well. The whole thing was just one big mess, enough to justify a new trial at a minimum. However, the side issues and their implications were a mess that, thankfully, someone else would have to clean up.

Back at Redmond, plans were being turned into action. Out of all the members of their entourage, Craig was the quietest and least talkative of them all. He liked to observe what was happening around him and never aspired to be the center of attention. He became an inmate due to leaving a bar where he had too much to drink, resulting in the worst mistake of his life when he accidentally took the life of a pregnant woman on a dark road. Ten years into a twenty-year sentence, he spent his time trying to atone for his mistake, getting sober for the first time in his life due to God and no access to alcohol. In Redmond, he had become one of the most devout members of their entourage and a leader among them.

After losing a cellmate and friend to the Axeman, he vowed to send him straight to Hell where he belonged. In the first battle of what would become their war, Craig positioned his contingent of spirit soldiers between the columns of enormous water storage tanks. The Axeman showed up in the hallway near the water plant. A ghost soldier set the trap on re-con with a well-placed shot to his arm as a means to draw him into a fight before running away, waiting only moments before he was close enough to attack. His strategy may have been clear, but it was risky.

The plan involved forcing the Axeman into a gauntlet, hoping to fire waves of shots at him before he could get near the first contingent of soldiers to take them out. When the Axeman appeared within range, a yell went out that all could hear. "Fire, fire, fire." Upon hearing this, his men opened barrage after barrage on him. For fifteen minutes, he was in Hell, hemorrhaging spirits he'd accumulated over decades. The Axeman's rage grew with every wave of bullets as spirits tugged on his body, trying to break free.

Before he got close enough to swing his axe or tap into the power of the spirits trapped in Redmond, Craig's first contingent of spirit soldiers retreated and the second contingent engaged. His power waning, the Axeman realized his losses were mounting as the imprisoned spirits slipped from his control. He hurled his axe in one sharp movement, the whistling flight ending with a loud clang and a satisfying metal tear as a breach opened in a water tank. Then he reached out his hand to compel his axe to return to him through some supernatural force, only to do the same thing to the water tank on the right. As water gushed out of the breaches in both, it was as if Moses had parted the Red Sea in reverse, creating a wall of water with a violent *whoosh* and a chilling spray. Craig could only stand in amazement as the water froze in a flash, forming an impenetrable wall protecting the Axeman's escape. Despite his withdrawal, the battle echoed in his ears. The transparent wall of ice allowed the Axeman to stare back at his adversary, not saying a word, before turning to walk away. What he was staring at was Craig's inmate number and cell block number on his orange jumpsuit.

The angel observing the fight realized no need to grant grace because Christopher never got close enough to land a blow. He disappeared, and then so did the spirit soldiers. Eventually, Craig felt a sharp tug pulling him back to his body, and the world returned to him. Slowly, he awoke, his senses dulled, the world swimming into focus as if someone had pulled him from a deep sleep. The man in his cell was an unwelcome presence, and he couldn't bring himself to trust him. He stared at him while standing in front of the sink and mirror.

"Hey, man, you talk in your sleep."

"Still a little confused. What was I saying?"

"You were saying fire, fire, fire." Dismissing it as a crazy dream, Craig recommended he go back to sleep.

The inmates knew it, and the staff of Redmond knew many ghosts routinely roamed the prison halls. However, Jon and his friends would notice something odd the next night while out of their bodies. Very few spirits were walking around and roaming the halls. They only saw the random Civil War ghost soldiers in uniform walking by a cell. Sometimes, ignoring the inmate, they passed by. Sometimes, they stopped only for a moment to stare at the shocked man who saw or felt a presence before walking away, fading into the distance.

The birds flying over the prison seemed to sense it, and the ghosts who haunted the prison knew it. A war was being fought based on the fierce skirmishes they observed without being seen. Jon strategically placed his soldiers under the command of his friends in key positions throughout Redmond. Then they lay in wait for the Axeman.

All was silent save the distant whisper of the wind, a serene and calming atmosphere. In an instant, all hell broke loose. Gary tested Jon's theory by saying Christopher's name three times while looking into a mirror in one of the Redmond inmate bathrooms. Only the steady drip of water from a nearby faucet was audible for the first few minutes.

His contingent of spirit soldiers stood ready, waiting to fire with the slightest order. These spirit soldiers may not have seen action during the Civil War. They may not have fired their weapons in a single battle. Gary could somehow sense their desperation to prove themselves, because many of them had died during training due to disease or other reasons long before any battle took place. They knew this was their chance to fight, their chance to make their deaths mean something.

The minute Christopher appeared in the mirror, Gary scrambled out of the line of fire, his heart pounding in his chest. Without hesitation, he promptly issued the order. "Fire, fire, fire." In quick succession, his soldiers unleashed volley after volley of bullets.

Shots rang out as Christopher stepped out of the mirror and through the wall, taking enormous fire while intimidating the hell out of Gary, if not his men. The fight raged on, lasting only minutes. Like a bull staring down a matador, the Axeman charged the line of men standing there in a two-by-two formation. Gary watched in horror as his line broke, and his men scrambled to reload. Swinging his ax in a rage, the Axeman took out soldier after soldier in close quarters combat, despite taking incoming sporadic fire. In staggered succession, one soldier fired, then another as one soldier struggled to fight hand to hand.

Regrouping when reinforcements arrived in force, a soldier sacrificed himself to buy time for the others to attack. Gary, sensing the time was right, issued the unmistakable order to his spirit soldiers. "Unleash hell, fire!" With rifled muskets loaded and ready, shots rang out as Christopher made his retreat, walking through a wall as the last bullet twisted through the barrel, hitting the wall just seconds after the Axeman walked through it.

Once the chaos cleared and his contingent of spirit soldiers disappeared, Gary thought he was alone with his thoughts when a spirit of light and spectacular brilliance took form. Standing before him was an inmate, a ghost from the old Redmond Reformatory. He could tell by the old uniform from pictures he remembered seeing in the warden's office. The black and white pictures on the wall captured moments frozen in time, each telling a unique story. At first, the spirit struggled to speak as though he had forgotten how to, but then found the words.

"I'm an innocent man, but not without sin, killed by the Axeman in the Old Redmond. While there, he captured my soul, and with it held me prisoner along with many, many others. Your courage, along with the help of other spirits, freed me. For that, I will be forever grateful, but know this: The war you and your friends are waging is not over. You are getting close to winning because he's growing weaker, battle by battle. The number of souls he's losing compared to the ones he's replacing them with, he's running out of time. This will make his defeat all but inevitable. So, keep on doing what you're doing."

Then an angel appeared, standing next to an open door that miraculously appeared. Sensing he had run out of time, the ghost walked through it and vanished. Moments after, Gary found himself pulled back to his body, a little disoriented about where he was and how he got there.

The next day, miles away at the Ohio District Court of Appeals, Attorney John Merit prepared to argue on behalf of his client, Jon Bowman, for a writ of habeas corpus, surprised by the speed at which the court took action on his filing. The judge's interruption during opening arguments brought him a sense of calm amidst the tension, signaling a favorable decision through one question to him. A barrage of angry questions directed at the state attorneys filled the room, the air thick with tension, each sharp word a jab, leaving a bitter taste and scrutinizing the potential bias present during the trial proceedings.

Judge Franklin was one of the most respected jurists serving. After the beleaguered state attorney asked and answered all his questions, the judge patiently leaned back in his worn leather chair, the smooth leather a welcome contrast to his tense muscles, and reflected on what he had heard. "Gentleman, we seem to have a poisoned fruit problem." Then, sitting up in his chair, he said, "I'm ready to rule on this case now. However, I'm inclined to wait to allow counsel for the state the time they need to prepare special paperwork."

Looking very confused, the state prosecutor responded, "Your Honor, what special paperwork?"

A huge grin stretched across Judge Franklin's face as he forcefully announced their loss, the sound echoing in the silent courtroom. His precise legal thinking provided a solution that salvaged their reputations, his words carefully chosen to deflect blame. He implemented a multifaceted strategy combining preservation and confidence-building measures to uphold Ohioans' trust in their justice system.

"Oh, the paperwork you file with the state legislators to release funds for compensating the wrongly convicted."

"Your Honor, that paperwork is of utmost importance. Under the statute, according to the law, to receive compensation, an unjustly incarcerated inmate must have endured a minimum of two years of wrongful imprisonment."

"If I rule on this case now, Mister Merit, your client would not be eligible for unjust incarceration compensation since it's been exactly two years. No one wants this young man behind bars longer than he should be. However, considering allegations of bias involving my fellow jurist and a member of law enforcement, causing many of them to take early retirement to avoid criminal action against them, I believe bias negatively impacted the trial. It's in the interest of this court to see that justice is served. The public must have faith in our system of justice.

"Mister Merit, we need to see the video of the officer planting evidence. If you produce that, it eliminates the need for a new trial and exonerates your client. Come back in six months, and I'll sign this writ. However, with an overwhelming number of judicial vacancies, it may be another year before my caseload is manageable. Hang in there; seeing this man walk out of prison a free man on TV is essential for everyone to witness."

"We'll make a note of any objections."

"You wouldn't be doing your job, Mister Merit," he said, his voice sharp, "if you didn't object, but that's my ruling. We're adjourned." And with the bang of his gavel, that was it.

Merit exited the building, disoriented, but the smell of fresh coffee from a nearby shop lifted his spirits. Mister Jackson's strained and urgent voice conveyed the event's gravity as he relayed the details and emphasized the critical need for the video. Knowing Jon would be safe in Redmond eased his mind. Despite the technical loss, he saw it as a win. He went home to get some needed rest, knowing he would have to go to Redmond to brief his client.

Meanwhile, at the capitol, Darnell informed his boss of everything discussed with Mister Merit. "Sir, it's only a matter of time before Jon's release. How are you going to tell him he's a dad?"

Leaning back in his chair in deep thought, Kimbell said, "That, my friend, is an interesting question. Perhaps we'll have to get a friend of his involved. We're better off dealing with this through his lawyer. Darnell, since you've talked to him, this is something I'm going to be leaning on you to help me with."

"I understand, sir. I'll stay on it."

Hours later, as the sun set on Redmond, the inmates prepared to end their day. Then a series of odd events was set into motion, culminating in hallucinations that shocked inmates and guards alike. It started when a Native American appeared in D-block, walking around as though he was outside, aiming his bow and arrow on the hunt, searching for the nearest buffalo straying too far from the herd. To the stunned inmates, the vision was as sharp and distinct as the face of the inmate in the opposite cell, every detail crystal clear. He was wearing traditional garb with jet-black hair and a single feather sticking out of it. Though among the dead for decades, he walked around like a man frozen in time. Despite being a spirit that only a few inmates could see, a wave of icy terror washed over those who could, their screams and desperate scrabbling at their cell doors plunging the entire block into pandemonium.

The reaction was different after walking through many walls to reach the C-block. The lockdown limited inmate involvement. Making matters worse was the fact that the guards were understaffed. Shouts and crashes from a D-block riot had forced the senior officer to reassign guards from C-block. What happened next astonished inmates and guards who helplessly watched. A small group of inmates out of their cells, mostly sweeping and mopping the floor, spotted the Native American. Upon seeing this spirit, the inmates reacted like lunatics, swinging wildly at him. After he appeared to lie on the ground dying, they started punching the ground, screaming. They punched until reaching near exhaustion. The entire scene made no sense and a puddle of red covered the floor.

The spirit had disappeared. What they were striking was a hallucination or a phenomenon defying human understanding. The other inmates watched as the men repeatedly slammed their fists into the concrete, punctuated by sickening thuds until their hands were raw and bleeding. When their heart rates slowed to normal and the adrenaline faded, the pain overwhelmed their nerves, almost paralyzing them. That's when the degree of their insanity hit them. The other inmates looked on, stunned.

The guards took their time to escort the inmates to the infirmary. Once there, they explained what had happened. The doctors' jaws nearly fell to the floor until their training kicked in, making them put their feelings aside to help patients.

As the spiritual battles raged on with Jon and his friends, they never understood whether they were winning or losing. They just tried to take things one day at a time. It was the same attitude they had to serve their prison sentences. For them, it was the only way to stay sane in an insane place.

Chapter 17. Heaven or Hell

Jon sat at the rectangular table in the chow hall, listening to the murmur of conversations washing over him like a distant wave, but he remained in a daze. He was physically in the room but mentally absent, lost in a world of his own making. Lost in the details he'd uncovered about Christopher in the prison library.

Something the angel said stuck with him, and he couldn't shake it. Two liars framed him, sending him to the gallows for a crime he didn't commit. It was a cruel injustice. Another statement stayed with him. "You will know when the time is right." The question of Christopher's connection to Redmond hung heavy in the air, hinting at a complex and possibly hidden past. According to some old, yellowed newspaper clippings, a lynch mob had assembled and killed him in Athens County, Ohio, on November 21, 1881. *What if there was no direct connection, only an indirect one?*

What if Redmond, with its shadowy alleys and whispering winds, was a supernatural beacon for restless ghosts and mischievous spirits? A sort of central station for ghosts, a place where the air crackled with unseen energy and the whispers of the departed echoed in the silence. What if Christopher was drawing strength from the trapped spirits, their tormented energy a tangible force he could feel coursing through him? He channeled their strength to serve his boss with unwavering loyalty while simultaneously sustaining his life, defying the natural order that should have claimed him. A huge smile crossed Jon's face as a sudden realization dawned on him. What if he was no longer in Redmond, unable to access the potent spiritual energy trapped within the ancient stones? With each passing moment, his power should diminish, rendering him a less formidable opponent.

He couldn't resist the pull of the mystery, and despite the grim atmosphere, Jon found himself back in the prison library, its silence broken only by the rustle of pages. A strange, unsettling feeling washed over him—the sensation of a missing puzzle piece, a crucial detail somehow lost. What sparked the inferno of rage that blazed within Christopher, leaving him trembling with fury? Why did he primarily choose to target white inmates? After frantically searching through news clippings, his fingers tracing headlines, desperate for a clue, the answers he sought appeared before him, a minor victory in his quest. Tragically, Christopher was among thirty black men lynched in Ohio during that period. As he read on, the story unfolded like a vivid movie in his mind. He became so engrossed in his work that his eyelids grew heavy, and he fought to keep them open.

Sleep-deprived for days on end hunting, Christopher seemed to have caught up with him. Struggling to stay awake, he eventually succumbed to his body's need to rest. He simply could no longer stop his eyes from closing. He soon discovered he would learn more from visions in his dreams than from reading a book. Falling ever deeper asleep, he entered a world he no longer recognized. He found himself back in 1881 Ohio, the sounds of horse-drawn carriages and distant church bells filling his ears. He'd become Christopher Davis in the days leading up to his arrest. As Christopher, he noticed a subtle shift, a change in the rhythm of his life, like the hum before a storm he couldn't change.

It was cold, but not snowing hard. The air hung heavy with a damp chill, carrying the scent of pine and wet earth. A slight chilly breeze blew through him, causing his teeth to chatter and sending shivers down his bones as scattered snowflakes fluttered in the air toward the ground. He was the shadowy figure near a tree, looking at the window outside the Georgian-style house, standing there with his axe in his hand. He took a moment to look at a reflection of himself in a barrel of water. It wasn't his face that he was seeing, it was the face of Christopher Davis. He knew this from the picture in a newspaper clipping.

Shaking off the odd feeling it brought out in him, he realized it was a dream, albeit a very realistic one. He was only an observer in Christopher's body, seeing his life unfold through his eyes. He continued looking up into the window, seeming to have an unshakable focus on it. Waiting on something, or more importantly, someone. A woman appeared wearing an almost see-through Victorian laced nightgown. She stood there a few feet away from the window. Close enough to be seen, but not close enough to see out of it. She seemed to know he was there, or she at least sensed it. She wanted him to see her, and she especially wanted him to lust after her.

She had intentionally left the door cracked open, an ever-so-subtle invitation for someone or something to come in, tempting him. Putting his axe down, the dull thud echoed as it leaned against the weathered frame of the back door. After admiring the breathtaking panoramic view, he felt a sense of peace. Though his instincts screamed at him to turn back, he pushed open the heavy door and stepped inside, the silence unnerving. This game of seduction had been going on for months now. After she hired him as her farmhand and handyman, he proved himself handy in more ways than one. Then one day, hidden amongst the trees, unseen eyes watched their every move. Two men, their faces reddening with rage, watched the unfolding scene. Hiding in the bushes, being careful to avoid being seen, they lay in wait until the coast was clear and the couple was inside the house, completely distracted.

Then they made a beeline to the back door. They quietly opened it and went in. The last man in grabbed the axe leaning against the door frame. The mood was ominous as they walked around the house's first floor. It was so eerily quiet outside that all of the birds flew away, seeming to sense that something troubling and tragic was about to occur. Inside, the two men quietly went upstairs to the master bedroom, where groans of pleasure could be heard throughout the hallway.

The men burst into the room, catching the couple by surprise in a very compromising position. The air was thick with the scent of flowers from a nearby pot. The first man in the room grabbed the woman from her partner's embrace as he struggled mightily to hold her. The second man in was calm and collected, smiling ghoulishly, holding Christopher's axe. He could tell it was his from the initials on its wooden handle. Jon felt like a puppet experiencing Christopher's perspective, the events unfolding in slow motion; a detached spectator, he could almost hear the muted soundtrack of Christopher's inner world. He was entirely at the mercy of the puppet master, unable to resist their pull.

His body jerked and spasmed, his limbs flailing in an unnatural dance. The sensation was unnerving—a complete absence of self-determination. The man stood there, radiating an aura of cold calculation; his icy gaze, like chips of glacial ice, pierced through the room. He traced the initials he'd carved there years ago while staring at his axe, its worn handle smooth beneath someone else's calloused fingers. The glint of steel in the assassin's hands, icy and unforgiving, reflected the growing dread in his heart; the air itself crackled with the anticipation of violence. He knew this was a fight for survival—a kill-or-be-killed moment, his heart pounding a frantic rhythm against his ribs, each breath ragged and shallow.

Using the distraction caused by his lover's struggle against her captor's grasp, a brief window of opportunity presented itself, her desperate pleas adding to the confusion. He saw his chance and seized it. With a deep breath, he moved the weight of the potential consequences heavy on his shoulders. Desperate, he tried to grab the ax to save himself when the unthinkable happened: a loud crash followed by an unnerving silence. His move had caused the man to swing the axe just as his accomplice lost control of the woman he restrained. The razor-sharp edge of the axe cut deep, somehow seeming to merge with his lover's stomach.

He watched, horrified, as the life slowly drained from her body as she lay on the bed, dying. Blood splatters covered them all as she bled out within minutes, held there by the man with the axe for what seemed like an eternity, until his partner returned with the sheriff and two deputies. Christopher was forced to wait in the custody of the two deputies while the two men talked to the sheriff. The longer they spoke, the angrier the sheriff got. When he finally walked over, the conversation was one-sided, more yelling than talking. "Boy, what in the hell were you thinking? Raping a white woman in my city, then making matters worse by killing her? You'll hang for this, I guarantee it. Oh yeah, you're going to hang."

Refusing to plead for his life out of stubbornness while trying to tell the sheriff the two men lied to him, his voice trembled, trying to contain his rage. A sense of futility washed over him; deep down, he knew it was a pointless endeavor. He was a black man in a place and time where justice didn't exist for black men. Especially for one accused of having relations with a white woman. Who would the sheriff believe, him or the two white men? There was no contest. He meticulously observed how the events unfolded, taking in every detail—the whispered conversations, the nervous glances, the subtle body language. The fabricated evidence against him sent a shiver of cold fury down Christopher's spine. This gave him the insight he needed to understand where the rage was coming from.

If getting arrested and taken into custody wasn't painful enough for Christopher, the ride by horse-drawn carriage to the jail was excruciating. He sat in a cramped jail cell, the air thick with the smell of mildew and despair, waiting for the circuit judge. The sheriff knew he wouldn't last long. The news of his accusations spread like wildfire, causing a palpable tension to settle over the community. A lynch mob formed swiftly, and the sheriff knew he didn't have enough deputies to hold them at bay.

Oozing cowardice and a complete dereliction of his oath to uphold the law, he left the station. He walked hastily away, his two deputies following close behind. He conveniently left the jail unlocked and unattended. The keys to Christopher's cell were carelessly strewn on his desk where the mob could easily find them.

Sitting in the Allen County jail was a terrifying experience, especially for a father of two who had never been in trouble in his life. He sat alone in the small cell, the rough stone walls closing in on him. He was in a very lonely place, but the lynch mob made sure he wasn't lonely for long. They showed up, gathered in a crowd, squeezing into that tiny room, yelling profanities at him. He had a feeling of sheer terror as one man grabbed the keys off the sheriff's desk to unlock his cell. Sweat rolled down his face like a waterfall. The heat from the stove in the room's corner warmed the room too much. This was made worse when all the people crammed inside.

Jon was experiencing fear through Christopher's eyes as the mob dragged him out of his cell and beat him to within an inch of his life. They stopped just short of killing him to ensure he lived long enough to be hanged. It occurred to him then just how much of his lover's blood he had on his shirt and overalls, an insignificant detail that seemed unimportant at the time. Later, it would become a constant source of rage and a reminder of the unfairness of his fate, serving as an additional source of his rage. Rage that would burn like a fire, starting as tiny smoldering embers, only to grow over time to engulf his soul.

Riding past the scattered houses with the mix of trees along the way, he watched the colors of the leaves and the various shades of orange and yellow as the sun set on the horizon. When they finally arrived at the spot where Christopher would spend his last moments alive, his thoughts turned to his children. His sons, alone and vulnerable, would have to fend for themselves as orphans, facing an uncertain future.

A crowd had already gathered in anticipation of what was about to occur. The mood of the crowd was the opposite of what it should have been, considering a man was about to lose his life. They were jubilant and festive. The tree they stood before seemed to be a hundred years old; it somehow stood apart from the other trees surrounding it. The gruesome and deformed appearance was likely due to the innocent men who lost their lives on its branches. The base was black from the dried blood of too many men who watered its roots with their blood. The ancient oak, its bark deeply furrowed and textured, held a thick, worn rope tied to one of its lowest, sturdier branches. The noose at the other end swung back and forth in the wind. Just seeing it initially caused his heart to skip a beat. Then, it gradually beat harder and faster, and he feared it would burst out of his chest.

Then the realization set in of just how short on time he had to live. Gathering his last ounce of courage and strength, he didn't pray to God to deliver him from his fate. No, Christopher did the opposite. He cursed God for depriving his children of their father. He cursed the gathered crowd, which was only there to gain enjoyment from his suffering. On that chilly night in November, he vowed to torment forever all those who lived there. He made a blood vow to torment all those who had a hand in his death and their descendants. The sins of the fathers, like a lingering shadow, he was determined to visit upon their children.

The inexplicable deaths began after Christopher died, each one more horrifying than the last, marked by gruesome scenes that sent shivers down everyone's spines. The whispers began almost immediately, all pointing to the same person, but that's a story for another time. That's how the legend of the Axeman, Christopher Davis, was born. There's a saying in the Bible that God knows and sees all; through his insidious minions, the Devil worked in much the same way. With his keen eyes and perceptive nature, the Devil knows and sees a lot too. The sharp sting of certain words echo long after they're spoken, making silence a far wiser choice. Christopher's dying vow, a desperate, guttural scream, reached the ears of the Devil's minions, causing them to stir in the shadowy depths. The instant it happened, an icy dread washed over him, sealing his fate.

The crowd's murmur died as he stood, their eyes like magnets drawn to his, the silence thick with unspoken tension. The rough hemp of the noose scraped against his skin while placed around his neck. Then calloused hands worked to tighten the knot until it was firm and secure around his neck, the air growing tight in his chest. When the shrill whistle pierced the air, signaling the start, the wagon lurched violently, throwing the man off balance. He sat heavily, one arm raised, his wrist aching and turning as he tried to relieve the stiffness. Holding the worn leather horsewhip, its braided texture rough against the driver's fingers. A sharp swat on the horse's rear sent it forward, its tail swishing. The sudden gust of wind caused Christopher to lose his footing, sending him dangling wildly over the edge, the ground a dizzying distance below. Choking on his saliva, his body convulsed, a desperate fight for air as his airway narrowed. His body shook as he gradually lost the will to continue fighting. Soon afterward, the noose broke his neck.

Christopher's death would only be the beginning of a new dark journey after his spirit left his physical body. Dragged before the judgment seat, in the blurry, in-between realm, the shimmering pearly gates of Heaven mocked him from just beyond his reach; he could almost feel the cool, ethereal air on his face. Devilish minions opened a fiery doorway to Hell, daring him to traverse Hell, to have a conversation with a snake. Beyond the doors that appeared on fire but never

seemed to burn up, the path led to a prison sitting on an island surrounded by lava in the crater of an active volcano.

After walking for an eternity, they finally came to a massive door,
which automatically opened as they got closer. Passing through the
courtyard to enter a smaller door, they eventually reached a room
with a giant door and a huge lock. The door handles appeared to
be intertwined snakes that were on fire but didn't seem to burn up.
There were also three symbols on the door that looked like gold and
seemed to represent elements of the Bible. The first represented God
the Father. The second represented God the Son. The third represented God the Holy Spirit. Near these was an inscription: *king of the
snakes, lord of the fallen, 666.* After a cursory glance around the room,
two of the Devil's minions then took him to a smaller room to the left,
the air thick with the smell of sulfur and fear. A giant snake lay on the
floor, curled in a ball on a plush layer of blue and red pillows.

It would be the oddest conversation he would ever observe. Jon,
still seeing visions unfold through Christopher's eyes, watched as the
giant snake made Christopher an offer he couldn't refuse. The snake
crawled, raised its head, and then slowly opened his eyes. It took him
a few moments to look at his guest, leaving Christopher with the impression that he was trying to decide whether to talk to him or eat
him. Then it spoke: Hate, rage, and revenge are the feelings I sense in
you. These feelings flow through you. If you serve me, I will help you
get the revenge you seek. The body you see before you, this shifting,
fluid form, is one of countless I can assume.

"The spirit who stands in my presence seeking revenge. Should
you accept this role, your service as my emissary will continue until
the end of existence, a solemn and unending commitment. When elements of the Book of Revelation come, trumpets will blare, and the
sky will blaze with celestial fire. A time when man no longer walks
God's creation with dominion. In this lonely time, the fallen will rule
over the living, and my offspring will hold sway, their presence a
chilling reminder of the devastation. To be of the dead and remain

among the living, you must spill the blood of the living. Stealing their souls to become part of them."

An icy chill ran down his spine.

"Gaining strength also means gaining power, a force that resonates within both of us. Your soul is mine, and every soul you claim also becomes mine. This deal binds your very essence, a chilling pact sealed by your consent." The air growing heavy with the scent of brimstone and fear. "Is this deal clear to you?"

Making an ever so slight nod of his head, Christopher said, "I agree with this deal. I agree to serve you. So long as my revenge comes swiftly, and those who murdered me die slowly, consumed by pain."

Following this bargain with the Devil, a palpable sense of unease settled over the room, thick like a suffocating blanket. A nervous flutter filled his chest as he wondered, curious, what might happen next.

"Since you're already among the silent, motionless dead, and your own body is now dust and bone, a piece of your soul, a shard of your very being, will be required in exchange for mine." A brilliant golden glow enveloped him within seconds, lifting him five feet to eye-level of the giant snake, its scales shimmering like polished emeralds in the dappled sunlight. Then, a piece of his essence, a shimmering ball of brilliant light, separated from him, and the snake absorbed it, lying in front of him.

Suddenly lowered to the ground again, the snake moved over ever so gently, enough to reveal a pulsating, living ball of little snakes. One of them slithered in his direction, moving away from the rest. Moving with the speed of lightning, the snake, a coiled spring of muscle and scales, shot out, slamming into his stomach, and his new body partially absorbed it, the remaining half thrashing and writhing until it vanished. As the process finished, their minds fused, a powerful wave of shared understanding surging through them, a rush of sensations like an electric current. This link was a horrifying connection; his boss, the Devil, could see everything, hear everything, and know everything—a chilling intrusion into his thoughts and perceptions.

Suddenly, an angel appeared, and with the snap of his fingers, it all faded. Jon was awakened from the most vivid dream he had ever experienced by a prison guard who stood over him, shaking him.

"Hey, man, you were sleeping so hard, I felt sorry for having to wake you. I would've let you sleep a little longer if it were up to me. But it's time to go."

"What time is it now?"

"It's seven o'clock, almost time to eat."

Jon scrambled to his feet, knocking over a nearby chair to return the books he was reading. He couldn't wait to tell the guys—his chest ached with the excitement of sharing what he'd learned.

After gathering in the chow hall, he answered detailed questions from all the guys around the table. All the men listened intently, then grew silent.

Craig spoke up, raising an important question. "How weak is Christopher now?"

"That's what we don't know, and absolutely need to find out."

Craig told them how he once overheard a guard talking to another guard about an odd video he watched from a part of the prison that was considered a blind spot. The guard described how he was sitting in the Emerald City control room. He had said he was watching the monitors and saw an inmate lifted off the ground, his body suspended nearly five feet in the air. Then he was thrown across the room like a rag doll, only to be impaled by a mop handle nearby.

"Do you guys realize how much power it must have taken to do something like that? I've been stuck in here for a long time and have seen many things. The old-timers told me those stories were common years ago. They were even pretty frequent months ago, but suddenly they stopped. I haven't heard much lately. Which makes me wonder, what changed? Better yet, what did we change? So, gentlemen, I ask again, how weak is Christopher now? We need to know, and hopefully, we can find out tonight."

So Jon, after going back to C-block and waiting for lights out, lay in his bed looking up at the ceiling in his cell, as he did so many nights before, when an odd feeling came over him.

After falling asleep, an angel appeared with the job of helping him leave his body, staying by his side to observe him and the others as they went about their mission. Sitting up as a transparent specter of himself, he emerged from his body with an odd feeling that this time was different. A strange feeling came over him: he was going to lose someone. They had been careful and lucky up to this point. However, he feared their luck from their past skirmishes might eventually run out.

\#

Taking up their positions in their assigned spots in a carefully conceived strategy to soften the Axeman until he was weak enough to defeat, they watched and waited until Christopher appeared in the oddest place: a water pipe concealed by a wall weakened by below-zero temperatures during the polar vortex. This caused this pipe to leak gradually until it eventually burst. Water flowed everywhere, creating a mini lake in the hallway intersecting with the C- and D-blocks.

The Axeman eerily emerged from the water, like walking from a lake to shore, dripping wet and on the hunt for new lives to take and souls to consume. Craig and his spirit soldiers stood ready at the midpoint in the narrow hallway from the C-block. Holding their position at the intersection connecting all other wings. The moment Christopher appeared, a hail of bullets only a ghost could see ripped through the air, narrowly missing him. A fierce battle raged for nearly half an hour, the clash echoing through the hallway.

The Axeman, hemorrhaging spirits at a rapid pace, attempted to tap into the power of the spirits trapped in Redmond, only to find that he no longer could. Reaching out his hand, he attempted to compel one of the spirit soldiers to come to him. It only partially worked, resulting in the spirit soldier being temporarily paralyzed, then released.

Finally, he attempted to disappear and then reappear in another location. He could, but it was more difficult than usual. Fading in and out, blinking like a light bulb about to go out, the Axeman knew something wasn't right. He realized he was like a battery losing its charge, and he felt a sudden, sharp depletion of energy, his muscles trembling. Screaming out, a raw, guttural sound filled the air, fueled by frustration and rage. It was like a ripple in the stillness, a tremor only the departed could sense, a faint echo from beyond the veil.

One of the Devil's minions heard his desperate cry for help echo through the air. Unlike the angels, who were bound by rules to observe, intervening only to hear those seeking grace, the Devil's minions were bound by no such laws. Sacrificing its own existence, this spirit transformed into some form of dark energy and merged with the Axeman, recharging him just enough. Then, a chillingly clear yet somehow distant voice gave him an unrefusable order, a command he couldn't ignore. It came sharp and gravelly, leaving no room for argument. "Vanish from this fight, becoming unseen, then reappear in C-block." He did as he was told, melting away only to reappear before Craig's cell.

His boss talked to him again with a raspy voice, but this time as though he was standing right next to him. He ordered him to enter Craig's cell and take possession of his cellmate's body and sit by Craig's breathing but motionless body. Then, with all his strength, he ordered him to smother Craig with a pillow to silence any potential screams, like an anaconda chokes its prey without reservations or remorse.

Chapter 18. Mercy or Death

Standing in that narrow hallway with his contingent of spirit soldiers by his side, Craig had a mind-boggling sense of unease. He suddenly experienced an overwhelming struggle to breathe. Confused, he thought, *No way I'm short of breath, my spirit's out of my body!* He knew something wasn't right.

That's when the angel standing near him as an observer spoke up. "Craig, your spirit doesn't need to breathe, but your body does."

After the angel pointed this out, they both disappeared, then reappeared in front of his cell. Inmates in the cells next to him and across from him were still asleep. Peering into his own cell, it was dark, but the light from the hallway illuminated the room enough to see, and what he saw terrified him. He was looking at his cellmate sitting next to him as he slept, his hands pressed down hard on a pillow covering his face, suffocating him.

The angel realized Craig was going to die a horrible death he was powerless to stop. He knew he had to do something, but what? With Craig on the brink of death, the angel watched him gradually being pulled back to his body. Craig's cellmate hastily stopped, sensing something. As the angel looked directly at him, he initially only saw Craig's cellmate with a ghoulish smile. However, once he looked closer, he saw the face of the Axeman possessing his cellmate's body. Realizing he had little time, he tried to help Craig in the only way he knew he could, telling him, "Seek, and you shall find; ask, and God shall grant you grace. Those who believe and seek divine grace will find their faith rewarded with God's boundless mercy."

So, mustering every ounce of strength he had, Craig was narrowly able to utter the words the angel needed to hear. "My faith in God may be weak, but I know his mercy and grace is everlasting. I beg for his forgiveness for all my sins." With this plea, his heart pounding in his chest, he felt a sense of anticipation wash over him as he hoped God would hear his prayers, allowing him to enter Heaven, where his soul would have peace. Not long after uttering those words, a jolt shot through him, yanking him back to his physical body.

He gasped, regaining consciousness, only to find himself in a terrifying, desperate struggle for survival. Each moment was a chilling reminder of his mortality, his heart pounding in his chest. He tried in vain to loosen the grip on him. It would be nice to say he survived, that he put up a valiant effort to save his life and won. However, that would be a lie. He did put up a valiant effort, but his cellmate overpowered him. He flailing for ten minutes until he had no more fight left in him. His cellmate's enormous arms were too strong for him to move, no matter how hard he tried.

Craig became just another victim on a long list to die at the Axeman's hands. He was the first and only member of their entourage to die in the prison war. He fought with all his might, but life ebbed away, leaving him still and lifeless. His spirit left his physical body for the last time, this time with no help from the angel, who was still there as a guide. Even though he lost his battle to stay alive in a noble cause, he knew their war wasn't over yet. So he stayed around, determined to see Christopher, the Axeman of Redmond, defeated, and ensure he burned in Hell.

Meanwhile, in another part of the prison, they continued to follow their nightly routine of hunting the Axeman. As the first light of dawn touched the horizon, they returned to their bodies, trying in vain to get enough sleep to function the next day. They were careful to act natural, avoiding any suspicious behavior that might reveal their secret. They woke up to the morning count separately, not realizing one of their own was gone. Each man felt a little groggy from the night before.

Each inmate stepped outside of their cell, waiting for the senior guard to walk by and observe the line. Once their inmate number was called, the usual routine was to repeat their number, confirming that they were present and accounted for. On this day, two inmates were missing from the line, which was an enormous problem and out of the norm.

When Craig's inmate number was called, there was no answer. Everything ceased. The guards focused on that spot where an inmate was supposed to be standing as the guys looked over nervously. They hoped and quietly prayed that their friend was alright, that he was still in his cell because he was sick or still asleep. After a brief time, a guard screamed, "You're holding up the show, and that comes with consequences. I'm warning you, come out here now, or I'm coming in to give you a hard thump on the head. You're messing up my schedule, and I'm not happy."

Everyone knew something was seriously wrong when there still wasn't a sound. It was so quiet you could hear roaches scurrying around on the floor. The guard looked at his list and realized the next man on it was also missing. Craig's cellmate was also not standing there. Walking hastily to the cell in question, the guard found one of the missing inmates sitting on his bed clutching a blood-stained pillow.

Craig's cellmate was sitting there, rocking back and forth, repeating, "I didn't mean to do it. The Axeman made me do it. I didn't mean to do it. The Axeman made me do it," while staring at the bed across from him. The guard took a quick look around the room, making a brief assessment, then bent over to check the pulse of the inmate on the bed. He knew within moments that the man was gone.

Observing the cell, he reasoned that Craig had only been dead for a few hours based on the fact that rigor mortis had set in a little. That was something he learned from his older brother, who was a forensic pathologist. Craig's body was cool to the touch, the stiffening of his muscles was clear. He had no pulse, meaning no blood flow. Alarmed, he immediately ordered guards over, his voice sharp and urgent. One secured Craig's cellmate, holding him in place. Another corrections officer got a camera to take pictures of the cell and the inmate in question. Outside the cell, the senior guard, his expression a mask of weary cynicism, remained vigilant, eyes never leaving the prisoners, a palpable stillness in the air.

He began methodically going through a checklist of procedures—his heart pounding, his mind racing to address the unfolding situation. He first ordered C-block temporarily placed on lockdown, well aware that the inmates, their stomachs rumbling with anticipation, were eager to get breakfast. A heavy sigh escaped his lips, the weight of his fate pressing down on him. As Craig's cellmate stood in the cold, echoing hallway, the fluorescent lights humming overhead, the senior guard noticed something. Visible bruises on the arms of Craig's cellmate that would seal his fate.

"Hey, how did you get those bruises on your arms?"

"I don't know."

The wounds were deep scratch marks, still red as though they only recently stopped bleeding. The question hung in the air, heavy with the weight of its obvious answer—one he already knew. When the investigators arrived, he instructed them to focus on one key detail. He insisted they meticulously examine the victim's fingernails, looking for trace evidence—perhaps a skin cell, fiber, or dirt—that might link them to Craig's cellmate.

As guards led the inmate to the interrogation room, the heavy metal door clanged shut behind him, echoing through the sterile hall-

way. The other inmates watched intently from behind the bars of
their cells, trying to figure out what happened. When Jon and Gary
saw the Ohio Highway Patrol officers show up, they instantly looked
at each other, thinking as one. A silent communication flowed between them as if their minds had melded. A shared understanding,
heavy with unspoken dread, settled over them. With bowed heads
and sorrowful expressions, they both made the sign of the cross. The
sight of Craig's body, stiff and pale, removed from his cell confirmed
the inevitable. His once vibrant face was now marred with a stillness
that chilled them to the bone. Their friend was gone, but now free
from Redmond...or so they thought.

Watching now as a free spirit, Craig observed the events unfolding
in confusion. The angel, who had never left his side, offered guidance
and an explanation. "I couldn't stop the Axeman from taking your life.
I could only prevent him from taking your soul. That's why your spirit
is still here for the time being. In the silent, lonely space between
Heaven and Hell, a place of chilling winds and unseen presences, you
await the judgment of your life. Here, a divine council will convene,
weighing your deeds and actions, deciding whether you can enter the
pearly gates of Heaven or are condemned to burn for eternity in Hell,
a horrifying fate of unimaginable pain and suffering. What you do
here matters and will determine your fate."

As the investigation ended, relief swept through the inmates as
they headed for a breakfast of surprisingly decent scrambled eggs. The
official announcement of their friend's death silenced the gathered inmates, and each man felt the weight of the loss. While trying to figure
out how he died, a million questions raced through their minds. The
day seemed to fly by, as did the sunset. The chow hall was hushed for
dinner as the empty chair weighed on everyone. Each man had the
same feeling of profound loss. They all remembered the times they
had with their fallen comrade while also thinking that they could all
be next, and the chilling possibility settled heavily on their shoulders.

As day turned into night, the mood seemed ominous. Many in the entourage thought this night might be their last. When the lights suddenly went out in a brief coordinated succession, their eyes slowly closed, and they fell asleep, preparing their minds and toughening their spines for the fight ahead. Their spirits and the ghosts of their spirit army assembled in the Redmond reception area.

Jon learned that massive water pipes lay beneath the fountain in front of the prison, supplying it and the prison itself with water. He thought this was the best strategic position to launch an attack. He deduced that the Axeman's approach might be from the direction of the old, moss-covered fountain because of the lack of attacks there and knowing he usually arrived from the water. Angels provided key information that their efforts had paid off up to this point: they had successfully weakened the Axeman to the point of sending him to Hell.

Every word was a carefully selected jewel, precisely conveying the most crucial details focused on his imminent defeat, and specifying his probable location and reasons for showing up at that location was essential. "The Axeman will come to you. Stay vigilant, and above all, stay ready. Because once he knows he's on the verge of defeat, he will aggressively run toward an attack instead of away from one."

Facing the water fountain, which amounted to a mini pool of water at the prison's main entrance, they were taking their positions when someone caught their attention. The moon reflected off the surface of the water, and Craig's spirit appeared, giving them the last advice he could give. "Don't fear death; be more afraid of the consequences of a life not lived well." He explained to them how he died and confirmed what the angel had already told them. "The Axeman is so weak that a demon had to recharge him after our last fight before he killed me."

After the talking ended, everyone retook their positions, waiting for a sign that signaled the Axeman's arrival. Then, one minute before midnight, a shadowy figure emerged from the fountain as though he was climbing an underwater staircase, dripping wet with his axe in hand. It was dark, but not pitch-black; the moon reigned high, illuminating the night sky and making their target clear. The burden to lead weighed on Jon as the five contingents of spirit soldiers steadied their aim. A heavy silence descended upon the crowd, punctuated only by the occasional nervous cough as they waited for the order. Jon suddenly screamed one word: "Fire!"

Volley after volley of almost invisible musket balls tore through the air, the metallic shriek of lead whistling a deadly song. While many hit their target with speed and accuracy, a few rounds strayed, flying off into the distance. The battle raged for nearly two hours in an almost circular firing squad, almost totally preventing the Axeman from getting close enough to land a blow. Spirits tugged on him, struggling to leave his body, fighting to gain their freedom. A magnificent glow illuminated the darkness emanating from him toward the sky, causing the clouds to part and the spirits to be pulled upward in a circular whirlwind. Then, an explosion of light occurred. There was no fire, and it left behind an unsettling peace instead of the typical devastation—no heat, smoke, or ashes. The explosion faded, and there he stood—not the Axeman, but Christopher Davis, looking exactly as he had on the day he died, his youthful face a stark contrast to the disfigured and deformed terror of Redmond Prison. To his shock and everyone's surprise, he appeared as the man he used to be.

There was a ceasefire after the explosion to see how events would play out. Three of the Devil's minions suddenly appeared to transport Christopher back to the one place he feared ever having to see again: that old disfigured tree where his life ended so many years ago. He didn't want to be there. Jon, Gary, Craig, and the others joined Christopher, who was waiting for them, accompanied by the angels who watched over them.

Seeing Christopher standing there with his axe in hand, the angels spotted three black and deformed-looking branches on the ground nearby. They told Jon and his friends to pick them up and pointed out their sharpened edges. The angels said they should use the branches to stab him. The men stood there looking confused, and Gary raised the question. "What in the hell are we supposed to do with these? How are we supposed to take him out with these funny-looking sticks? He's got an axe, and he's enormous—that's a problem."

One of the angels responded with a smile as bright as the sun. "If you've read the Bible, you know Goliath was a giant compared to David. But David somehow defeated Goliath with God's help. Just a slingshot and some rocks. The branches you've got there. It may seem like Christopher has an unfair advantage, but you're mistaken. Those branches, gnarled like ancient claws, are from the same misshapen tree you're standing beneath. The same gnarled oak tree, its bark scarred and weathered, where they hanged Christopher so many years ago. Stabbing him with those branches will drain him of his remaining power, weakening him enough to be sent back to the fiery depths of Hell. He'll be stuck there for a while."

Forming what amounted to a triangle, Jon, Gary, and Craig faced Christopher from three sides. Despite being a giant of a man with a menacing appearance and intimidating demeanor, they were determined to show no fear and stared him down. Gary and Craig stood behind him like cats, ready to pounce.

Swinging his axe wildly, they realized it was big and bulky. They were careful to avoid its sharp and lethal curved blade, and they observed how it made him slow and predictable in a fight. So they attacked him where he couldn't see it coming. Distracting Christopher face-to-face, Craig caught his axe after he swung it. Having nothing to lose since he was already dead, he tightened his grip on it just long enough for Gary to stab him in the side below his ribs.

Spotting his chance, Jon stabbed Christopher right through the heart. Craig, now sensing Christopher's weakness after releasing his hold on his axe, carefully watched him as he eventually dropped it, fatally wounded. He tried to walk, but staggered around like a bird with a broken wing. Craig wanted to look Christopher, the spirit responsible for his death, in the eyes before stabbing him in the neck with the last stick and sending him to Hell.

Gasping, Christopher Davis, the Axeman, let his axe fall with a heavy thud. The impact sent vibrations up his arms as a demon with burning eyes settled onto its handle. The object vanished, only to reappear mysteriously on a wall-mounted display inside the imposing structure of Redmond Prison. A long time in the making, the Axeman's defeat finally arrived. The angels watched in stunned silence, broken only by the air changing once they'd won. The glint of golden chains flashed in the dim light as they swiftly secured them to Christopher's weakened wrists, the rough metal biting into his pale skin. Then a door appeared, hovering a few inches off the ground.

The door blazed, an inferno seemingly defying destruction, leaving Jon, Gary, and Craig speechless. The crackle and pop of flames filled the air. Jon and Gary, with heavy hearts and lumps in their throats, had to say a tearful farewell to Craig, embracing him tightly one last time. It got still and heavy right before he entered that otherworldly place for his judgment. Then, with a jolt, they returned to their physical bodies, the familiar weight of their limbs a welcome shock. It was a silent victory that no one would know they won.

Before receiving a rough shove and suffering the indignity of being frog-marched by the angels into Hell, suffering through the sounds of infernal screams which echoed around him., Christopher received a revelation in a vision that reduced, but couldn't extinguish, the rage and anger in his heart. The two angels, Samuel Davis and Paul Davis, watched over the prison chapel with unwavering dedication. Christopher saw a vision of his sons, who couldn't have been over thirteen years old. Hiding on a nearby hill concealed by bushes, they watched people make their father stand on a rickety old uncovered wagon. They watched in agony as another man put the noose around his neck.

Somehow, sensing his sons nearby further tormented him. His fate was inevitable as he wept uncontrollably. He made only one request of

God. "Lord God almighty, please don't let this be my sons' last memory of me." Unsure if there was a Heaven or Hell, he begged the Lord to grant his request.

Two angels appeared, temporarily blinding and distracting the boys from the event on the ground below. "You two shouldn't be here watching this. Remember what you learned in church. Close your eyes and pray for your dad's soul. Ask God to take away some of his pain and anger." The boys did as asked and then went home to a community that found out what had happened and raised them as if they were their own.

The gathered mob hanged their father. Secretly, his sons would watch them put a noose around his neck, but they never actually saw their father die. The vision also revealed they prayed for God's mercy on his soul, even though he'd cursed him.

That was why Redmond Prison and its immediate vicinity formed a chilling confinement for the Axeman. He was stuck in that creepy prison, always smelling stale air and sensing the despair in inmates. When the vision stopped, they dragged him to Hell. This visit, however, was markedly different. The air hung heavy with the stench of sulfur, the sounds of torment echoing differently than before. Rows of cages surrounded the castle, its dark stones contrasting with the fiery glow of the volcano, the sounds of caged creatures echoing eerily. The countless columns of cages extended as far as the eye could see, their metallic gleam dull in the dim light, a low humming sound vibrating through the air. Periodic bursts of flame shot up from the lava, scorching the unfortunate souls trapped within, and the air filled with the smell of burning flesh and sulfur.

At that moment, God reminded him that terrible decisions paved the road to Hell, each one echoing with regret, and the air filled with the screams of the damned. Led down that narrow path, a chilling premonition settled upon him, the oppressive silence and looming shadows amplifying his fear. The only way to reach the castle on the desolate island was a narrow, treacherous path that wound its way through jagged rocks. Surrounded by rivers of molten lava in the crater of an active volcano, he could feel the earth's heat radiating from the ground and smell the sulfurous fumes. This would be his new home, a fiery, sulfurous Hell he never wanted, not for a moment.

The following day, Jon woke up in his body, feeling extremely happy about what they had accomplished as well as sad for those he lost along the way. For reasons he couldn't explain, he just had an odd feeling that things would get better. Especially when, during breakfast, a guard showed up just as the guys were aggressively stuffing their faces—it was pancake day, one of the few things a man had to look forward to on the inside. Every inmate had to find the little things that made it worthwhile to go on. When the guard walked up, he was very to the point. "Inmate 70664," he read, "Bowman, Jon?"

"Yes, sir," he replied promptly.

"The warden wants to see you."

"Do you know what it's about?"

"I don't know. All I was told was to bring you to the warden's office because you don't belong here."

One hour before the inmates of C-block sat down to eat breakfast, three visitors had arrived to see Warden Hudson. They had been there before, so after making their way to his office, they greeted his secretary and requested an urgent meeting with him. He agreed when he realized who it was: Agent Coleman, State Rep. Townsend, and Attorney John Merit.

"What can I do for all of you this morning?"

"No, it's more about what we can do for you this morning." Agent Coleman took a DVD from a manila folder he was carrying under his arm, placed it in the DVD player, and turned the TV turned on. "Jon Bowman's innocent." As the traffic stop video played, the warden felt a knot of tension tighten in his stomach, his eyes glued to the screen. Meanwhile, Agent Colman provided frame-by-frame commentary. "Warden, keep a sharp eye on Jon's location to the officer and be aware of the surrounding environment. He's by the front tire on the driver's side." With a stern look, the officer reached for the car door handle, about to begin the search.

"The driver didn't know the officer was reaching into his pocket. There were two bottles of pills. He swears he knew nothing about those opioids in his car, and this video proves he was telling the truth. Not to mention, he knew nothing about the drug itself. They never found his prints on the drugs, only the arresting officer's."

Warden Hudson looked at Agent Coleman, then turned his gaze to State Rep. Townsend. "Let me make sure I got this right. From what you're saying, and what I see in the video, tainted evidence is at the heart of this problem?"

"Warden, that's exactly the message we're trying to convey."

The warden sat down in his chair, slumping over his desk and placing both hands on his face in deep sadness. "How do you tell a man he lost nearly four years of his life for no damn reason?"

Rep. Townsend stepped over to him, placing her hand on his shoulder, and said, "First, sit him down and play this video. Then you should be brutally honest with him. Tell him that the justice system failed him. Then tell him about those who serve in it who, once they realize their screw-up, scramble to fix it! They know our justice system isn't perfect. Despite this, these dedicated men and women also know they must fix mistakes once they become known. We can only hope to compensate him for his lost time. Those who work in the system must atone for the error in another way."

"Agent Coleman, can you provide any additional evidence to the judge to support the release of this inmate? What reasons do you have for wanting this guy released early? Let me be clear: I can't release anyone without a judge signing off on it."

"Well, the arresting officer is being charged with planting evidence. Many young men who fit the same profile as this young man should be enough. That's combined with testimony from drug dealers who this officer arrested. Drug dealers who will say he robbed them will also be an enormous help. The individuals arrested by this officer have agreed to testify against him. They will state on the record that he robbed them, along with under-reported cash seized and contraband found, testifying that he falsified police reports."

That's when Mr. Merit interrupted them. "Warden, that should be enough for a new trial at a minimum. Although, my goal is a writ of habeas corpus and a complete exoneration."

Once Jon and the corrections officer cleared all the doors and locks, and the tedious verification checkpoints within the prison, they finally arrived at the warden's office. The warden and some familiar faces were there to greet him.

"Am I in trouble? My lawyer has never met me in the warden's office before."

"No, you're not in trouble. We have a video you need to see."

Jon looked at Agent Coleman. "Do I have to answer more weird questions about this prison?"

"No, we don't have any more questions for you this morning; it's just something to show you."

"Oh, well, you should know there haven't been as many strange deaths of inmates in here. Although, I have some bizarre stories about the history of Christopher Davis, who's connected to all of those strange deaths."

The warden spoke. "When you arrived at this prison, I reviewed your record, and you explained why you were here. I told you that my gut told me you didn't belong here. I said that because your file didn't have a whole hell of a lot in it. Do you remember that conversation?"

"Yes, I do, sir."

"I also told you it was odd for a United States attorney to file a friend of the court brief on your behalf. Well, young man, I need you to watch a video."

Chapter 19. Freedom

As the video began playing, the room grew silent. Only the video's background noise was audible. Everyone in the room waited, a hush over the crowd, punctuated only by the ticking of a grandfather clock and Jon's shallow breaths. He watched the video from start to finish, closely scrutinizing each detail until it ended. Then he revealed what was on his mind. "Well, I'll be damned, I knew it." Looking directly at Agent Coleman, he said, "I think you should take out your notepad for this.

I've replayed that day over and over again in my head, trying to remember everything that happened. It occurred to me that there was a gap in my memory. I remember standing near the front tire of the car. The other officer arrived, and I frantically explained, the words tumbling out, that the drugs weren't mine—someone must have planted them. Months after the stop, I had trouble remembering what happened in between. I was terrified those cops would shoot me. It was all I could do to keep my cool. I was trying not to do anything stupid that would get me killed.

"Look closely at the video—the passenger window's down. I knew one of those officers planted those drugs. I only had two joints on me that I got from a party I attended two days before the traffic stop. I used one the day after the party with the vaporizer found in my car. I heard the siren from the patrol car behind me, and I carefully waited

241

to throw the second joint out during a bend in the road. A wave of relief washed over me as the officer's car disappeared from my rearview mirror, the flashing lights fading into the distance. I doubt the officer ever found the small joint on the side of the road amongst the overgrown weeds and tall grass.

"All he saw was the vaporizer, which had weed residue in it. That's why I got busted—it let the cop search my car. My prints are on the vaporizer, but not the bottles of opioids—I never touched them. I never touched drugs other than Mary Jane, so I knew nothing about opioids. There's no chance that the officer discovered any weed, let alone opioids, in my car. I only had one joint and was smart enough to ditch it. So he never should have found two bottles of opioids."

That's when his attorney spoke up. "I've heard enough, we're getting you out of here." The wheels in his mind had already been turning, racing with the possibilities this new information provided, focusing on the potential legal strategies it afforded his client, given its absence from the original trial. He realized he could file an amendment to the motion already submitted to the Ohio State Court of Appeals for a writ of habeas corpus.

Mr. Merit then handed him a pen and some paper. "Jon, I need you to write about everything you told us. Young man, you're going home based on what I now know. I have a clear picture of what actually happened that day. You won't go home immediately, but you will get out of here soon."

After everyone cleared out of the room, guards returned him to his cell, still shaken by the revelations.

Meanwhile, miles away in a cold courtroom, former officer Anthony Donovan sat at a table with his lawyer, deep in thought about the wreckage of his life. He sat there wishing to return to a younger version of himself. A period when he was fresh out of the police academy in that clean uniform, those spit-polished shoes, and a nice hat. He was ready to take anything criminals could throw at him. He wished he could go back to that specific point in his life so he could punch that naïve young man in the jaw, prevent him from becoming corrupt and jaded. He had no wife or kids, and the job had become his life, and now that was gone, leaving him with nothing.

The longer he sat there, the more people filled the courtroom. Some were reporters, and some were observers curious to see how the justice system worked. He didn't recognize many faces, but in the end, that didn't matter. When the bailiff walked in, saying, "All rise," the room immediately went mute. Judge Mason walked in, an older man with almost entirely gray hair, a sharp legal mind, and a firm but fair temperament.

Getting down to business after shuffling some papers around, he addressed both attorneys. "Gentlemen, I hear you've worked something out on this matter between the two of you."

"Yes, Your Honor. They nodded in agreement.

Looking at the deputy US attorney, the judge said, "Why don't you enlighten the court about this possible plea agreement? I stress the word potential, because I don't need to remind you of my discretion to accept or reject this plea. I just feel it's necessary to ensure justice is served."

"Your Honor, I have carefully reviewed and comprehend every aspect of this agreement's terms. With a heavy heart, former officer Anthony Donovan will plead guilty in court to planting evidence in the case against Jon Bowman. The specifics of his actions, revealed in court, will undoubtedly paint a grim picture. He'll insist the police search turned up nothing illegal on that young man. He alone planted the drugs found, and he filled out the paperwork, each false claim a deliberate act. His supervising officer's unwitting affirmation of the report lent it a false sense of authority. He has agreed to serve four years for each count charged. A sentence he will serve at Redmond Prison that will run concurrently, amounting to only four years due to the fact that he was a law enforcement officer for nearly 25 years. These factors, along with others, produced this sentence. We believe this plea will deliver justice. We offered this plea deal because we also need his cooperation in other matters."

Judge Mason leaned back in his chair, weighing what he just heard. "I'm inclined to sign off on this plea deal, but I need to know something. To what extent is former officer Donovan's misconduct limited to incidents involving traffic stops?"

"Your Honor, the new district attorney is thoroughly reviewing all traffic stops he was involved in, observing any potential civil rights violations or irregularities. Because of his questionable reputation, the more cautious members of the department subtly but effectively blocked his promotion. He could not work on significant cases without supervision."

As time moved on, Jon grew restless, wondering if he would ever get out of Redmond. Two months had passed since that meeting in the warden's office, and still no word. The wait was excruciating. The renewed hope of freedom was a powerful, bright beacon in the darkness of his prison cell, more potent than the cold, hard reality of his confinement. As the days bled into weeks, that initial hope dwindled, replaced by a growing sense of despair, like a wilting flower under a harsh sun. He felt like a man slowly dying from an unknown, unseen virus—lonely, hoping to live, afraid to die, while praying for a cure.

Five guards interrupted their dinner, creating an unsettling silence. The senior guard had a clipboard under his arm, while the others had documents. The senior guard spoke. "Men, we have been watching you for some time. Speaking collectively, I can say that you've all made our jobs easier since you've been here. It's a tough gig, having to be the boss in a place where everyone would rather be somewhere else. So, I'm happy for days like today when I can bring positive news to inmates serving time."

He called off names on his list, along with their inmate numbers. Once he confirmed they were the ones he was looking for, he said the words all inmates wanted to hear: "You're paroled!" He congratulated them, methodically down the list, reading name after name, then paused. Everyone thought he had lost his place. Jon thanked the guys leaving for helping him survive, telling them all how much he would miss them and wishing them well. He wondered how he would survive without them.

That's when the guard reading off the names found his place again. "Who is Jon Bowman, Inmate 70594?"

A hush fell over the table.

"I'm Bowman, sir."

"Inmate Jon Bowman, 70594, you served nearly four years in prison for a crime you didn't commit. The now former police officer in your case stipulated in open court that he planted the drugs found in your car. Your lawyer submitted a record of this statement and video surveillance from the FBI to the Court of Appeals. This morning, the judges, with a few strokes of their pens, granted and signed a writ of habeas corpus, clearing you of all charges, voiding your sentence, and releasing you."

All the advice he had gotten up to that point was to be tough, show no emotion or weakness while in prison. However, tears rolled down his face at that moment, and he just couldn't stop.

Partially shocked by this revelation, the guys sat in their chairs out of respect. In the ultimate display of respect, they used their food trays and the table to make a clapping sound. Once the other inmates realized what was going on, it spread like a wave. The guards had their rules, and the inmates had theirs as well. It's what inmates did for each other when they found out a man served years behind the walls for a crime the poor slob didn't commit.

Within hours, true to their word, the guards prepared him for release. For the strangest of reasons, he would miss this place. Not the prison, but the inmates. That's when the Warden approached with a somber expression, a stark reminder of Redmond's unwelcoming nature, delivering news that felt like a punch to the gut. "Young man, I got a weird call from a social worker about your friend Freddie. She said he passed away peacefully, with only a handful of family members around. According to her, he did not commit suicide. She said this three to four times."

"What did he die of?"

"He had a stroke and died in his sleep. The doctors say he didn't feel a thing."

"Warden, I appreciate you telling me this. Despite the challenges facing an ex-con, he was determined to build a new life outside prison. He was adamant about not committing suicide. He said being free, even for a minute, was better than prison, no matter how used to it he was. In our last conversation, the guys told him that if he survived twenty-five years on the inside only to off himself because he couldn't take life as a free man, we would find his grave, urinate on it, and then curse him out. That explains that phone call." He had to laugh himself.

"Young man, you never belonged here, and I sure never want to see you back here. Do we understand each other?"

"Yes, sir," he said, smiling as he watched the cars pull up out of the corner of his eye.

When the warden walked away, Jon couldn't help but look up at the sky. He took a few minutes to admire the breathtaking view, the fresh air filling his lungs, and the weight of prison lifted. It was a spectacular vista with clean air and vibrant, intense colors, as though God knew the significance of that moment in time and made it picture-perfect. The blue sky with sporadic clouds thrown in floating high in the distance, the trees swaying gently in the breeze, their leaves whispering secrets to one another. Birds flew back and forth, their calls echoing through the trees. He just couldn't help standing there, taking it all in. He basked in the sun's warmth shining on his face and smiled.

A black sedan pulled up, honking its horn. He couldn't tell what the make of the car was, but it seemed very familiar to him. Then it hit him: his lawyer had a car like that. Squinting, he strained to see the driver through the dark windows, but to no avail. When the power window slowly rolled down, the man stared back at him. This man, with his unwavering integrity and silent competence, had earned his utmost respect and appreciation.

"You don't wanna hang around here, man. Do you need a ride?" he said, grinning at Jon. He got in the car as the V-6 engine roared with the slight push of the gas pedal, and the vehicle sped away.

A comfortable silence filled the car for a few minutes, broken only by the gentle hum of the engine. Then Mr. Merit asked, "Are you familiar with State Representative Kimbell?"

"Unfortunately, due to a lack of opportunity, I haven't yet had the chance to get to know him properly and build a meaningful relationship. The only knowledge I have of him comes from the stories, filled with both admiration and fear, that I've heard. He's been an influential and respected leader for years. I know his daughter better. She's my priority; I need to see her before anyone else."

Mr. Merit spoke carefully, guarding his words. "You know, he took a special interest in your case because of other similar cases. I can take you to see her now if that's where you want to go."

Jon was both eager and nervous. "It's not out of your way?"

"No, no, I've got plenty of time."

The relatively long drive from Redmond wound through Ohio's rural landscape; the rhythmic thrum of the tires on the highway was accompanied by the wind rustling through grass fields. Finally, the sounds of nature gave way to the cacophony of the city—a symphony of car horns, distant sirens, and chattering crowds. The slow blur of buildings outside faded as he stared from the window, lost in a world of his own making. He stared at the unrecognizable landscape, a stark contrast to his memories of just a few years ago; the sights, sounds, and smells were foreign. He still recognized enough landmarks to know where he was going, but a lot seemed foreign, as if he were on an alien planet. The closer they got to their destination, he became more nervous. Would she recognize him, let alone miss him?

Mr. Merit seemed strangely confident that she still lived at the address he gave him. Once they finally arrived at their destination, the car slowed, pulled into the parking garage, and parked. Reaching to open the door, Jon realized just how nervous he was. His hands were so sweaty that it caused his grip to slip a little while trying to open it. He had dreamed of the day when he could look into Michelle's beautiful brown eyes, when he could hold her again, his arms wrapped around her waist, pulling her closer. He had dreamed of the day he could talk to her face-to-face as a free man.

Beads of sweat popped on his brow as he stammered a frantic explanation for his disappearance, his words a jumbled rush of half-formed sentences. He tried rehearsing what he would say to her in his mind before they arrived. Even the best-laid plans don't always go according to a plan. Standing at her door, a terrifying thought entered his mind: What if she had forgotten about him? Worse yet, what if she had gotten married?

He knocked on the door, trying hard not to panic, periodically looking back at his lawyer standing in the hallway. The door suddenly cracked open. The woman who appeared seemed shocked to see who was standing there. When she came to her senses, she opened the door a little wider to reveal a breathtaking sight. Jon stood there with his mouth open, stunned to near paralysis at the gorgeous woman before him.

A sharp, clear voice cut through the silence, crying out from the background, "Mommy, Mommy, cartoons are on!"

"Wait, wait, you're someone's mother?!" The words hung in the air, a shocking revelation. A gasp escaped his lips as the shock struck him, leaving him speechless. "When did this happen?"

"Well, this isn't something I can explain to you in a hallway." With a gentle push, she opened the door, revealing the warmly lit interior, and invited them in. "You really should sit down; this is going to take a while." However, before she could even breathe to start, his interruption stopped her in her tracks.

"I'd like to ask you another question. Your beauty was always natural, effortless, like a wildflower swaying in the breeze. How can you look even more beautiful now after becoming a mother?"

A hush fell over the room, and Mr. Merit turned, his smile crinkling the corners of his eyes, and looked at Jon. A silent nod and a brief head inclination conveyed his complete agreement. He lightly elbowed him in his rib without saying a word.

Taking a few minutes to stare at him, a slow smile of appreciation spread across Michelle's face, her eyes lingering on his features. "High praise like that can open unexpected doors and lead to incredible opportunities. It feels like ages since someone offered me such a sincere compliment; I've longed for that feeling again. I've tried my best as a mom. Being a single mom is hard, but my parents help. In the last few years, compliments from men have been as rare as a blue moon."

Thinking fast, his mind raced, and he blurted out the first thought that popped into his head. "A woman as wonderful as you deserves compliments every single day."

"Saying stuff like that can get you places you never thought you'd go. Jerry told me what happened to you. I wanted to see you, but he told me it was a terrible idea because of who my dad is. He was right, so remind me to thank him."

"I didn't want my mom visiting me in Redmond, and especially not you. Thinking about you helped, especially that last day. Holding your hand, chatting with you, being near you. That's what helped me stay sane in there."

The room grew silent again as Mr. Merit listened to the conversation with a huge smile. He continued to elbow Jon in the ribs when he heard statements he liked. Michelle just stared at him, smiling. She looked at him as though peering into his soul. "I think there's someone you should meet." She turned to look at the room at the far end of the hallway. From the living room, he could see a cracked door, and light flickered on the wall from the TV.

Michelle raised her voice a little to ensure it carried enough to be heard in the next room. "JB, there's someone here who wants to meet you." Within minutes, a rambunctious three-year-old sprinted from the room into the wide-open arms of his mother. Jon looked at the little boy intensely, trying to get a sense of who the father might be. The more he looked at him, the more it occurred to him that the boy was a mirror image of himself at that age.

Trying to suppress his suspicions, he asked a few more coherent questions. "So what's your name?"

"My name is Jon."

"Really? I have the same name as you do. How old are you?"

He responded by holding up three fingers rather awkwardly, then said with a huge smile, "I'm three."

Making swift calculations in his head, Jon thought to himself, *I've been gone nearly three years. It's possible.* Not missing a beat, he said, "I know your mother loves you and is very proud of you. It was nice to meet you."

After Michelle hugged her son, she told him he could finish watching cartoons. With a quick sprint, he was gone.

Jon, with a massive smile on his face, looked at Michelle. He couldn't help but ask the obvious question that any logical person would ask facing a similar situation. "So, who is his father, and where is he?"

Evasive and highly intelligent, Michelle was a force to be reckoned with. She answered the question in a way that demanded another question. "Oh, he disappeared a few years ago."

"Michelle, I need you to be a little more specific."

"Well, he disappeared a few months before my son was born."

"I disappeared a few months before he was born. Exactly how much fun did we have the last time I saw you?"

"Well, we had a little too much fun. The best way I can answer your question is like this: If you ever want to see that little boy's father, all you have to do is look in the mirror."

At that moment, he could've been knocked over with a feather.

Mr. Merit, who was still sitting next to him, had been told beforehand. He put his hand on Jon's shoulder and whispered in his ear, "Young man, you survived prison, and you can survive this."

Still in shock, Jon reached into his pocket, pulling out his wallet. He pulled out a picture of himself, and his smile widened as he gazed at it, lost in a happy memory.

Mr. Merit suddenly mentioned a friend specializing in paternity tests, just to leave no doubt, given the circumstances. "I mean no disrespect, Ms. Kimbell, but this situation is unusual."

Michelle confidently spoke up, "He is well within his right, to be sure. That little boy is his. I'm more than willing to submit to any paternity test."

Jon handed Mr. Merit the picture he was holding. His emotions were overwhelming him and tears rolled down his face. "That picture captured me when I was three, with a huge mischievous grin on a sunny afternoon."

Mr. Merit took the photo and studied it.

"Damn, the resemblance is remarkable, even down to the smile. It's like God went back in time and made a clone of you."

Looking at both of them, Jon decided. He showed maturity with a well thought out answer, "Based on what I've learned today, I don't need a test to tell me he's mine. You should do the test not to satisfy me, but to ensure that my little boy grows up knowing who his father is. Knowing that his father loves him, cares about him, and will be involved in his life. If the test proves that he's mine—the dates match our time together, my arrest, along with the period to carry the pregnancy to term—if those things match up, and based on what I've learned, I think they will, I have to be involved in that little boy's life. I know what it's like growing up not having a father and the difference it makes in having one, even if it's a stepfather. Let me tell you, having lived it, the lack of a father's presence leaves a painful and lasting void. Dads are crucial in raising children, so for the sake of the child, I believe you can't exclude them unless they pass away. Unless the father's actions show a lack of respect for the privilege, then they shouldn't be involved, especially if they're a sorry excuse for a father. That's why so many guys are in prison. I found out while in there.

"Wow, this has been a fantastic day! I'm released from prison. Looks like I could be a father. Plus, I gotta explain this to my mom, which is another thing. Seriously, what more could happen?"

Mr. Merit, sitting next to him, looked at him with a grin. "So what's your plan now that you're out of prison? Now you've got someone else counting on you."

"I'd initially planned to stay with my mother, relying on her comforting presence and home-cooked meals until I was financially stable. My goal is to graduate. I have to finish what I started. I gotta find a job and explain to anyone who'll hire me what happened to somehow explain the holes in my resume."

"That's a decent plan, but I think you can do better. Returning to school to finish what you started is the best part of your plan. The rest of it could use some improvement." He reached into his inside jacket pocket and pulled out an envelope with Jon's name on it. The letter had bold writing on it with the raised state seal.

Jon studied the envelope and noticed where it came from: *State Rep. Kimbell, House Judiciary Committee of the State Legislature.* "What's this?"

"Just open it."

A letter with a check from the state treasury was in the envelope. $210,500 to Jon Bowman.

"Jon, in the state of Ohio, that's your compensation for false imprisonment. It's fifty-two thousand six hundred and twenty-five dollars for each year spent behind bars. So that amount times four is where the check's number comes from. The first part of your plan should be to call your mother. You'll have to explain that a little boy needs to see her. Finding out about a grandson she didn't know she had is something she must find out from you. Then, you need to ride with me to a bank to open a checking account so you can deposit that check. That letter, a tangible testament to your wrongful imprisonment, is irrefutable evidence—keep it safe. The bank may need that documentation to verify it. Then, we will return to the leasing office of this apartment complex to get the key to your apartment. We've handled everything, you don't have to worry about a thing. You need to be close to your son to spend time with him. Eventually, he will get to know you and trust you. When the test confirms that he's your son and you agree that the time is right, only then should you tell that little boy that you're his father. A bond is a delicate thing you shouldn't rush, and trust has to be earned.

Then you have to thank State Rep. Kimbell privately and during a press conference for that check. Usually, that process takes years, but with his help and the help of others, it only took months. He did this for you because you deserve it. He also did it because he needs your help to restore faith in the Ohio justice system. This will go a long way to assure him that his only daughter and grandson will be in excellent hands with you. Any relationship you may want with Michelle going forward depends on that."

"You know, since the first day I met you, you've always given me sound advice, not just as my lawyer, but on other things. How did you become so wise?"

"Son, there are many things you can learn from turning the pages of a book. But there are many things you can only learn from living your life. Everyone stumbles at some point, sometimes tripping over their own two feet, other times over unexpected obstacles. Sometimes, unfair mistakes happen, forcing you to rise above them. The critical point is, did you learn something from those mistakes?"

Jon felt a strong sense of unease, mostly because his stomach was turning in knots from the bowl of mixed cereal he ate before arriving.

It tasted fine going down, but now it was coming back to scare the hell out of him like Jason scared all those counselors at Camp Crystal Lake. What should he say to his mother? *Hey, Mom, I'm out of prison. I love you, and I've just found out that you may have a grandson?* Ultimately, he knew he just had to get on with it. He looked at Michelle, a silent moment passing between them before he spoke.

"Hey, can I use your phone for a few minutes?"

"Sure, you can use it. I'm curious to know how your mother will take the news. We had to tell my mom together, it was a two-person job."

With a serious expression, Jon asked, "You truly went there with your mom?"

"Yep, we double-teamed her."

That made him more nervous than he already was. Pushing past his fear after being handed the cordless phone, he dialed the number and waited patiently for the soft, familiar voice of his mother to answer.

"Hello, Mrs. Darlene Freeman?"

"Yes, who may I ask is calling?"

"Oh, I'm just calling to see how you're doing."

"Oh my God, when did you get out?"

"Mom, how did you know it was me?"

"Trust me, young man, moms know their babies. Why am I just hearing from you now? Where are you?"

"Well, I planned on coming to see you first but ended up seeing a close friend who told me some surprising things. Mom, are you sitting down?"

Chapter 20. Peace & Judgement

"Well, who is this friend you chose to see before seeing your mother? For nearly four years, I waited, my heart heavy with worry and my prayers unceasing for your safe return."

"I met this fantastic woman at school."

"You've got some explaining to do, young man."

"Mom, things have been crazy since I got released from prison."

"Who is this woman, and why haven't you told me about her before?"

"I kept it a secret only because I didn't know how things would go with her. I'm telling you this because I was with her the night before my arrest. Well, you know what happens after nine months, right? Especially if you don't take precautions and wear a raincoat?"

"Jon Bowman, are you seriously telling me I might have a grandson or granddaughter walking around somewhere I've never met?"

"Yes, Mom, that's precisely what I'm saying."

Repeated screams of "Oh my God" echoed through the phone and filled the room with her unmistakable reaction of joy and excitement. Her joyous screams were so loud that he had to pull the phone away from his ear for a moment, the sound waves almost painful. When she finally stopped screaming, the questions came in a flurry.

"Have you laid eyes on the child?"

"Yes, Mom, I've seen him."

"So, a grandson, huh?"

"Yes, Mom."

"Tell me about him."

"You know that picture of me at age three, the one I keep in my wallet; it's a little faded around the edges. Mr. Merit, my lawyer, is here. He's convinced we're so alike, it's like God cloned me. He suggested a paternity test to remove all doubt, saying it's the only way to be sure. We both agreed to submit to this test to eliminate questions or doubts."

His mother quietly listened, and when he finished talking there was a brief pause filled with anticipation. "Jon, the minute you know with absolute certainty that he's your son, I damn well better know too. Do we understand each other, young man?"

"Yes, Mama, you will be the first person I call. I thought you would be mad."

"Jon, you are my son and I love you. Why would I be angry? I've been alone for far too long. I've hoped for this day and prayed for it. This came sooner than expected, and I thought you would be married first, but I'm not complaining. My one consistent wish was that God would let me live long enough to be a grandmother. If true, you gave me the best Mother's Day and birthday gift ever. I want to see both of them as soon as possible once you know."

"Yes, Mama, I promise I'll arrange it as soon as I know."

The week that passed seemed excruciating, waiting to know the results. When the phone call came, Mr. Merit was very professional and they gathered in his office to find out the results. It was like slow torture, like sitting in a chair watching as someone was pulling out his fingernails with pliers.

Mr. Merit pulled out a folder with only five or six pages. Silence hung heavy in the air, broken only by the rustle of papers as his lawyer intently scanned the documents. Then, looking at Jon with a smile, he asked, "So what's your favorite sport?"

"Now seems like an odd time to ask that question."

"No, it's very relevant. This report says you need to check out local Little League sports and read up on fatherhood. You're the boy's dad."

Sitting beside him, Michelle exhaled, breathing an enormous sigh of relief. She was always confident that he was the father; he was the only man she had been with. It was just the relief of knowing for sure. The confirmation in black and white on paper gave her peace of mind and the assurance that she could tell her son who his father was with no doubt or reservations.

Being a man of his word, Jon remembered the promise he had to keep. Borrowing Mr. Merit's phone, he had to call his mother to relay the exciting news to her. It occurred to him that events were playing out exactly as they had in Michelle's apartment. He dialed the number, she answered the phone, and he told her the results. Everyone in Mr. Merit's office could hear a loud, joyous scream that caused him to hold the phone away from his ear.

When she finally stopped screaming, overwhelmed, he struggled to tell her that he needed time to tell the boy he was his father before introducing him to his grandmother. He had to know him before he could tell him about her. It wasn't easy to ask, but she agreed to be patient and wait.

Weeks after his release from Redmond Prison, the shock of finding out he had a son had set in. A month later, he was outside the Ohio Legislative Building. There was a podium with a single microphone. He stared at it while carefully staying out of sight of the reporters waiting for politicians to appear. A crowd of reporters and ordinary Ohioans stood patiently, waiting for the new leadership team to appear. He was nervous because he was a guest speaker on a topic that this crowd wasn't expecting. The crowd was eager to learn more about the scandals gripping the capital.

Everyone was stunned when the new House speaker, judiciary chair, and Ohio Supreme Court chief justice walked out along with a young man and other unfamiliar faces. A nervous energy filled the air. The Ohio justice system faced a crisis of confidence when the exoneration of 23 wrongfully convicted men exposed deep flaws in the system, sending shockwaves throughout the state. Trust in the system plummeted, only to be made worse by the resignations of high-level public officials.

As State Rep. Kimbell introduced him, Jon felt nervous. His clammy hand slid on the microphone as he fumbled with it. His speech was a crucial first step toward restoring faith. Looking out at the gathered crowd, scared out of his mind, he battled his fear, slowly piecing together words, then a phrase, until a profound truth emerged.

"My fellow Ohioans, today you're sad. Today you're angry, and today you're worried. You're worried because it could have easily been you. If you are a young black man in Ohio, have a family member who is black, or deeply care for a black man like me, it could have easily been you or someone you care about stuck in a cell, deprived of freedom for a crime you know you or they didn't commit. Like me, it could have easily been someone else who looks like me sitting in a courtroom. A prosecutor's pointed accusations and a judge's silent scrutiny may feel like heavy weights pressing down as the scales of justice turn. But hey, we shouldn't give up hope.

"I can say that because there are those still working in this system who get up every day trying to do the right thing. People inside this system are trying to fix mistakes when they find them. As one of the 23 wrongfully convicted people, my freedom is directly because of the hard work and dedication of those who tirelessly seek and correct mistakes, a testament to their commitment to excellence. Thanks to the Ohio FBI, politicians, and public servants who give a damn, today I'm a free man with renewed hope. Even though sometimes justice is blind, there are people in this system helping her see the truth."

Receiving enormous applause, Rep. Kimbell leaned over with a smile. "Young man, are you trying to take my job?"

"No, sir, I have no interest in politics."

"Well, politics may be interested in you."

"I have more interest in your daughter and grandson than anything else."

"That reminds me. I heard about the paternity test results. We need to discuss your plans for both of them."

"Sir, we can have that conversation anytime at your convenience."

"That's awesome. After church, I'll have my wife arrange a family dinner with roasted chicken and her famous mashed potatoes. Did you grow up attending church regularly?"

"Yes, sir," Jon replied. "Due to my dad's incarceration, my mother made sure we attended church regularly. She didn't know any other way to raise a boy that ensured he would become a decent man. The deacons and elders in my neighborhood were role models, and some of the older inmates at Redmond helped."

"Young man, I like what I hear, but you still have work to do if I'm going to trust you with my daughter and only grandson."

"I understand, sir, and I don't blame you. You should know they are both worth the effort, and I don't mind hard work."

"Thank you for agreeing to do this press conference. Heads up, you could be in the news! That speech was excellent! I'll see you on Sunday."

The press conference, a flurry of carefully worded statements designed to quell the unrest simmering in the streets, ended as suddenly as it began. Sure enough, Jon made the evening news, his face illuminated on the screen, the anchor's voice narrating his story.

The following day, Rep. Kimbell got a surprise visit from fifteen of his district's most respected black religious leaders. His secretary brought them to his office conference room. Another member of his staff told him they were waiting for him and who they were. He walked in and shook their hands, greeting everyone warmly and respectfully. He needed those religious leaders on his side if he wanted to get re-elected, just like any politician would.

"So, ladies and gentlemen, why do I have the honor of meeting with all of you today?"

When Darnell got word of what was happening, he tiptoed into the room and sat in the corner. Then, the group's most senior and respected member took the lead.

"First, we're here to pray for you. A member of my congregation saw your wife coming out of a doctor's office who only treats cancer patients and told me about it. Second, another member of my congregation saw your daughter in the emergency room when your grandson was born. We have seen none of you in church in a while. I thought it was odd you never got your grandson christened. We understand now why you haven't recently visited all of our churches dealing with these scandals. What I don't understand is why you didn't tell me your daughter was pregnant and your wife was dealing with a serious health scare, let alone why you didn't bring your grandson by to see me. You were married in my church, and I performed the ceremony. What's going on with you? We all saw you on the news yesterday. Everyone agreed that the press conference was necessary and helpful. Everyone was furious before it, to the point of the younger members in our churches and the community around them thinking, 'Let it all burn.' Who was that young man who gave that fantastic speech? He possibly prevented a riot."

"Ladies and gentlemen, that young man is the father of my grandson."

The entire room fell silent. The older pastor in the room responded by saying, "Well, I'll be damned. We didn't see that one coming."

Rep. Kimbell, usually the rock of strength that everyone else in the black community leaned on, sat there with tears rolling down his face. "I was dealing with the risk of losing my wife to cancer, combined with my daughter being pregnant and the father of her child in prison. The truth came out later, unveiling slowly like a creeping vine, its tendrils wrapping around the hearts of those involved. After nearly four years, we finally got that young man out of Redmond Prison. Four years filled with the harsh reality of prison life, the echoing silence, and the ever-present fear. All because one corrupt cop planted drugs in his car and many others. The revelation that our system is systemically racist is something that everyone in this room is well aware of. To make things worse, those jerks profited from our community's imprisonment, and top officials covered for each other to keep the cash rolling in.

"Sometimes, life feels like a runaway train; one minute, everything is fine, and the next, you're overwhelmed by a chaotic mess of problems. I was facing a personal and political issue. My daughter was pregnant by a man in prison. It was a mess, so we kept it under wraps. No one discussed it until we dug deep and found a lot of corruption, especially with these for-profit prisons. They were targeting our young people. We're already losing too many young brothers and sisters to the criminal justice system, as it is due to nonsense."

As he leaned back in his chair, Rep. Kimbell broke down. "Too many things were coming at me, and I didn't know what to do. You're right, I got married in your church. I should have come to you for help if it got too stressful."

The other pastor asked, "Will we ever have peace in this country? When will the U.S. treat us fairly?"

Then another pastor asked, "So, what do we tell everyone—our church and the black community?"

A heavy silence descended on the room as Rep. Kimbell reclined in his chair.

"We need the truth."

"Okay, there are only two instances when the black community and their leaders can trust this country. We shouldn't trust the United States to act in our best interests. That's about as likely as Hell freezing over. The second event would be Jesus' returning if the events in the Book of Revelation are to be believed. Smacking us all with the Bible, saying the world's gonna end. Tie up any loose ends you may have. That, my friends, is a key moment, and the only time our community should trust this country to do right by us, when it's trying to save itself from itself. A nation that has historically caused us pain and disappointment finally acting in our best interest. Only when the United States is trying to save itself from itself. So answering your question, the conclusion the black community and its leaders should come to on the trust question is not only no, but hell no."

The room erupted in arguments and screaming.

"That's not true; that's a pessimistic view."

The more conservative-minded pastors yelled, "We can't tell them that. We shouldn't tell them that," while the more progressive-minded pastors screamed back, "We've gotta tell them the truth. This community has been dealing with terrible conditions for too long. We've got to tell them the truth. Our condition is far worse than any other racial group in this state and the nation. We're doing the worst in any statistical category of measurement we look at."

Eventually Rep. Kimbell interrupted them. He was slightly biased in favor of the more progressive-minded pastors, while also trying to be fair to the more conservative-minded ones. He started by explaining why he held such pessimistic views, raising his voice and asking all of them to quiet down.

"Ladies and gentlemen, on a federal and state level, in terms of money and resources, this country doesn't care about us. That's the bitter truth. America shows who and what it cares about by revealing who and what it spends its money on and where it spends its money, and that's not on us. To unite the black community and pool our community's collective wealth, we have to tell them the truth about the circumstances we find ourselves in. I know I haven't left all of you with much to be hopeful about, but it is what it is. There's one thing I'd like to ask you to do for me as you leave here and return to your respective churches. Pray that I'm wrong about what America thinks about us, and how it feels about us, while preparing the masses for the possibility that I'm right."

One month after the meeting in Rep. Kimbell's office, on a bright Sunday morning, dressed in their best clothes, they arrived at Michelle's parents' house, waiting to pile into the car to go to church together. It was a cool seventy-five degrees with a pleasant breeze. Jon stood there smiling like a proud father, watching LJ tugging on a clip-on tie that he didn't want to wear. He reminisced about doing the same thing at that age. Little man earned the nicknames Little Jon and LJ to avoid confusion since they shared a name. It was a picture-perfect day to spend with God. It would also be a perfect day for a christening ceremony.

Jon finally arrived at one of the oldest churches in Columbus, its weathered stone and stained-glass windows whispering tales of a century's worth of worship. Stepping inside, he loved the bright colors and surprising design, the red carpet, along with the matching pews and pulpit. He felt the weight of his first church visit since being released. Service started with the choir and then the pastor's sermon. LJ slept through most of it, waking up for the christening. Standing there near the pulpit in one of the most respected churches in the black community felt like a dream Jon didn't want to wake up from. His son was standing there, holding his hand, wondering why everyone was looking at him.

When the pastor walked over, Jon picked LJ up, cuddling him, revealing how much their bond had grown. The pastor placed his fingers in holy water and then marked the cross on LJ's forehead. This caused his mother to whisper that he couldn't take it off, at least for a while. The whole church stood up to pray for him. When the service ended, they all returned home to eat Sunday dinner. The table groaned under the weight of food—mountains of steaming rice, glistening platters of roasted meats, and bowls overflowing with colorful vegetables. It was a joyous occasion no one would soon forget. Then, moving to the couch, LJ sat down between Michelle's parents with a book in his hand. His grandpa opened the book and started reading while Jon and Michelle sat on the loveseat across from them.

Jon leaned close, his breath warm on Michelle's ear as he whispered sweet nothings, causing her to giggle uncontrollably like a schoolgirl while her mother watched with a careful eye. "Honey, who do those two remind you of with their playful teasing and laughter?"

He glanced away from the book and felt the worn pages on his fingers. "They remind me of us twenty-five years ago. We may have to get a head start on planning a wedding for those two."

LJ surprised both of them. "Mommy and Daddy have been doing that all the time."

Confused and surprised, Mr. Kimbell asked, "Little man, who told you that's your dad?"

"My friend Freddie told me. No one can see him but me."

Mr. Kimbell raised his voice to get Jon's attention. "Hey, Jon, do you know someone named Freddie? Because he told LJ you're his dad."

Jon stopped his conversation with Michelle. "Did you say Freddie told LJ that I'm his dad?"

"Yes."

Looking directly at LJ, Jon asked, "What else did Freddie tell you?"

"Freddie said you should write a book about what happened to you at Redmond. He said you should tell the story of how you beat the Axeman. When you finish writing the book, he said to tell you to put two copies of your book in the Redmond Library. He also told me I should ask you how to play chess when I get older."

Jon looked directly at Mr. Kimbell. "While at Redmond, Freddie, an older inmate, helped me survive. He passed away just before I got out. We played chess nearly every day until he got out."

Standing up and pulling himself off the plush loveseat, Jon took a few steps forward before kneeling on the worn rug. "LJ, come over here for a minute." He looked directly at his son. "You are my son, and I'm your dad. I will always love you." He gave him a big hug. "Little man, do you know you have two grandmothers who love you? That's your mom's mom," pointing at Mrs. Kimbell, "and your grandma. Tomorrow, you're going to see your second grandmother, my mother. They both love you a lot, and your second grandmother has been waiting to see you for a long time."

The next day, LJ woke up to a room filled with images of astronauts, the solar system, and the planets. Like his dad, it was a reflection of his personality. He had a curious mind. That's why LJ got up and knocked on his mom's door. Waiting for permission to come in, he could hear muffled voices and the sound of shuffling feet inside. After a few minutes of struggling, he finally heaved himself onto the high bed, his muscles burning, until he finally found his footing. He crawled between his mom and dad, his heart pounding, to blurt out a single, urgent word. "Grandma! Is it time to see Grandma?"

Smiling at him, Jon said, "Yes, little man, we'll visit your grandmother. But we must eat breakfast first."

After breakfast, they all piled into the car to make the drive. Buckling LJ up in the back seat as he looked out the window, Michelle conveniently walked to the passenger side while looking at Jon with a grin.

He looked back at her, confused. "Wait, I thought you were driving."

"I was until I looked at your driver's license and realized it's still valid. You've been avoiding this because of what happened to you. If you're going to take LJ to the park to play with other kids, you must overcome your fear of driving."

Knowing she was right, he got into the car, turned the ignition, and pulled off. The drive was so relaxing—he got to listen to Michelle more than he talked. LJ, ever the curious child, spent the entire ride quietly observing the world outside the window. His eyes traced the blurry landscapes, the whoosh of wind against the glass a gentle soundtrack to his journey. He was amazed at all the interesting people, buildings, and sights that passed by.

Once they arrived at his mother's house, Jon couldn't help but emotionally stand in front of it. It had been nearly four years, which was too long. A hesitant series of knocks sounded on the door. The door cracked open, then opened wide as his mother stood there smiling, trying to understand how much he changed. "You've grown a little, gained some weight, and you're a little taller and older, but you're still my son." She hugged him tight, loving the feeling of his arms around her.

Tears of joy rolled down her face, and when the hug ended, she stepped back to look at the woman he was with. Introducing her, Jon tried to say all the positive things he could think of to describe her, but his mother interrupted him. "She's a beautiful woman, but more importantly, she's the woman who gave me a grandson. There will always be a special place in my heart for you. He doesn't have to tell me about you. He knows me well enough to know better than to bring just any woman here to meet me. I look forward to getting to know you better."

Then she stooped to look at her grandson.

"So, who is this little boy you brought to see me?"

"Oh, that's your grandson."

She gave him a big hug while kissing him on the forehead, then wiping it off. A dog's sharp, insistent barking echoed from another room in the house. A brown Labrador retriever ran down the hall into the living room, wagging its tail, making a beeline to LJ and licking him like crazy while wagging his tail. Jon looked at his mother, confused.

"Mama, when did you get a dog?"

"I got him two years ago from a shelter. The name on the adoption papers says his name is Cujo, but I've seen that movie and refuse to call him that. Besides, he's more likely to lick you to death than bark at you. I call him Dino because, for some odd reason, he likes to watch cartoons."

"Well, Mama, why didn't you get a dog for me when I was LJ's age?"

"You made my life way more interesting. Watching you learn and grow while guiding you through life until you become a young man. The pain of letting you grow up and leave home was immense. Especially knowing you faced a world that might not appreciate you and a country that didn't deserve you. Also, another mouth to feed would've been brutal on my already tight budget as a single mom. We would've gotten you a dog when I married your stepfather, but he was allergic to them. Since you've been gone, and your dad passed away, the story changed. I've been alone for far too long. I've had that goofy dog for two years now."

LJ hugged Dino and gave him a gentle head pat. "Dad, we need to visit Grandma a lot more."

His grandma looked at him, all smiles and grins. "Your son is bright, and I'm so happy and proud to be his grandmother."

As a prisoner in Hell, Christopher sat wondering if escaping was possible. Compared to the prisons of the living, the sheer hopelessness and the crushing weight of despair made this a hundred times worse. Looking out of his window, the view was horrific. The sky was light red all the time. While the sun was high in the sky, it was a dark reddish orange. Worst of all, it always seemed like it was on fire. As sulfur filled the air, the fires of Hell burned day and night without interruption. Christopher's fall from grace was long and hard.

It didn't matter that he was one of the Devil's emissaries. He had failed his given job, to steal the souls of the living, allowing his boss, the Devil, to gain strength to break free of his chains and reign not only in Hell, but also to have dominion over the Earth.

Despite his most recent setback, the sting of defeat taught Christopher a harsh lesson about the consequences of failure. There was no such thing as special treatment in Hell. The heat of the place scorched him during the day. As soon as night fell, flames roasted him some more. He could feel the intense heat on his skin, smell the acrid smoke, and hear the crackling fire. Demons appeared without warning, added to his torment, their unpredictable visits bringing unbearable agony and a palpable aura of dread, the air thick with the stench of brimstone.

Those demons forced him to relive his death again and again, repeating the flashbacks every day as though it was Groundhog Day, reliving the worst moments of his life every hour for sometimes twenty-four hours. This was sometimes combined with the torture of roasting him, which went on for weeks. He was dead already, so there was no need for breakfast, lunch, or dinner breaks. Days bled into each other, each one grimmer than the previous, and he just had to put up with it.

However, always in his spirit, he knew the time would come when the lock on his cell would weaken. That's when he would be the one doing the torturing. Time seemed to pass slowly, maybe to prolong a soul's pain and agony. Then one day, the temperature in his cell dropped to an almost bearable level. Curious to find out what was going on, he stood up to look out of the door window, careful not to touch the door handle out of fear of being engulfed in flames.

Chapter 21. Epilogue

Secured by the celestial power of the angels, the lock pulsed with a faint, ethereal glow, making it impossible to open. A wave of heat radiated from the door, so he carefully only opened the window. He saw a king cobra slithering on the floor in a zig-zag movement from the enormous cell he suspected the Devil was locked in. The snake eventually made its way underneath the door of his cell. Rising to nearly eye-level, the snake's forked tongue moved in and out of its mouth before it said a word.

"Mr. Davis, Hell is the worst because time has no meaning here, and your punishment never ends. That is for some of us. However, in your case, my friend, you are in Hell because you failed. You're not out there hovering above the lake of lava like those other unfortunate souls. Be glad you're not out there engulfed in flames. You're in here because you've shown that you're a sadistically efficient killer and thief. Until those damn angels showed up and stopped you. Our boss doesn't reward failure, but your record impressed him. You know who I mean. We're not allowed to say his name, so we just refer to him as little as possible. We usually think of him as an absentee landlord. He likes it that way.

"Who else do you know that's not a fan of sticking their nose in other people's business? He didn't stop those racist a-holes from murdering your girlfriend. That absentee landlord didn't intervene to stop that mob of racist a-holes from murdering you. He was getting angrier and angrier, the fire burning inside him, fueled by each infuriating word he heard. He punishes those who steal souls, sending them to a fiery Hell, a place of screams and torment. You'll get out of here only if you serve the boss. Your axe remains in Redmond Prison and through it you can take the lives of the living. Though trapped, this place offers a chance to regain your strength and escape. Despite being here, you can use it to kill, taking the souls of the living to gain strength.

"Only our boss can send you back if you serve him. Don't forget the deal you made. Don't forget whose side you're on. Remember, our eyes are always upon you, watching your every move."

The conversation ended, leaving a sense of unfinished business hanging in the air. It was odd to say the least. Then the snake slithered away, making it halfway across the floor before disappearing under the cell door, leaving only an icy whisper.

After the snake left, Christopher sat staring at the wall in his cell. He simply couldn't stop thinking about the many ways he could torture and eventually kill the unfortunate inmates he came across once freed. Feeding on their fear while gaining glee from seeing their pain.

He sat in that scalding dark cell, staring at the wall in the Devil's castle. The thought gnawed at him, a relentless, intrusive presence that dominated his every waking moment. He could see nothing but the lava lake, its surface a sea of molten rock glowing with an infernal heat. He stood there, paralyzed by fear, the chilling sight before him making his breath catch in his throat. As periodic flames shot up, scorching the poor souls in their cells above the lava lake, the air filled with the smell of burning flesh and sulfur. Christopher stood, looking out the window.

Reaching his ears were the constant moans and screams of the suffering. The more he listened, the angrier he became. His fists clenched, his jaw tightened. The hunter sharpened his cunning, his thoughts filled with increasingly creative yet brutal methods for pursuing and ending his prey's life, each plan more calculated than the last. He didn't realize the Devil across from him shared a psychic link with him. His mind was a maelstrom of furious thoughts, all swirling around a single, obsessive idea.

"The body may die, but my spirit lives on. The grave may possess my bones, and God may chain my spirit in Hell. But know this: every door has a key, and every prison has a release date. I'll be back."
Christopher Davis

Former officer Anthony Donovan arrived at Redmond Prison a few months after pleading guilty to planting drugs on many innocent black men. Approaching the enormous walls of the prison, he was groggy from the weird dream he had woken up from. It unfolded like a short movie. In the dream, as he got near the inmate reception entrance at Redmond, an old tree stood that could have easily been a hundred years old. It had an odd presence that got everyone's attention; even the bus temporarily stopped near it. The branches and silhouette of the tree looked like something that could've easily terrified small children on Halloween.

On every branch except one, he thought he saw what looked like black men hanging with ropes around their necks. He would swear to it on a stack of Bibles. The scene, when recounted to black inmates, caused them to replay the song "Strange Fruit," by Nina Simone, in their heads for the rest of the day. He also described how, on the one branch without a hanging man, a single owl stood there just staring at him. It talked to him, saying the same thing over and over again. "You will die here," the raspy voice hissed, the words echoing in the chilling silence.

He later learned that the other guys on the bus saw men hanging from that tree too, but they got a different warning. Some were told they would die in Redmond, while others were told they would survive, but not as the same men who walked in. The owl showed those with blood on their hands flashes of their future, a horrifyingly vivid vision of how painfully they would die. He couldn't imagine what was worse, being told you're going to die or being shown how painfully you're going to go. After this odd vision, he knew Redmond Prison was a place to survive, not one to be reformed at. He also didn't understand the owl's warning until months later because, as an officer, he never used his gun to kill anyone.

The days became weeks, and the weeks became months. Being an ex-cop in a prison with inmates he may have put there was a terrible position to be in, one that made it impossible to make friends. However, since he only planted drugs on black men, he knew his only option to make friends was with the Skinheads. But they refused to trust cops, and that included ex-cops; the distinction made no difference to them. Their position changed after two years into his four-year sentence when a guard approached him.

"Hey, Donovan, you got a visitor."

He was escorted through the various doors and locks to the visitor's room. A man in a sharp black suit with a brown leather briefcase sat patiently waiting for him. When he entered the room, he stood up, shook his hand, and sat back down, then opened his briefcase. He took three photographs out, placing them on the table. "Mr. Donovan, my name is Mark Paterson, and I am an assistant district attorney conducting a civil rights investigation of your traffic stops. Do you recognize the men in these photos? Do any of them ring a bell?"

"Yes, these are three of the many men I planted drugs on."

"Excellent, I can now close my investigation. I appreciate the honesty. I know these are mistakes in your life that you want to get past since they landed you here. However, I've got good news and terrible news for you."

"What's the bad news?"

"The unfortunate news is that the three men in the photos are dead. One man died by getting shanked in the recreation yard before we could clear him of the false drug charges. Another man committed suicide before we could clear him of his charges. The last man had a medical condition that could have been better treated and managed had he been on the outside, but took his life in prison. As far as we're concerned, you've got three bodies on you. We believe these three men would still be alive if not for you. Due to your plea deal, you're granted immunity, shielding you from prosecution for these deaths—that's the good news. The black guards of Redmond know about my findings and will no longer treat you like an ex-cop. The white guards will offer you some protection, but the black ones will not. You've got two years left. You may need to let this guard who escorted you here leak this to the Skinheads in exchange for some protection. They'll never trust you, but they may understand enough to help you survive to see your release date."

Donovan lowered his head after hearing everything, then looked up. "Thanks for the advice."

The meeting ended abruptly, and the guard escorted him back to his cell.

The next day, in the recreation yard, he was standing near members of the Aryan Brotherhood but mingling with non-affiliated ones when two men approached him that he didn't know.

"Hey, Donovan, my boss needs a word with you."

Knowing he was in no position to turn down a sit down with the leaders of the Brotherhood, he followed them. They brought him to two men he only knew by reputation.

"Don, do you know who I am?"

"Yeah, I know you're a man who commands much respect here. I know your name is Bill, and your number two is Tom. I also know you've got an excellent street pharmaceutical business."

"We heard about your problem, and we may be able to help each other. We've got beef with the Chicanos, thanks to a dead brother who flipped to save his ass. He was talking out of school to the DEA."

"I heard about the Redmond Civil War. I heard it was terrible."

"That business problem was a disaster, and we must avoid repeating it."

Tom asked, "Tell me about the drugs you were planting on black men. That wasn't all of it?"

"No, it wasn't. I sold most of it to the Brotherhood and disposed of the rest by framing black people. I was making a killing—way more than I ever imagined. It was the best! Getting busted was a chance I took, but I wasn't about to snitch. I kept changing my drop locations to stay safe so nobody knew who was who."

Tom looked at Bill. "This could work. He could be our go-between with the Chicanos. He has everything to lose and nothing to gain by double-crossing us. He may also help us prevent the police from interfering with our business. And if he double-crosses us, we can turn him over to the black inmates. If he double-crosses the Chicanos, they can do the same."

The sit-down ended, and within a blink of an eye, he was lying on his bunk waiting for lights out, trying to think about how to survive another day.

Gary Washington had become the alpha dog without trying to or seeking the status. He helped black inmates get things that made life easier on the inside. He arbitrated inmate-to-inmate arguments that flared up from time to time, and, in doing so, he made the guards' jobs easier. Perched on the top bench of a bleacher stand with a 360-degree view of the yard, he observed everything. At the same time, he was mentoring a younger inmate in Freddie's tradition, now on a rotating basis due to having a total of five younger inmates to mentor. He was also flanked on four sides for added protection with what amounted to a small army, but was actually a mutual defense alliance.

His new number two was sitting one bench below him while he played chess with a mentee. A guy whispered something in his ear, and he whispered what was told to him in his boss's ear. Talking to his mentee, he said, "Chess is sort of like the game of life, and in it, you're encouraged to think a few moves ahead, making the best decision possible to win. I just learned something about an inmate named Anthony Donovan. It seems Mr. Donovan, an ex-cop who planted drugs on black men and was responsible for the deaths of three of them, just made an excellent chess move. Pay attention, young man. The black inmates and guards wanted to move on him, but now we can't.

"Seems Donovan weaseled his way into being a middleman for the Skinheads and the Chicanos. Now he's untouchable for the time being. Everyone agrees that if we move on him, it will piss off the Skinheads and the Chicanos. Spread the word that Anthony Donovan is hands-off for now and say why." Then, looking at his young mentee, he asked, "Have you heard the word indispensable? It means that something is vital. That's what Anthony Donovan made himself into. Instead of an individual who is vulnerable and alone, he transformed himself into an asset that is valuable and needed."

The chess game ended, and everyone went inside for dinner. When the day was over, there began the wait for another day. Every day, inmates hope and pray that their next move is the right one, never one hundred percent sure it is.

#

Anthony Donovan worked for three months back and forth, taking messages between the two sides. Coded messages that the guards knew about but weren't able to break despite their best efforts. Business was terrific; it was so good that what they were doing amounted to running a mid-sized company making millions of dollars. The only problem was they were selling illegal products and running it as a company from prison. As a reward for Donovan's hard work, the Chicanos arranged for him to get a job in the prison garden. Once this happened, Anthony Donovan's time among the living was short.

The ghosts of Redmond visited him repeatedly. He tried not to let them prevent him from doing his job as a go-between because he knew that's what kept him alive. He was struggling to maintain his cool with the Chicanos and Skinheads while seeing ghosts every night as he slept. Working in the prison garden, he gained some peace from his routine and the spirits. It was something different to do that he appreciated, and something better to see. However, after lights out, it took him a while to fall asleep. His body seemed to know it was better to stay awake.

Soaked in sweat, tossing and turning while asleep, he saw three blurred figures that, over time, came into focus. It was the three men he framed who died. They tormented and tortured him all night without a moment of peace. He woke up in a cold sweat, screaming and thrashing. Guards rushed to his cell, alarmed by the commotion. "Ghosts are trying to kill me! Ghosts are trying to kill me!" he screamed repeatedly until he was taken to the infirmary and eventually calmed down.

The following day, he tried to go on as usual, but no one believed he was alright. The black inmates had him under observation for months and knew the ghosts were getting to him, and he would eventually crack under the pressure. Time on this day went by at a snail's pace, but it would go by fast on any other day. Making his way to the prison garden, he felt as though he was sleepwalking through life. In a flash, he saw a vision of a man sprawled on the ground. A plume of blood drenched the back of his orange prison jumpsuit. The victim's obscured face prevented identification.

Arriving in the garden, his task for the day was digging holes, dropping seeds in them, then moving to the next spot. A low, indistinct murmur in the distance rapidly escalated into a heated argument, the rising volume carrying on the wind. Two men were arguing about something and he only glanced over to look for a few seconds. Then he refocused on his work, ignoring the heated words and frustrated sighs of the arguing men. One of them did the same, but the other man in the argument decided not to let bygones be bygones and grabbed his shovel and, using all the strength he had, he threw it.

With a blur of motion and a metallic whine, the shovel transformed into an axe as it arced through the air.

In its new form, it became more aerodynamic, spinning in the air and, amazingly, gaining speed. Continuing on its path, it flew like a guided missile. Bystanders watched, astonished, as it missed its initial target and stabbed its actual target, Anthony Donovan, in the back. Blood soaked his white t-shirt underneath his orange prison-issue jumpsuit. He felt an enormous sharp pain that hit every nerve in his body, then suddenly nothing. When his spirit left his body, he stood over it. His vision near the tree from when he arrived at Redmond Prison instantly returned to him.

He had seen the image of a man face down, sprawled out on the ground, with an axe stuck deep in his back. He now realized he was looking at himself because the inmate ID number on his orange jumpsuit was the same one in his vision. Worst of all, the initials *CD* were etched into the axe handle wedged into him, which sent shivers down the spines of those gathered around Donovan's lifeless body. The sight of the blood, still wet on the wood, added to their unease. Then, the axe suddenly disappeared, adding to the mystery of how this odd event happened in the first place.

\#

The following day, Jon Bowman opened the front door of a house he now shared with Michelle and his son. Stooping to grab the newspaper, still appreciating the view as a free man, a headline leaped out at him, leaving him speechless. On the front page, the headline read, "Ex-cop Anthony Donovan Killed in Prison by Axe." When he walked back into the house, the phone was ringing.

"Hello, Jon, did you see the newspaper's front page this morning?"

Recognizing the voice, Jon said, "Mr. Kimbell, I've seen it."

"Well, please tell me what's going through your mind."

"Well, sir, stupid reasons tragically ended the man's life. Also, this may seem like an odd time to ask this question, but I would like permission to ask your daughter to marry me. Second, I have to write a book about my experiences in Redmond Prison and make two copies available to the prison library. The newspaper's front page showed a picture of an axe; the initials etched into it match Christopher Davis's. He will come back. Me and my friends beat him once. But someone else will have to beat him again."

The Axeman's Poem

- One, two, he will come for you.
- Three, four, there's no locking your door.
- Five, six, get a crucifix.
- Seven, eight, there's no staying up late.
- Nine, ten, he will kill again.

Publisher Information

<u>Publisher Information</u>

- www.steelepublications.com

- herberts@steelepublications.com

- https://steele-publications-nqm-shop.fourthwall.com

  - New Titles

Herbert S McKinney is a Florida Atlantic University graduate with a degree in Interdisciplinary Studies and a Political Science minor. He's spent time working on a Master's Degree in History at Texas Southern University. Reading about, learning from, and writing on various historical topics has always fascinated him. As a result he's always maintained a love for all history in general, but African American and African history in particular. This is along with a a love for and focus on African American Leadership, political science, economics, finance, investing, and sociology. All while exploring creative writing as a pursuit and Historical Fiction as an interest.